Midnight in Malibu

Rebecca Randolph Buckley

R. J. Buckley Publishing
San Tan Valley, AZ

www.rjbuckleypublishing.com

"MIDNIGHT AT TRAFALGAR"

"Rebecca Randolph Buckley provides a cast of characters who struggle with chaos and who must conquer their weaknesses in their quest for happiness. Her book is highly recommended for those readers who enjoy colorful scenes, realistic characters, and endearing life drama."

David S. Rosenberg, *Author of "The Hungry Dragon"*

". . . thoroughly enjoyed my trip through London and on to Cornwall with the characters this author has so skillfully created. Her description of Rachel fits a few ladies that I know, and it was a fantastic bonus to imagine any one of them being Rachel as she becomes caught up in a romantic fantasy in the beginning of the story, but later comes to realize that perhaps happiness lies in what you've known and been comfortable with all along. There is just enough suspense and intrigue in this story to keep you turning the pages to find out what happens next! I can't wait for the sequel to this book as Rachel goes off again in search of . . ."

Anne Elwick, *Author - "We Don't Say Goodbye"*

"MIDNIGHT IN BRUSSELS"

". . . finished first four novels and I think the third was my favorite. I was sorry PB was killed off and was a bit irritated at Rachel for not recognizing how she felt sooner! But with the way she globe trots, and with her independence, she should probably just stay single. I have to admit, I wasn't crazy about the vibes between Rachel and PN . . . glad you didn't go there. (You're not going there, are you??) Although I won't hold my breath on her getting married to MB and staying married! I liked the storyline of Amanda; it was a good progression of her; from learning to [sew] from her [mother] and grandmother [when she was a girl] to becoming her own designer. Very believable, since having nothing will often make a person creative and resourceful. Looking forward to "Midnight in Malibu."

Stephanie Thomas - *Troy, Texas*

Works by Rebecca Randolph Buckley

NOVELS - Rachel O'Neill Series

Midnight at Trafalgar
Midnight at the Eiffel
Midnight in Brussels
Midnight in Moscow
Midnight in Malibu

COLLECTIONS – Short Stories and Plays

Love Has a Price Tag
Bits & Pieces of Me
My Dramedy
The Shoe's on the Other Foot

© 2012 by Rebecca Randolph Buckley

First Printing September 2012

For information about special discounts for bulk purchases, please contact the publisher at: rjbuckleypublish@aol.com.

ISBN: 978-0-9838343-7-3

Library of Congress Control Number: 2012918468

For my son Barry and his wife Kellie
who both share my fondness for Malibu . . .

"Whether lying beneath the big Montana skies,
Walking the moonlit beaches of Malibu,
Gazing at the midnight Manhattan skyline,
Afloat on the River Seine,
Leaving one's heart in Russia,
Or building a nest in Cornwall,
Love and life are forever beckoning,
For we're never too old to dream."

Rebecca Randolph Buckley
www.rebeccabuckley.com

PART ONE

Allegra McAdams

Chapter I

Sounds of shattering glass and porcelain, thuds and crashes of books and artifacts hitting the floor, papers in file drawers being shuffled, ransacked, and tossed made Allegra McAdams bolt from her Edwardian four-poster bed.

The double doors that led from her bedroom opened directly onto the catwalk above the foyer below. She was afraid she might be seen by the intruders if she went out that way, so she hurried through her dressing and bath area into a closet. At the back of the closet there was a secret door that opened into an adjoining study. Inside the study, one would never have known it was connected to Allegra's suite through a hidden door behind a bookcase.

Once inside the study, Allegra crept through its double doors into the corridor leading away from the catwalk. She pressed her back against the wall, glancing back around the corner and down at what appeared to be flashlight beams bouncing off the walls in the downstairs library.

The massive, carved entry doors that opened from the portico and colonnade were ajar. She could see the reflection from the outside lights shining onto the glossy marble floor of the foyer.

She quickly turned and hurried to the last bedroom at the end of the corridor. Why she chose to hide there, she didn't know. Maybe it was because it was as far away from the marauders as she could get in the part of the house where she was trapped.

Once inside, Allegra crawled underneath a giant medieval bench below one of the windows and began praying that the perpetrators would not find her. She peered around the folded edge of a seventeenth-century Aubusson rug that was draped over part of the bench, hanging to the floor.

She scrunched up even smaller, attempting to disappear into the stale darkness beneath her shelter. The added mustiness of the centuries-old rug gave her a strange feeling of safety.

She heard footsteps coming up the marble staircase.

A light flashed on in the hallway beyond the guestroom door that was slightly open. She hadn't closed it securely.

Damn! Please, please, God, don't let them come in here, please!

Allegra was terrified. She was afraid to move, afraid she'd make a noise and was wishing she could stop breathing. She could always find her cats in hiding by listening for their purring. Her heart was pounding so loudly she was sure it would be heard same as purring if the burglars came into the room.

Now someone was in the room next door. She heard the door open.

All she could think of was how her mother must have felt. She wondered if this was how it had happened to her. She covered her mouth tightly with both hands, holding back the sobs of fear and memories that suddenly filled her head.

Her thoughts jumped to her coffee cup. She should have brought it with her. She always drank coffee as she read in bed, and the cup still sat on the bedside table. The home invaders would surely feel the warmth of it and know that someone had just been there. She could bet they had discovered it by now and were looking for her.

It was quiet again. No movement going on. They were listening for her purring, she just knew it.

How she wished that the outside staircase leading from her bedroom veranda to the patio below was usable. The age-old wooden stairway had rotted and fallen away, and was in the process of being rebuilt. She'd hired a contractor to design a more secure winding staircase with stone steps, but he hadn't begun the project yet. So there was no way she could have escaped from the second floor of the mansion while someone was on the first floor.

There was only one curved stairway, indoors, leading down from the catwalk that circled the second floor perimeter above the foyer. Other corridors branched off from it to all the second floor rooms. The stairs leading up to the third floor weren't safe either. They needed to be repaired, so hiding up there was out of the question.

Downstairs, off the entry, were the library, an office, and a reception room next to a spacious sitting room. A formal dining room was straight across the foyer under Allegra's bedroom leading to a family room and a kitchen towards the sunroom and indoor pool. Beyond that were the gardens and outdoor pool that were the determining features in buying the Malibu house. They were the deal clinchers for Allegra.

She wondered how many burglars there were, and whether or not they were male or female.

Burglars are usually male, she thought as her breath quickened.

The thought of a home invasion had always terrified her. ADT was scheduled to install a more effective and extensive alarm system the following Friday, but that was a week away. The burglars must've been able to disarm the existing one, it was so outdated. Her mind was racing. She knew she had locked the doors and windows. She checked them before she went to bed. Yes, they must've disarmed the security system.

The problem was she'd left her cell phone recharging downstairs on the kitchen counter, a big mistake. She hadn't thought to try the house phone in her bedroom. There wasn't one in the guest room, but it didn't matter. She figured they would have cut the lines before entering. Professional burglars would have done that.

Now she could hear movement again, more doors opening and closing.

Oh, how she wished she'd listened to her big brother! Arlie had been nagging her over the phone just that week to buy a gun, but she couldn't bring herself to do it. Now she was thinking that she should have listened to him. She'd sure as hell feel much safer if she were lying there pointing a loaded revolver up at the bastard prick when he found her. If she survived, she was going to buy a gun.

Three houses had been broken into on Hollingsworth Drive during the past month in the upscale gated community of Malibu Colony where she lived, which was why her brother had begged her to buy a gun. Burglars were drawn to the area for the valuable pickings. Supposedly security was patrolling more than usual, but obviously not, for they hadn't prevented this break-in.

Someone opened the guestroom door slowly and switched on the light.

Oh God, please don't let this happen to me!

Tears filled her eyes again as she blinked hard and fast to clear her vision and block out the thoughts of her mother trying to thwart the advances of her own killer just two years before.

Now she could see a man's shoes through a space between the hanging folds of the rug and the wooden floor. They didn't look like the shoes of a low-life crook. They were shiny dress blacks, patent leather, like those worn with a tuxedo. In fact, there appeared to be a satin stripe on the side of the pants leading up from the man's ankles, same as on a pair of tuxedo slacks.

He's wearing a tuxedo?

She pressed her body back against the wall, making sure there was plenty of space between her and the front of the bench. Allegra silently thanked her mother for passing on her small genes to her. She had been 4'11" and weighed 98 pounds – same as Allegra.

God, why didn't I listen to Arlie and buy a gun?

The McAdams family had always been a gun family, so it wasn't like she didn't know how to use one. She'd handled guns since she was a preteen when she was living at home on the ranch in Montana. She and her brothers had been taught by their father how to shoot when they could barely hold a gun up to aim. Allegra was a crack shot and usually won first place, if not second, in shooting competitions with her brothers and friends in those days. But ever since her mother had been brutally beaten, raped, and shot to death

6

with her own gun, Allegra didn't want a firearm near her. She felt if the gun hadn't been in the house that night, her mother might still be alive.

"Allegra, are you in here? Allegra?"

Her heart stopped. "Connie? she squeaked, but didn't move. Her body was still stiff with fright.

Connie moved towards the small voice and bent down to lift the edge of the Persian carpet. "Yes, it's me, darling. Here, let me help you out of there." He lifted the heavy ornate bench as if it was made of balsa wood and set it behind him.

"I was leaving the Hildreths' anniversary party, saw your light upstairs, and then noticed that your front door was standing wide open. Are you all right?" He helped her to her feet.

Allegra wiped the tears from her eyes as she stared up at the tall, handsome Englishman. She clung to him and sobbed, "I was so afraid, Connie. I didn't know who was in the house. Did you see them? I was afraid they were going to come up here and find me. It was awful! All I could think of was my mother. I was afraid they were going to kill me, too."

"Someone was downstairs before I came in, darling. They must have heard me come up the walk because the French doors in the office were wide open. They must have gone out that way. Saw no sign of anyone, but could hear them running down the driveway. I called the police on my cell as soon as I saw the damage downstairs."

Allegra was listening, but couldn't speak. Her face was burrowed into the ruffles of Connie's silk shirt.

With his arm still holding her close, Connie pulled his cell phone from his inside jacket pocket and punched a number with the thumb of the same hand. "Gladys? Yes. I'm at Allegra's. Will you please send Trudy and Carl over to spend the night with her? Someone has broken into her house. Yes, tell Carl to arm himself. The police are on the way, yes. Thanks. Are Eric's rooms ready? Good. I'll be home soon."

"I don't need any babysitters," Allegra sniffled. "I'll be alright."

"But it'll make me feel better," Connie insisted. "I need to make another call, do you mind?"

"No, go ahead." Allegra reluctantly released her grip on Connie. She went to the stairway landing and flipped the switch, lighting the four chandeliers hanging over the foyer. She could see that a rare Ming Dynasty vase, usually atop a pedestal, was now shattered to smithereens on the marble tiles - the crashing sound she had heard. She could see strewn papers and books on the carpet just inside the library. She sighed heavily and looked back into the room where Connie was still talking on the phone.

Allegra had had a secret crush on Connie ever since she moved into the neighborhood and met him at her first Home Owners' Association meeting. He had greeted her at the meeting that welcomed new residents to the community. She melted at the sight of him and even more so when he took her hand and held it for what seemed like forever but not long enough. She wished it was forever. But he was at least twenty-five years older than her, and besides, she was sure she wasn't his type. She didn't feel sophisticated or fashionable enough for him. She was just an inexperienced girl from a ranch in Montana, had never had a serious relationship, while he had his choice of all the beautiful women in the world, according to the tabloids.

She fantasized about him anyway, she even wrote a character based on him in one of her film scripts. He either didn't see the movie or didn't connect with who it was. She never mentioned it, and neither did he.

Usually she would go to the parties thrown by her neighbors on Hollingsworth Drive, hoping he'd be there, and he usually was if he was in town. But she hadn't gone to the Hildreths' party that night.

Hollingsworth was a community made up of quite an assortment of residents. There was a top model, two lesbian movie starlets who had bought a house together, a famous comedian turned dramatic actor, several film and television producers, two writers other than herself, an Academy Award actor, a jewelry store family, a clothing designer, and a successful building contractor. And then there was Connie Brown, a philanthropist from Britain.

"Come," Connie said as he put his cell phone away, "Let's go downstairs and wait for the police. I'll pour us both a glass of Scotch, if you don't mind."

Allegra nodded. "Sounds good to me. I'm still a bit shaky."

He took her hand and put his other arm around her as they went down the stairs into the library that housed an elaborate bar.

"How did you know I was in that guest room?"

"I didn't. But the only doors that were open were the doors from the room next to your bedroom and that guest room. I thought that if you had fled, possibly you were in the room where the other door was ajar. Just a lucky guess." He reached for a bottle of Scotch. "But I checked all the rooms, anyway. As I recall, this is your favorite single malt?"

She was surprised he knew. "Yes, it is. How did you know that?"

"I've been to enough parties in the Colony with you present to see what you drink. Last one was at our 'girls' engagement party." He grinned and winked at her. "Nice party. I've never seen so many women. The men were outnumbered ten to one."

Allegra laughed. "Well, that's what happens when two women become engaged. They invite all their female friends. Were you uncomfortable?"

"Not in the least. I adore Millie and Julie. Did it bother you?"

"No, of course not. My youngest brother is gay. Doesn't bother me at all."

"Here you go, darling." He handed her an old-fashioned crystal glass half full of the golden liquid.

"Thank you, I really do need this."

"I thought you might." He lifted his glass to hers and said, "To finding the bloody culprits and locking them up forever."

"Hear, hear!" she responded and took a big gulp of the drink. "Okay, I think I'll sit down now. My legs are feeling a bit wobbly."

"What am I thinking? Of course you're wobbly. Come," he said as he set his glass on a cocktail table in front of the leather sofa and then guided her carefully to the seat. "There you are. Now what's this about your mother being killed?"

She told him that her mother's murder had never been solved. It hadn't been a burglary; nothing was taken from the ranch house. She said her father had died three years before that, so her mother had been running the ranch with the help of Allegra's oldest brother, Arlie, and the ranch hands. Her youngest brother had been living in New York City since before her father died, so he hadn't been there when his mother was killed. Allan and his father didn't get along once Allan's effeminate ways and his homosexual tendencies became more obvious. So he took off to New York to find himself.

She told Connie that Arlie had been pleading with her not to send Allan any more money for he'd already gone through his trust fund. Allan had been more of a mama's boy, not a daddy's boy like Arlie, and had always felt like a misplaced member of the McAdams family. He had artistic abilities, but hadn't quite found his niche in New York City, so he partied instead, ran with the jetsetters, traveled all over the world, and eventually lost most of his money in one quick money-making scheme after another.

Suddenly she realized how she'd been rambling on, spilling her guts about everything. It embarrassed her. "I'm sorry. You don't want to hear all this. Sorry." She stood up to freshen her drink.

"Oh, damn, the siren. They're here." Connie stood. "I'll meet them at the door. Just relax, take a deep breath and collect your thoughts. They'll want to question you." He left the room before she could say anything else.

As he waited outside the open front door, Connie could still feel Allegra's tiny, curvy body pressed against his. He had trained his thoughts on something else so she wouldn't know how she'd aroused him. He had wanted to hold her close ever since he first met her. And more still, he had wanted to kiss her. She was like a little dream angel to him, someone unaffected by the crassness and brashness of the Hollywood scene. How she managed to stay apart from it all, he didn't know.

Even at the gatherings and parties on Hollingsworth—and he went to as many as he could in hopes of running into her—she never clung to or climbed all over the studio execs, producers, and directors like the others. She never pitched her scripts at parties like the others either; she never asked for favors. She was cordial and behaved like a well-put-together young lady. If only she weren't so young and innocent. He knew she would never be interested in anyone his age, and surely not him. She didn't even need his money, so he couldn't win her over that way. How he wished it were different. She was about the same age as his son Eric, he figured.

His thoughts switched to his son. He was arriving tomorrow afternoon from England where he'd lived for the past eight years with his grandmother. Eric had telephoned the week before. It was the first time in four years Connie had heard from his son, although Eric's grandmother gave Connie monthly reports. Eric had been a problem child.

Connie took a deep breath of the cool night air and faced the policemen coming up the walk. "Right this way, gentlemen. She's in the library."

Chapter 2

Allegra McAdams had moved to southern California when she entered USC Film School. That was ten years ago. Her first two screenplays became successful films and she bought a modest home near Wilshire Boulevard where she lived for several years before finding and falling in love with her present abode - an estate that had once belonged to the silent film star Marla Scott. Marla wasn't as famous as Greta Garbo and Gloria Swanson, but she had married a prominent film producer and they had built one of the most luxurious mansions on Hollingsworth Drive in the '30s. Although it was smaller than the mansions that came along later, it was in the heart of exclusive notable residences. Allegra was lucky, buying it at auction for a little over four million.

Living in La La Land was a far cry from growing up on a cattle spread in northwest Montana, but it suited her. Although she loved California, she missed the ranch, missed the simple life and realness of it, and she was always happy to take a few weeks off and go home in between manuscripts. In fact, she was wishing she was in Kalispell at that very moment as she lay awake in the dark.

"Good morning, Miss Allegra," Trudy said as she came through the door and opened the draperies to let in the bright sunlight. "How you feeling?"

"I'm a bit weary, but other than that, I'm feeling good. And you? Are you and Carl comfy in your rooms?"

"Oh yes. Thank you, Miss Allegra." Trudy grinned widely, secretly knowing that they shared the same room instead of using both of them. "You have a beautiful home here, Miss Allegra," she said as she continued opening the draperies on all the windows. "It's a lovely spring day, ma'am. Birds are a chirpin' at the top of their lungs. Can I do somethin' else for you, ma'am?" She stood and waited for an answer.

Allegra threw back the covers and stood on the fluffy Flokati rug next to her bed and stretched. "What I need now is a good cup of coffee. Would you have one with me, Trudy?"

"Oh, Carl and me have had ours already, Miss. And I don't drink more than one every mornin'. Why, I'd be spinnin' on my head if I did. It gets me all worked up. But we made a fresh pot of coffee for you as well as your breakfast. I hope you like biscuits. You want me to bring it up here, or wait till you're dressed and come downstairs?"

"You didn't have to make breakfast. I usually just have coffee in the mornings. And I'm not used to being waited on. I do it all myself. I only have a housekeeper who comes in twice a week."

"You livin' in this big ol' house by yourself, and no one to help you? Well, then, I'm glad we did it for you, Miss Allegra. Why don't you have servants, ma'am? In this big house, I would think you would need them. My sister Callie is available; I know you'd love her. She's no bigger than a minute, like you. She just moved here from New Orleans. All my family is here in California now. We all lost our places during Katrina and most of us still are flounderin'. Where do you keep your linens, Miss? I'll change your bed and do your laundry while I'm at it."

"Oh no, please. You don't have to do that. The housekeeper does it when she comes. Really, now. And tell me some more about your sister Callie, I may take you up on that offer. But first, let me get dressed. I'll meet you down in the kitchen. You can tell me down there. Okay?"

"Alright, Miss. Is there anything else I can do for you before I go back downstairs? Do you need help dressin'?"

Allegra was overcome with the old-fashioned politeness and sweetness of the young black girl standing before her. She felt like Scarlet O'Hara in *Gone with the Wind*, felt the charm of the old South through Trudy's genuine kindness. "That'll be all, Trudy. Thank you."

Trudy actually curtsied and backed through the doorway. It was all Allegra could take. She felt transported to a different time and era. She giggled in spite of what all had transpired the night before and the memories that had been conjured up in her usual nightmares.

Her cell phone rang.

"Hello?"

"Good morning, Allegra."

"Connie! How are you this beautiful morning? Did you get any sleep at all?"

"Not much, but I don't need much sleep. How about you?"

"I did sleep some, yes. And I must say, you have quite a jewel in Trudy."

"I thought you'd like her. Keep her for a few days. I've a house full of servants at the moment, since my son is arriving today."

"Oh no, I wouldn't dream of it. She told me about her sister Callie. I may hire her. She needs work."

"Oh yes, you'll love Callie. She's worked a few of my parties. Yes, she's a good choice. And I'm sure if you need more staff, Trudy can supply them. Her whole family is in L.A. now."

"Yes, she told me. Hurricane Katrina."

"Unfortunate tragedy. So, have the police come back this morning? They said they would."

"I don't know. I just got up and am going downstairs now."

"Well, let me know if you need me. Even though my son will be arriving, I'm sure he'll be off on his own. Pretty independent, you see. By the way, I'm having a little get-together for him, welcoming him back, inviting a few of his old friends and some of the neighbors. Another excuse for a party. Will you come Friday night at eight?"

14

"I'd love to. Will it be formal or casual?"

"Casual."

"I'll be there."

"Wonderful! I'll see you then, unless you need me in the meantime. You have my cell number. Have you called the security company number I gave you?"

"Not yet, but I will."

"Would you like me to call them?" he asked.

"No, I can do it."

"Well, if you decide you want me to do it, call me."

Allegra sighed. "Alright, I will, and I'll call you if the police want to talk to you."

"Okay, bye now."

"Bye." She closed her eyes and held the phone to her ear for a few moments even after he hung up. His voice sounded sexy over the phone.

After breakfast with Trudy and Carl, for Allegra insisted they sit down and eat with her, Allegra took her laptop to the patio by the outside pool and began writing her new screenplay. Just the day before she'd decided to take some time off before starting the next one, she had been thinking of going to Montana for a month. But all that had changed now. She was inspired. She wasn't going anywhere. Plus she wanted to finish remodeling the house, along with being suddenly drawn closer to Connie. Both reasons were enough to keep her in Malibu.

She leaned back in the cushioned wicker chair and took a deep breath, the fragrance of climbing wisteria, lilac and roses wafting on the breeze. Carl had cut fresh roses and put them in a glass vase on the table beside her while she was writing. She hadn't seen him on the patio at all; he just suddenly appeared with the bouquet and set them on the table. Trudy followed with a fresh pot of coffee. They were spoiling her in the short time they'd been there. She loved their company.

15

Her mind was forming a plot, this time a departure from the previous detective stories. She wanted to write a love story - a simple love story. Maybe a period piece. She loved British history. Maybe something to do with early British history. But then again, maybe not. Her thoughts shifted to Connie Brown. He was British, although it was difficult to place the accent. His was more of a worldly accent, didn't sound pure British.

"Miss Allegra," Trudy interrupted. "The po-leece are here to talk to you. You want them to come out here?"

"I'll come in." She set the computer on the table and followed Trudy into the house.

Detective Worthy greeted Allegra with a hand shake and a bright grin. He introduced himself and his partner, Detective Johnson. Both were young, in their thirties most likely, as far as Allegra could tell. *Probably early thirties,* she thought as she showed them the damage in the library.

"Is there anything missing? Or is it hard to tell in this mess?" Detective Worthy shook his head as he took in the room of chaos.

"Well, my neighbor and I both agreed that they were definitely looking for something. I don't think they were vandals, and as far as I can see, nothing of any value is missing. They didn't find the safe. Maybe that's what they were looking for. They certainly cleared the bookshelves, though, didn't they? The antique vase in the foyer was broken to bits, but that's about all the major damage. Can we start putting the books back on the shelves?"

Detective Worthy reached down and picked up a leather-bound book with gold inscription. "You've quite a collection here."

"Yes, most of them belonged to the previous owners. I bought the house with the library intact. Strange, but then I guess the heirs to the decedents didn't want to bother with the books. Some of them must be valuable; there are some signed copies and first editions in the lot. Do you think the burglars might have been after one of the books since they didn't go into any other part of the house?"

"Could be. But I'm more inclined to think they were looking for a safe. That's how it's been happening in the other homes that have been burglarized in this area. They're after money or jewelry. They don't even bother with electronics."

"I'm glad I had the safe moved, then. They would have never found it. But I wonder what made them think it was in the library."

"The best part is that you were smart enough to get out of harm's way."

"True, and I'm going to buy a gun now. I think I need one to protect myself, just in case. I've been foolish in not doing it already. My mother was murdered in Montana with her own gun two years ago and ever since then I've been afraid to have one around. But it's time."

"I don't know that that would be the best thing to do, Miss. Do you know how to handle one?"

"Hell, yes! I'm a crack shot and I've won shooting contests up in Montana and all over the northwest. I'm a ranch girl; I was raised holding a gun, owned my first one when I was nine. In fact I used to do trick shooting. Would stand on a galloping horse and shoot at moving targets. So you don't have to worry about me. I can hold my own with the best of them."

Both detectives raised their eyebrows and glanced at each other as she was talking.

"In fact, my dad's collection of guns fills a room the size of this library. I should have some of them shipped down here. I just might do that. My brother Arlie doesn't need them. He has his own collection. Yes, that's what I'll do." She smiled mischievously and added, "I could display them in my bedroom and the parlor next to it."

"Well, that ought to hold the burglars at bay, not to mention the suitors," Detective Johnson said through a wide grin.

They laughed.

Chapter 3

Allegra couldn't decide what to wear to Connie's party. She'd been trying on outfits for an hour and still hadn't found the right one.

"How about this one, Miss Allegra?" Trudy was holding up a short rust-colored silk dress that was almost the same color as Allegra's long wavy hair. "This is your color, you know. And I saw some shoes in there that match this dress."

It was Trudy's last day at Allegra's. Her sister Callie was arriving in two days as well as their cousin Ben. Both were going to live with Allegra and 'take care of her', as Trudy had said. She told Allegra that Ben was a big man, 45 years old, and he could help with the remodel of the house and do some odd jobs that Allegra wanted done. So with Callie and Ben and the housekeeper Esther and the two gardeners, Carlos Ramirez and his brother Juan, it was becoming quite the little ethnic community.

"Yes, I like that dress. I keep forgetting about it. It's casual enough, a shirt dress. Okay. Perfect. Thanks, Trudy."

"Don't mention it. You gonna wear your hair down or up in a ponytail like usual?"

"Down, I think. Makes me look more mature, don't you think?"

"Ha! That's funny. Most women want to look younger. Why is it you wantin' to look older? Why is that, Miss Allegra?" She cocked her head and grinned mischievously. She had seen the way Allegra had been looking at Connie Brown when he came over and helped put the books back on the shelves in the library. Trudy saw a bit of chemistry between them. But her boss made a quick exit after the job was done, maybe too quickly, even though Allegra had invited him to stay for dinner. His excuse was that he needed to get home and discuss something with his son. Poor excuse, in Trudy's estimation. His son wasn't worth the trouble. Eric was disrespectful of his father and didn't show any appreciation to anyone. She'd be glad when he went back to England.

"Is Eric like his father?" Allegra pulled the dress over her head instead of unbuttoning it. She fastened the belt.

"No ma'am! He ain't like his daddy at all."

"How old is he?"

"About your age, I guess. You better watch out for him, Miss Allegra. There's something wrong about him that gives me the willies. A look in his eyes, you know? Something's just not right with him. My Carl says the same thing."

"What do you mean, exactly?" She sat at the dressing table and brushed her hair.

"Well, I can't put my finger on it. His daddy bends over backwards for him, gives him everything he wants, but Eric doesn't show no appreciation. He's rude and ungrateful, talks about his daddy behind his back, making snide remarks. It just ain't right. And he lives over there in England with his grandma, doin' nothin'. Hasn't worked a day in his life. Sends invoices to his daddy for his living expenses. Can you imagine that? And his grandma ain't much better. She gives him all the money he wants, too. They've spoiled that brat, yes they have."

Allegra chuckled at Trudy's seriousness. "Well, you know how it is with the wealthy. They just hand everything to their kids not realizing how important it is for them to learn how to make their own living. My father didn't do that with the three of us. He tried to teach

19

us the value of a dollar. We all had to work for our allowances growing up.

"Of course my brother Arlie has always been pegged to run the ranch. It's always been his. But my other brother, Allen, poor Allan, he couldn't find his way, wasn't cut out for the ranch. Then when he left, he ran through his trust fund in no time flat. He lives in New York. The last time I sent him money, Arlie jumped all over me. But I couldn't let him just die on the vine, you know? He's my baby brother. Maybe that's how Connie and his mother feel about Eric. Maybe Eric just doesn't know how to take care of himself, like Allan. It's a hard call sometimes."

Trudy nodded. "I suppose you're right, Miss Allegra, but I jes don't understand people like that. We all have to work for a living. I always have. Even if I had lots of money, I'd still work," she said as she brought the matching patent leather shoes to Allegra. "Here you go."

"I'm going to miss you, Trudy."

"You'll like Callie, you will. She's jes like me, only a younger version, and half my size. She wears her hair in braids all over, with beads. And I know you'll like Ben. He's our favorite cousin. Maybe a little simple-minded, but he's fearless and good with his hands and is loyal. You'll be happy with them both, Miss."

"I'm sure I will be."

"And you know, I was thinkin', if you might one day want to get a different housekeeper, one that lives in, my auntie Talutha is the 'crème' of the crop. She cleaned houses for some of the richest people in New Orleans and she's here too, looking for work. She lived at a famous doctor's house for seven years before Katrina came. She could come to work for you on a moment's notice; I'd make sure of that."

"You mean she'd live in?"

"Yes, ma'am. She'd need to live in. She'd work for her board and keep. She doesn't ask for much."

"Well, I'd give her a wage, too. I wouldn't ask anyone to work for nothing. I'll think about it, Trudy. It would be nice to have someone here all the time. Does she cook?"

"Oh my goodness, does she ever cook! She is the best cook in our family. She even learned how to do the gourmet cookin' when she was at the doctor's. They paid for her classes."

"No kidding? That settles it then. Tell her she can start in two weeks. I'll have to give Esther two weeks' notice. Okay? Actually Esther isn't all that much of a good housekeeper, so this will work out great. And Callie can help her."

"Oh, Miss Allegra, that makes me so happy. You don't have any idea how happy. Between you and Mister Connie, I'm gettin' all my family placed. He's been helping me get them here from Louisiana and has been paying for them all a place to stay until I can find 'em jobs. Some of his friends have hired some, too. I'm so happy I could cry." She wiped her eyes with the hem of her apron.

"Oh no, don't cry, Trudy. You'll make me do it and then my mascara will run."

They both laughed through their tears.

Chapter 4

What Allegra thought was going to be a small gathering of Eric's friends turned out to be a gala. There had to be at least 300 guests in Connie's ballroom, and Allegra discovered that the Brown mansion was more than a mansion.

It was a palatial estate that stretched unendingly, it seemed. She couldn't believe the size of it. She'd seen the columned entry and the front of the house set back from the gate on Hollingsworth Drive every time she drove by, but she had no idea that the structure was U-shaped, extending farther back on the property on two sides, four stories on all three sides, surrounding gardens fit to be included among the grandest in the world.

It certainly had to be the grandest in southern California, a best-kept secret for sure. Allegra had seen nothing like it. The gardens were superb. She loved gardens, got that from the genteel side of her family: her mother's.

As soon as she arrived, Connie gave her a tour. After an hour of him telling her its history and pointing out important works of art, she was overwhelmed and suggested he get back to his guests, said she didn't want to monopolize his time, said she'd roam on her own and would meet him back in the ballroom. She was actually tired of hearing about it, too much information to absorb all at once.

So he excused himself and she continued on the journey through the Brown Palace, as she silently dubbed it.

I have never seen anything like this in my life! She looked up at the massive portraits of what had to be Connie's British ancestors lining the staircase. *So many of them. The frames alone have to be worth a fortune.*

"So, what do you think of our little family?"

Allegra turned to the voice and was almost nose to nose with Eric, who was standing very close, two steps below her. She was surprised at how handsome he was. Trudy had neglected to tell her that. He didn't look like his father. His hair was blond, not black like Connie's, and his eyes were blue-gray, not cobalt. "Oh, you startled me!"

"Sorry. That one is my great grandmother on Connie's side, Lady Arlington. She was a grand old Dame."

"So you knew her?"

"Yes, for a short time. She died when I was seven. But I remember her. And I've heard Connie and his mother tell the tales." His broad grin revealed perfect white teeth and dimples in each cheek. His father didn't have dimples in his cheeks, but had one in the middle of his chin; a Cary Grant cleft.

"I think it's wonderful to have such a display of ancestors. It pays homage to them, actually. It's respectful. Not many people in America do that, you know. We have photos of our grandparents in frames in Montana, but not paintings, and maybe some of our great grandparents, but not as far back as these go. It's fabulous!"

Eric shrugged. "I find it rather boring. So, I understand you live on Hollingsworth Drive too?" He joined her on the step where she was standing and leaned against the wall, perusing her from head to toe.

Moving back to the outside railing, Eric was crowding her, she answered, "Yes, just up the street. But not in a palace like this. Mine is much, much smaller, was built in the '20s."

"I'd love to see it. These twenties and thirties mansions intrigue me."

"Sure. I mean— well, maybe you and your dad would like to come to lunch tomorrow, or one day next week. I'll ask him."

"You'll ask me what, my dear?" Connie reached for Allegra's hand and led her to the bottom of the staircase, away from Eric.

"Eric asked to see my house. Would the two of you like to come to lunch tomorrow or Sunday?"

Eric frowned. "No. I'm meeting up with some friends for the weekend." He turned and walked past them down the stairs towards the bar.

Allegra was puzzled at his sudden departure. "Did I say something—"

Connie smiled and shook his head. "That's just Eric. I think he wanted you all to himself. Sorry I interrupted."

Allegra smiled back. "I'm not sorry."

Their eyes met and held for a brief moment and then they moved, arm in arm, toward the ballroom.

Chapter 5

Allegra was dead on her feet. When her cheek hit the pillow she was nearly asleep already. As she lay there, she thought back over the events of the evening. She thought of Connie, his touch. She thought of his son Eric, who was a bit strange and scary.

Eric had come on to her very strongly as the party began to wind down and the guests were leaving. He insisted on walking her home, being very pushy, but Connie stepped in and took her arm. As they headed down the driveway, she had felt Eric's glare from the portico.

Now she was grateful Eric had said he'd be busy over the weekend and couldn't come to lunch, for she didn't think she could bear to be around him any more than she had to be. She felt sorry for Connie. His only son was downright rude. It was just as Trudy had said. He was a spoiled brat.

After she turned over on her side and pulled the comforter up to her chin, she remembered she'd left her cell phone downstairs again, and she'd forgotten to turn on the new alarm system.

"Dammit!" She threw the covers back and snapped on the bedside lamp. "I'd forget my head if it weren't attached."

Now she was wide awake again and feeling hungry. She thought she might have a turkey sandwich and some carrot juice while she was in the kitchen. And some potato chips. Yes, that sounded yummy to her. Trudy and Carl had the weekend off, and Trudy had left her a note about the turkey and trimmings she'd left in the refrigerator for Allegra to munch on that weekend.

"Wha—?" Her heart stopped as she came face to face with Eric standing in the kitchen. Her adrenaline rushed as she backed up through the kitchen doorway into the hallway. The door leading out to the patio was standing wide open. "What are you doing in my house?"

"I thought I'd come give you a proper goodnight kiss since you were whisked away by my father before I had a chance to express my desire," Eric replied in a raspy, breathy voice. "Your back door wasn't locked."

The look on his face was odd to Allegra.

He reached for her and grabbed her shoulders before she could do or say anything.

"Stop it, Eric!" She tried to get away from him.

"Just be still, I won't hurt you. You know you're attracted to me. Just a simple kiss. What's it going to hurt?" He pulled her tightly to his body, pinning her arms to her sides, forcing her to look up at him.

She struggled to break his grip and dodged his face as he tried to kiss her. "Stop it, Eric! I mean it! Let go of me!"

But that was not Eric's intention, not at all. He was used to getting what he wanted. In the struggle his body was pressing and rubbing against hers. Her body felt good to him in her skimpy little nightgown. The moment he had seen her standing in the kitchen doorway, his determination had increased. He could see her naked body right through the thin fabric. Although it never had been necessary to see a nude body to provoke him, that wasn't what induced his actions. It was the thrill of control, of being able to dominate another person. Especially a woman.

"Eric! Don't!"

He held both her arms behind her with one hand clutching her wrists. He fondled her breasts with his other hand while enjoying the fear in her eyes.

She spat in his face. "Your father will kill you for this!"

"My father will never know. You're not going to tell him. If you do, you'll end up like your mother."

A jolt shot through her brain. "How do you know about my mother?"

"Connie told me." He turned her and shoved her towards the stairs, still holding her wrists. "Go upstairs!"

She tripped on one of the stairs and almost took them both down, but Eric caught himself and grabbed her as she scrambled to get out of his reach. She fought him all the way up the stairs, cursing and yelling, but there was no way anyone but the two of them could hear her.

Once in the bedroom, Eric rummaged in a dresser drawer for something to tie her hands behind her back. He found a silk scarf and wound it around her wrists, securing them with a double knot.

"Now the fun begins," he said through a wild and slobbery grin.

"Are you crazy?" Allegra screamed at him. "What's the matter with you?"

Without saying another word he pushed her, face down, onto the bed, holding her down with one hand as he unzipped his pants.

"Stop it!" She screamed and kicked back at him, humiliation and terror ripping through her body.

He roughly spread her legs with his.

"Stop it, Eric! Stop it!"

Screams again. "No no! No, stop it! Help me, somebody! Help!"

More screams.

He repeatedly forced entry into her in spite of her body's resistance.

"You're hurting me! No! God, help me! Please stop . . ."

Her hoarse cries for help continued to resound through the high-ceilinged rooms of the 1920s mansion, but nobody heard.

The rape went on for over an hour. Eric used her to exhaustion—his and hers.

She had nothing left, no more resistance, no more sounds, no more tears.

He stood back for a moment to gaze at her lying unconscious on the urine, feces and blood-soaked bed, for he had left no orifice untouched. He was satisfied.

He untied her before he left.

Chapter 6

Allegra sat motionless in a tub of hot water for what seemed like hours after she finally forced herself from the bed and stumbled to the bathroom. When the water got cold, she let it drain out as she watched it spiral down the dark hole. Then she filled it up again with a new batch of hot water, watching the water gush from the faucet while still sitting numbly in the tub. She repeated the process over and over. Her mind was blank, her senses attuned only to the sound and sight of the water filling and draining the tub, filling and draining. She ignored the sick, searing, burning pain that spread through her lower extremities.

Empty the tub, fill the tub. Empty. Fill.

The sun was coming up. Pale light filtered through the blinds in the bedroom. She turned off the faucet and slid down until her head and face were under water, her eyes open, gazing up through the water at the blurry ceiling and crown molding. The water didn't sting her eyes; the only pain was still below her waist.

She wondered whether she should call a doctor or not. It didn't occur to her to call the police. She felt confused about what had happened to her. It felt surreal.

No, she wouldn't call the police, she couldn't tell anybody. How could she? Not because of what Eric said he'd do to her if she told, but because she couldn't hurt his father. Connie loved his son. It would kill him to know.

No, she wouldn't tell anybody. It was over, she had survived it, she was alive. But how could she ever look Connie in the eyes again? Would he be able to guess? No, Connie wouldn't in a million years believe his son was capable of anything so evil.

He is evil. He's evil! Her mind spun in circles, waves of terror hit her again.

She came up gasping for air and rested her head back against the oversized claw-footed tub.

As her head cleared, she felt as if she could stand up. She pulled the plug one more time. Maybe she should give herself a medicated douche. The pain was unbearable. Yes, that's what she'd do. She also had some leftover codeine and antibiotics from the treatment of an abscessed tooth a couple months before. She'd take those too. She could get through this by herself. She could.

She took the meds and drank coffee. She carried her coffee with her as she shuffled aimlessly from one room to the next, sometimes sitting and staring into space, sometimes standing and staring out a window. One minute she thought about calling the police, but the next minute she decided she couldn't. She didn't want Connie to know.

Every few minutes, anxiety flooded her, and she would whimper as the memories surfaced, happening all over again. Only for a moment, though, for she would shove them back down into that deep, dark place where painful memories are stored.

Suddenly a fear that Eric might come back threw her into a whole new set of terrors. She had to get out of there. It took all of her strength to hurriedly pick up the traces and residue of the assault. She rolled up the sheets and covers and put them in plastic bags to be disposed of.

Then she straightened her bedroom. She hadn't remembered so much being strewn about during the attack. Eric must have gone through her things after she passed out. Drawers were pulled out, cabinets opened, closet in disarray, as if he'd been looking for something. Not only was he a demonic sadist, he was a sociopath; a weird, strange lunatic. How could someone like Eric be spawned by Connie?

She felt like she needed to eat something, needed strength, so she went into the kitchen and quickly fried slices of wholegrain bread in a skillet of melted butter, just like her mother used to do for her when she was a child, comfort food. She needed to feel her mother's protective presence.

The coffee smelled good as the fresh pot brewed. She leaned against the kitchen counter, thinking of her mother while holding the plate of toast and watching the coffee dripping into the pot. She began to cry. She couldn't eat. She had to get out of there. The fear of Eric continued to increase. She would go to Montana immediately. She wasn't going to spend another night alone in the Malibu house.

She forced herself to eat a few bites of the toast, then she put the plastic bags of bed linens and her ripped clothing into the trash bins outside. She got dressed, packed a small bag, called the airline and then dialed Connie's cell number while waiting for the taxi.

"Hi Connie. Allegra. Good morning." It took all the strength she could muster to sound normal. "Yes, thank you. Uh, just wanted to tell you I'm leaving for Montana right away. Something's come up and . . . and I'm leaving. Yes, it is sudden. I know, but I must go. No, I've already called a cab. Would you please tell Trudy and Carl? And tell her that when Callie and Ben come tomorrow, to go ahead and show them the ropes. She has the key. She knows where they're to stay. And Talutha too. Yes, all three of them. Thank you. Well, I've got to go. No, I'm fine. Really. Yes, of course. And thank you, again, Connie. For all you've done for me. Okay? Got to go. Bye."

She hung up quickly, fell to the floor and wept.

Chapter 7

Allegra looked at her watch. She was surprised that her brother Arlie wasn't waiting to pick her up at the Kalispell airport. She stood on the curb outside the terminal and pulled her cell phone from her purse.

"You need a cab, ma'am?" An aged driver wearing a cowboy hat and what looked like new boots grinned widely, showing a perfectly formed set of false teeth, uppers and lowers. He had one of those square Randolph Scott chins, thin lips, straight nose, squinty eyes.

She had to control her reaction to him. He was comical with his clacking teeth, hat and boots. "No, I'm fine. My brother is on his way. Thanks."

"If he doesn't show up, well, I'm parked right over yonder, ma'am. Sometimes you can't depend on family much. So just wave your hand at me and I'll take you wherever you want. The name's Monty."

"Thanks, Monty, I'll do that." She dialed Arlie's cell number. It had been a long time since she'd felt the down-home naturalness and ease of the people in Montana, a far cry from those in California. "Hey, Arlie, where are you? I'm here. Yes, I've been waiting outside the terminal. About twenty minutes. No, don't worry about it. I'm fine. Okay, see you in a few."

She turned and went back into the terminal, carrying the small gym bag she had packed with her laptop and necessities. She still maintained a stash of clothing and personal effects at the ranch, which made it easy to travel back and forth, although she hadn't been doing much of it lately.

Arlie said he was running late because of a crisis, and would be there within the hour. He suggested she wait in the coffee shop and he'd meet her there.

As she entered the café, the counter person recognized her.

"Well if it ain't Leggie McAdams! How are you, honey?" A tall, well-endowed woman with bleached blonde hair bounced towards Allegra and gave her a welcome-home hug.

"It's so good to see your smiling face, Tammy Sue." Allegra let Tammy guide her to a booth near the counter and against the window. The pain in her abdomen had started up again. She reached for the Aleve in her purse.

"Honey, you're a sight for sore eyes. How long has it been now? A couple of years?"

"Seems longer. How about a nice cup of your fabulous coffee, and a glass of water? I'm waiting on Arlie."

"You mean that handsome brother of yours is coming into town right now? Boy, howdy! This is my red letter day for sure. Both of you together again." She went to the coffee machine, talking a mile a minute, and poured a cup for Allegra. "You know, I've been wondering about you lately. Arlie talks about you all the time. And your brother Allan, is he alright? I heard he was back up here a couple weeks ago, but I didn't get to see him."

"He was here? Arlie didn't tell me."

"I don't think Arlie knew about it, honey. You know they aren't the best of friends." She set the cup of coffee and the water in front of Allegra. "Yep, he flew in on United, Sandy told me. And flew out again the next day. I figured he'd drop by for a cup, but he sure didn't. Strange visit, just one day, don't you think?"

Allegra nodded. "Very strange."

"Well, you just sip on your coffee, got some more customers to take care of. You want something to eat?"

"No, I'm fine. Thanks, Tammy Sue."

"Oh, don't you mention it. It's always good to see you, hon." Tammy went back to the counter and greeted a newcomer to the café. She glanced back at Allegra, feeling that something wasn't right.

Allegra frowned as she took the painkillers and wondered why Allan had come to Montana just for one day. *Had to be for money*, she thought as she sipped the coffee. She decided to call him from the ranch the next day to find out.

Her thoughts involuntarily jumped to the night before. It didn't seem like it was only a few hours ago that Eric had raped her. She cringed at the memory and tears filled her eyes. She quickly wiped them away, along with the thoughts.

The first thing she was going to do was go to the family doctor and make sure she was physically all right. She wondered how she could make Eric pay for what he did to her without Connie finding out what a demon he'd spawned.

It wasn't like Allegra to be a victim. She was always the aggressor, albeit subtle, especially in the business world. She'd always been strong, regardless of her size, and nobody would think of attacking her like Eric had. It must have been because of the break-in. Maybe she'd exuded vulnerability that had never been there before. Maybe the recent memories of her mother's murder and her own paranoia had weakened her in the sight of others. For some reason she'd been feeling as if someone was out to kill her, too.

There had been a few other instances that hadn't made any sense at all. But then again, maybe it was coincidence, maybe it was all about Eric. Yes, that had to be it. She needn't feel paranoid. Anyway, she would talk to Arlie. Her big brother had always been able to help her through her worst fears and make it all better again. But she wasn't going to tell him about the rape. No, that was not going to happen. She was afraid of what he might do.

Arlie came bounding through the door. He was six-foot-five and muscular, with shoulder-length jet black hair flying back behind his ears. "Where's my pretty little sister, Tammy Sue?" He put his arm around Tammy Sue and kissed her on the cheek, then gave her a friendly peck on the lips. Of course he knew where Allegra was sitting. He'd seen her through the window before he came in and saw she was in deep thought. "There's the little darlin'. Come here, my little sweet pea!"

Allegra scooted from the booth, laughing, and was scooped up into Arlie's arms in the middle of the cafe.

He held her the way a groom would carry a bride across a threshold.

"Arlie! Put me down! You're embarrassing me," she said as she planted a kiss on his cheek.

"Ahhh, you're always complaining." He set her down on her feet. "You're getting smaller, aren't you? Or am I getting bigger?"

"I think you're getting bigger, especially around the middle."

"Well, come on then, let's go home. I've got lots to tell you. Where's your bag?"

"Right here. Just this one."

He slung it over his shoulder and took Allegra's hand. "Put the coffee on my tab, Tammy Sue. I'll call you about the barbecue."

"Coffee's on the house, don't worry about it," Tammy Sue replied jovially. "See ya."

They were out the door before he could reply.

During the 90-minute drive to the ranch, they talked about Arlie's new ideas about increasing the herds, and about Allegra's career and the burglary.

She didn't ask any questions about Allan's brief visit to the homestead. She decided this wasn't the time. She'd broach the subject at breakfast the next morning, but she was still doubtful about whether or not she would tell Arlie about the rape.

Once inside the ranch house, Allegra felt safe. She still couldn't go into her mother's bedroom, though. The door was shut as usual. Arlie had put up a brass plaque on the door saying *The Private Quarters of Our Dear Departed Mother. No Admittance.*

After the investigators had collected all the evidence in the suite of rooms that had belonged to Adele McAdams, it had been rearranged and preserved just as it had been when she had lived there. The housekeepers would go in periodically and clean and dust, sometimes open the windows and air out the rooms, but that was it. Everything was intact: memorabilia, clothing, jewelry, personal belongings. Nothing had been moved or removed.

"Your room is ready for you, little one. Go on upstairs, get settled in, and I'll meet you in the den after you freshen up. What's your poison? Still the same?"

"Yep, Scotch rocks."

"You got it, Miss Leggie."

They both went off in opposite directions: Arlie grinning, Allegra thinking about calling the doctor in Kalispell right away.

Chapter 8

Connie was puzzled about Allegra. He'd been around her more the week before she left than in all the time she'd lived in Malibu. A few weeks had passed and he was missing her dreadfully. They had been together parts of every day for one reason or another. He had helped her put all the books back on the shelves in her library, had taken her to lunch twice that week, and had sauntered over to her place a couple evenings and joined her for conversation over cocktails. And they were together again on that last night at the welcoming party for Eric. She'd been in Montana for nearly a month now, and he wondered when she was coming back. He decided to call her before his trip to Switzerland. Actually, he wanted to see her before he went.

Connie was glad Eric had returned to London. It had been harder to get along with him this time, more than ever before. Something was definitely wrong with the boy, Connie concluded. He wanted to get to the root of his son's tantrums and outbursts, but Eric wouldn't have anything to do with his suggestion about seeing a therapist. Each time he asked Eric what was bothering him, Eric would storm out of the house. The last time he stormed out, he left and telephoned from the airport, saying he was on his way back to London, and hung up on his dad. No explanation, no formal goodbye, nothing. Connie didn't understand his son at all. Never had.

Early on he thought maybe Eric hated him for divorcing his mother. Many times Connie had contemplated telling Eric that it was the other way around; his mother was the one who left. She ran away with one of her addict lovers. Connie took the blame, for he felt if he'd been at home more and paid more attention to Sally, maybe she would still be there. He'd loved her at one time; in fact was never with anyone else after they met and during their marriage. She was from a noble British family and had a promising career in fashion design. But soon after the marriage, when she got pregnant, everything came to the surface. As it turned out, Sally was an addict and bipolar, which had been kept from Connie. Her family knew all about it, but hadn't said anything to him. She cheated in their marriage, then deserted Connie and her five-year-old son. The real tragedy happened three years later when she died in a car crash. So Eric never knew the truth about her. Connie kept it from him all those years.

Originally Connie had sent Eric to his Brown Estate in England, the home of Connie's mother. But that didn't work out at all, so he sent Eric to live in London with Greta Moore, his maternal grandmother.

In the early days, Connie constantly traveled the world to take care of business, certainly not the best life for a young boy to be nurtured by strangers while his dad was away. But Connie had loved his son just the same. He felt guilty for missing all the important events in Eric's life, even though Grandmother Greta had been there for him. She loved Eric too. Connie was thinking maybe it was time to pay her a visit while he was in Europe. Maybe she could enlighten him about Eric's recent behavior. Yes, he'd do that when he finished business in Switzerland. He'd fly to London from Zurich before going to Australia and New Zealand.

But first he needed to go to Montana to see Allegra. And as luck would have it, he had a good excuse - a client in Missoula.

He dialed Allegra's cell phone number and waited.

"Hello?"

"Allegra, Connie here. How are you?"

"Oh my goodness! Connie! What a surprise! Is everything all right?"

"Everything's great here. Eric went back to London and I'm leaving for Switzerland. How about you? When are you coming home?"

Allegra was slow to answer because she wasn't sure what to say. She'd gone to the family doctor and had been treated for vaginal abrasions and bruising, making him promise to not report the rape, against his better judgment. She was beginning to feel normal again. The pain disappeared after three weeks, and now a month later, she had managed to accept what had happened to her. She was coping with the help of her therapist in Missoula, the same one that had worked with her after her mother died.

"Allegra? Are you there?"

"Oh, I'm sorry, Connie, I was distracted. So much is going on here at the ranch right now, so I'm not really sure when I'll be coming back to Malibu. Would you please ask Trudy to give me a call and let me know how my new house staff is getting along?"

"I can do better than that. I'll tell you myself, in person."

"In person?"

"I'm leaving for Zurich a week from Tuesday, and thought I'd leave a day or two early for a stop off in Missoula. I'd love to see your ranch, meet your brother. Is that possible?"

"Uh . . . well . . . I don't know— what am I saying, of course that's possible. But why would you want to go that much out of your way? We're all the way up in Montana. Why would you want to do that?"

"Actually I've a business associate in Missoula. So I thought I'd drop in on him to check things out. You know, it helps to appear in person and see for yourself when you're investing in someone's business."

"What is the business? Maybe I know who it is."

"I doubt it; he's new to the area. Anyway, what do you say to the weekend before? You needn't pick me up, I'll rent a car and after I've taken care of business I'll drive up to the ranch. I just need to know where it is."

"Okay. Do you have an email address, Connie? I can send you the directions."

"Yes. It's— "

"Wait a minute. Let me go to my desk." She hurried from the kitchen to her office. "Okay, what is it?"

"C L Brown at Onyx dot com."

"Got it. So what does the L stand for?'

"Langel. It's my mother's maiden name. Connie was my grandmother's name. I've been stuck with names belonging to women my entire life. At one time I thought about changing it, but figured what the hell." He laughed.

"Connie Langel is a good name. I'm glad you didn't change it."

"So are you all right, Allegra? It bothered me that you left so suddenly. Why was that?"

"I just needed to get up here and attend to some family business. So I'll be looking forward to seeing you next weekend?"

"It'll be early evening on Friday by the time I get to your ranch. Is that all right?"

"Absolutely. I'll send you an email with directions. See you then."

Chapter 9

Allegra was born in Eureka, Montana, where her mother and father had purchased a small ranch between there and Rexford. Both towns were less than ten miles of the Canadian border: Rexford on the Kootenai River in the timberlands; Eureka, five minutes from the border, on the Tobacco River surrounded by acres of State and Forest Service land. And both were known for unusual mild weather placing them in what was called the "Banana Belt" of Montana. The summer temperatures averaged in the eighties, the coldest weather being during the snowfalls of January or February.

Although the Eureka cabin she knew and loved so well and visited often was a thing of the past, Allegra still spent days at a time there when she could manage to hide away. It had been a favorite of her brother Allan too. He preferred to spend his nights at the Eureka place when he visited from New York, although there hadn't been many of those visits that Allegra knew of since their mother died.

Also the Eureka ranch was pretty isolated and quite a distance from everything, so usually Allegra stayed at the 150,000-acre Kalispell spread with her brother Arlie. It was closer to civilization and nearer Glacier Park International Airport. The actual town of Kalispell's population was 20,000, give or take. A small town by far, compared to L.A., but it was home to Allegra and her brothers.

Allegra's thoughts were interrupted by the sound of Arlie's heavy-booted footsteps on the wooden floor of the hallway outside the library doors.

He took after their dad, a big burly bear of a man. Father and son had been two peas in a pod, and Arlie always followed along behind their dad like a puppy. His death devastated Arlie, who was still recovering from it when their mother was killed. There seemed to be one tragedy after another in those few years. The year before their dad died, they had a hoof-and-mouth disease scare, as well as mad cow. Luckily they got through it all without losing their herd.

Bursting into the room, Arlie spoke loudly. "Leggie, I want you to come out of this room right now and go for a ride with me. You've had enough of this moping around, or whatever it is. It just ain't like you, baby. Now come on, go get your boots on and grab a hat and jacket. We're going out on Princess and Big Black. They need exercising."

He waited for an answer. None came. "C'mon now. I mean it." He reached for her arm and pulled her to her feet from the overstuffed chair she had been curled up in, covered with a blanket.

"Arlie, what are you doing?"

"Just what I said, we're going riding." He pulled her into the hallway. "Now go on, do what I said. I'll be waiting for you outside. Butch has saddled the horses for us. Skedaddle!" He slapped at her buttocks lovingly.

She shrugged and trudged up the stairs towards her room.

After twenty minutes in the saddle, Allegra was feeling the healing spirit of the wilderness. She hadn't realized how much she had missed the outdoors and the beauty of the foothills leading up into the pines. Acres upon acres of Christmas trees, she called them. They rode along the northern edge of Flathead Lake, which is a tad larger than Lake Tahoe. The McAdams Ranch extended north, east and west of the lake, across the valley and up into the Rocky Mountains.

"Leggie, what's bothering you? And don't say it's nothing, because I know better. You don't fool me at all."

Allegra thought for a moment as she rode along the lake's edge, staring straight ahead at the majestic mountains. "I can't tell you."

"Too late now. You know I'll drag it out of you, now that I know there is something going on in that pea brain of yours." Arlie pulled up to a stop and dismounted, leading the horse to the water's edge. "Come on down and let's have us a little heart to heart. That looks like the perfect boulder over there to sit for a spell, under that oak tree."

Allegra rode to the shaded boulder and dismounted. Her lower back, bottom, and abdomen were aching from riding astride the hard saddle, so she was glad to be able to get off and have a rest. She laid the reins loosely over a low branch and walked awkwardly to the boulder.

"All right now, out with it," Arlie said as he perched on the rock beside her.

She stared into his eyes for a moment, then lowered her gaze to her fidgeting hands lying in her lap. "I was attacked and raped the night before I came here, Arlie," she whispered, tears instantly filling her eyes.

Without hesitation, Arlie grabbed her and held her tight, his own tears following suit. "Baby, baby! No! Are you alright? Who was it? I'll kill the son of a bitch!"

"I—I don't know who it was, Arlie. He broke into my house the night before I came here, couldn't see him in the dark, and I'm sure he's long gone by now. I'll be all right, though. Doctor says I'm okay, just a few bruises, and I'm working on the emotional part of it. So don't worry. It's just a little hard for me right now, getting past it." Her voice quivered. "At least I'm alive."

"Did you call the police?"

She hesitated. "Yes, of course. They're . . . working on it."

"That does it. You're not going back to California to live in that dang house. You're staying home this time, Leggie. You're staying home with me so I can protect you. I mean it, no argument."

Allegra didn't say anything. Her mother hadn't been safe at the ranch. But what he said made sense to her. All she wanted was to

43

hide and do nothing. At the same time, she knew she'd have to go back eventually. Her work was in L.A.

On the ride back to the ranch house, Allegra asked Arlie about Allan's recent visit. He said he hadn't seen him and didn't know that he'd been in Montana, said he didn't call or come to the Kalispell ranch.

They both found that strange.

Chapter 10

Connie arrived at the Kalispell airport after a short flight from Helena, the capital of Montana. He'd taken care of some business in Helena the day before; his contacts from Missoula had met him at his hotel. He figured as long as he was in Montana, he might as well do some business, although that of course wasn't the primary reason for being there.

His first introduction to Montana came when he invested in a copper mine that belonged to his partner in a cattle ranch in the northeast region of the state, for he brokered stock from Scotland. In Connie's world, billionaires were the norm; they had their hands on everything. He hobnobbed and did business with the best of them. Especially those who owned land, and mined and cultivated creatures upon the land. Although his mining investments were global, he didn't focus on any particular mineral, for he was diversified in his choices. No one knew just how much he was worth, but the guesstimates were that, if the truth be known, he was right up there with Bill Gates, Warren Buffett, and the rising Mexican star Carlos Slim Helu - the three richest men in the world that year.

Connie didn't flaunt his wealth, although his Malibu palace was a blatant clue, but in general he was a very private person. The tabloids were always digging and would fabricate as many stories as they could when they were lucky enough to catch up with him in his travels and at charity events, always with a beautiful woman at his side. But generalities were all he allowed to be revealed. The personal intricacies of his life were pretty well guarded and secret.

He wasn't quite sure what was going on in his mind at the moment regarding his sudden bold need to seek out Allegra in Montana. He wasn't sure why he was pursuing her, for if that was indeed the case, it would be to no avail. He knew that. But something was driving him on. He was compelled to see her and talk to her before he flew to Zurich. She had left California too suddenly in his estimation, and he wanted to know why. It didn't make sense that she would do that without taking the time to see him first. He felt something was wrong and he couldn't shake the feeling.

A rental car awaited him at the Kalispell airport, and after he signed the paperwork, he drove off towards the McAdams Ranch, which was only a few miles northwest. Allegra had emailed him the directions, so he figured it would be easy enough to find his way.

She'd told him the entrance to the ranch was just beyond an outcropping of huge boulders and a copse of poplar, aspen, and spruce trees. She also said there would be a sign saying *Welcome to God's Country*. Her father had installed it when he first purchased the ranch those many years ago when she was a small girl.

While driving what seemed like miles beyond the sign, looking for the entrance of the ranch, he couldn't believe the size and the beauty of the surrounding terrain. He'd never seen anything like it. Some estates in England were immense, but nothing like ranches in Montana. The McAdams ranches, three of them, included 360,000 acres, counting the original spread further north, up close to the Canadian border. He'd met Ted Turner and Tim Bixseth who were among the biggest landowners in Montana, but he'd never heard of Alex McAdams or the McAdams Ranch until Allegra. As it turned out, McAdams owned more land in Montana than Turner or Bixseth. Allegra's father had been a cattle baron for nearly thirty years. Connie had gleaned that information from his business partners in Helena the day before.

The mountains on the horizon surrounding the land were majestic and seemed surreal, more like an oil painting one would see in a landscape gallery. In fact, he was thinking a few of the paintings hanging on his walls could be of this same mountain range. They were very similar. He also owned some Charles Russell paintings and some of his bronzes. He'd thought about visiting the C. M. Russell Museum in Great Falls, but he wasn't sure if he would have time. Evidently Russell's log cabin studio was part of the museum complex.

He saw it. The McAdams Ranch entrance loomed ahead, a unique arbor of sizable antlers of all types of animals, attached to a sculptured, heavy metal, ornate fence and security-gated entryway. Off the road into the distant foothills, he could see what looked like a sprawling, two-story log house surrounded by a masonry wall and more security gates. He wondered if that was the ranch house or the foreman's house.

He pulled up to the gate, reached through his open window and pushed the electronic button on the voice box installed on a pillar.

"Who's there?" a voice boomed.

Its volume startled him. "Connie Brown of Malibu, California," he answered. "To see Allegra McAdams."

The buzzer sounded and the giant gates opened inward. He drove onto the property, watching the gates close behind him in the rearview mirror. He noticed green dots of light flashing along the top of the gate, shooting out along the top of the fence in both directions as far as he could see. Electronic security, he figured, and it must have cost a fortune if it was all around the perimeter of the ranch. Surely not.

But then he could understand the precaution, given the tragic murder of Allegra's mother. He wondered if they would ever find out who did it. His business acquaintances at the meeting in Helena told him about it and how the circumstances surrounding the ordeal were a complete mystery. Nothing had been stolen, no sign of forced entry, and the actual killing was committed using Mrs. McAdams' own handgun that she kept by her bedside in a drawer. No prints were found on it, it had been wiped clean. She was at the ranch house alone that night, they told him. No witnesses. It had been a brutal rape that ended in murder.

Connie shuddered at the visual his thoughts conjured up, and what could have happened to Allegra if she had been there at the time. He believed whoever had committed that crime and other crimes like it should die a savage death. No mercy.

As he drove closer to the masonry wall and gate of the ranch house, he saw Allegra standing aloft in the gatehouse perched above the wall, watching him approach. He honked his horn and waved out the window, his heartbeat increasing the closer he got. *She is such an adorable little thing, in such a big, bad world.* His impulse was one of protection and caring.

The gate opened and he drove through, pulling to a halt just inside. He jumped from the car and with big strides reached the bottom of the spiral stairs coming down from the gatehouse before Allegra was even halfway to the bottom.

She wore tight blue jeans and a pink and blue plaid western shirt tucked into them. Her boots were tan with embroidered pink flowers down the sides.

He wanted to grab her and never let go. It was incredibly difficult to contain his feelings at the sight of her, and to keep his hands to himself. He'd never met anyone that provoked those emotions in him. There was something ethereal about her; fragile, but strong. She was like a porcelain doll in a glass case, untouchable and precious.

She seemed happy to see him too, but he detected a reserve that had not been there before. *Could be because she's on home terrain,* he told himself.

They did hug, however, but she pulled away after a couple of seconds, telling him to follow her up to the house. Her Jeep Cherokee was parked a few feet from the gatehouse.

He drove behind her in his rental car, although he would have preferred to ride with her. He was reeling with anticipation and excitement, eager to spend every single second as close to her as he could get.

He wondered about her reluctance to remain in the welcoming embrace they'd shared. It was very different than it had been in Malibu.

Chapter 11

Arlie McAdams was waiting in the Great Room with drink in hand when Allegra and Connie entered.

"Mister Brown. Connie, is it?" Arlie said as he extended his free hand, thinking it was strange that the man standing before him had a girl's name. "Welcome to the McAdams Ranch. Glad to have you here."

"Thank you, Mister McAdams. It's wonderful to meet Allegra's older brother." He shook Arlie's hand vigorously. "I must say, your ranch, what I've seen of it, is utterly magnificent. I can understand why Allegra loves it so."

"Would you like a drink?" Arlie asked. "Allegra? You want one too?"

"Yes, I'll get them, Arlie." Allegra went to the bar and while pouring a single malt, she looked at Connie. "Want one of these?"

"I believe I could handle one of those. Yes, please." He grinned widely at her.

"Good," Arlie said. "Then we can all toast and you can fill us in on what brings you to Montana, Connie."

"It's mostly business. I have a few business partners here."

Allegra handed Connie the drink.

"Thank you, my dear."

Connie's stationary grin at Allegra was not lost on Arlie. "So here's to life and all its little surprises," Arlie toasted with a raised eyebrow. Then he sat on a bar stool and cocked his head before speaking to Connie. "So you have business here? What kind of business?" He wasn't sure he bought what Connie said. Why would a man like him be doing business in Montana?

Connie went to the huge fireplace and perused the photos displayed across the mantle under the immense moose head with its intimidating antlers mounted above. "Cattle. Same as you, my friend."

Allegra did a double take. "What? You're into cattle? I didn't know that. Why didn't you tell me? Who do you deal with here in Montana?"

"A few of the biggest and best, I imagine. I invest, they play with my money. I don't really have a hand in the actual operation of their businesses. I'm a silent partner, so to speak. An investor, mostly, but it's a lucrative endeavor. How is business for you, Arlie? Is yours mostly cattle?" Of course he already knew the answer; he'd done extensive research on the McAdams family.

Arlie downed his drink and stood up to get another. "Yes, it is, actually. We've been importing bulls and improving our breeding lines. The steers are bigger and better, beef is top notch. And we've been producing some pretty damn good bulls and steers. Very profitable. I'd say we're doing good. So who did you say your partners are?" Still not quite believing him, Arlie needed some names.

"Oh, I didn't, actually," Connie replied. "I'd prefer to keep that to myself, if you don't mind. Up to them to reveal their investors, you see. But regardless, I do understand a bit about your business. And I'm curious how you make it work. Do you mind if I take a look at your operation while I'm here?"

Allegra spoke up. "I can show you around, Connie. No problem. Maybe you can give us a tip or two while you're at it since you're in the know." She winked at Arlie, aware that his hackles were rising. Nobody knew cattle and ranching better than he. Connie just didn't know that yet. And Arlie wasn't one to reckon with. You didn't want to be on his bad side by thinking you knew more than he did.

51

"So Allegra says you're from England. What part of England?" Arlie asked.

"Northumberland, between the Scottish border and Newcastle upon Tyne, the northeast side of England. You may have heard of Hadrian's Wall? In that area, near a village called Whitfield. We raise Aberdeen Angus cattle and ship breeders to ranchers around the world."

"You never said anything about that either!" Allegra said, looking back and forth at Connie and Arlie, while noticing the huge difference between the two men. Arlie was big and scruffy, tough and loud. Connie, in contrast, was slim and polished, a polite and soft-spoken gentleman. *Not even close*, she thought as she poured herself another drink.

Chapter 12

At breakfast the next day, Connie met the ranch foreman, Clyde Bennett, and his right-hand man, Trevor. The five of them carried on a conversation over a ranch breakfast of ham and eggs, fried potatoes, pancakes and biscuits.

Clyde sipped his coffee in between bites interspersed with questions. "So, how do you compare your Aberdeen Angus with the Belgian Blue and the Hereford Angus?" he asked.

"You do know the Hereford breed originated in England, yes?" Connie grinned.

"Yes, we're aware of that. I know all about the history of the Hereford. That's what we raise, you know. If you'd like I'll take you out later today and show you some of the herd. If you don't mind, Arlie?"

"Not at all. Be my guest. I have to run into town, so yes, that would be good." Arlie looked at his watch. "In fact, I better get going." He stood and reached for his Stetson hat.

"You have to go?" Allegra asked, frowning.

"Yep, duty calls. Got a date with a waitress." He winked at Allegra. "I'll be back in time for dinner, so I'll see you then." He left the room abruptly.

Allegra wondered if he was telling the truth about having a date with Tammy Sue. That would be a first. He hadn't dated anybody since his high school sweetheart broke his heart. They were all set to get married the summer after he finished college, but she got cold feet. The rumor was she was a lesbian. Allegra had heard she moved to Oregon and they never saw or heard of her again.

Clyde gulped the rest of his coffee. "Well, I have a few things to do first, so I'll be back around ten and we can take a ride around the ranch. You can go too, Allegra. You haven't seen some of the changes we've made."

"I'd love to, Clyde. Thank you."

She watched as Clyde and his head cowboy gathered their hats and took off in the direction Arlie had just gone.

"Well, they do take their business serious, don't they?" Connie leaned back in his chair and sighed. "That was too much breakfast for me, Allegra. I can't do that every day I'm here, I'll be as fat as one of the cows out there."

They laughed.

"Wait till you have one of our barbecue dinners. Steak and salsa, beans, corn on the cob, baked potatoes, French bread, way too much food too. Luckily my metabolism is up and running, or I'd be as wide as I am short. At least you have height to save the day. Room to pack it in." She grinned as she looked at the beguiling, handsome man across the table, momentarily forgetting what his son had done to her.

Connie's cell phone rang. "It's Eric. Do you mind if I take this call?"

Instantly her mood changed. "Go ahead." She hurried into the kitchen where she tried to control the shakes that had come over her. Then she went outside on the back porch so she couldn't hear any part of the conversation that was going on.

Connie was pacing the room. "No, Eric. I want you to go to Australia. I want you to work with Stuart for a while. Yes, I'm standing firm on this one. You are going to Australia and you are going to learn the business. No, there's nothing more to say about it. Abby has your ticket and you'll get money in Australia, not before.

54

Next Monday. I'll be there after Zurich, and Stuart will give me a full report."

Connie pulled the phone away from his ear, shaking his head after Eric hung up on him. He sat down at the table.

He just didn't know what to do with Eric. Even when he was a child, they had never bonded. He had tried, but had soon found out that it was hopeless. Sometimes it just doesn't work between parent and child, one of Eric's psychiatrists told him. He had wondered many times if maybe Eric wasn't his biological child. But of course he was.

Connie put his napkin on the plate as the cook and his helper came in and began clearing away the dishes.

"Did you see where Allegra went?" he asked.

"She took off to the barbecue pit outside the kitchen."

"Thank you. Breakfast was superb. Perfection!"

The cook grinned as he watched Connie head for the kitchen, then said to his helper: "Very different; ain't never seen the likes of him around here before."

"Is he what they call a *genteel* man?"

"Yep, guess so."

Chapter 13

Later that night after the ranch tour and supper, Allegra cozied up on the overstuffed chair in the Great Room to read a book, while Arlie and Connie were in Arlie's office engrossed in a heavy-duty conversation about cattle. She had watched the two of them all evening and listened to how they were taking to each other. Sometimes it seemed like a sparring match. Other times they laughed and joked. It reminded her of when her father was alive, felt comfy and homey.

She was glad to see Arlie warm up to Connie, letting his jealousies, if that was what it was, and his over-protectiveness of her fall by the wayside. She detected Arlie's annoyance over the way Connie had looked at her the day before when he first got there and how it had continued. Even she felt it, and avoided reacting. Things were different now. It wasn't like it was in Malibu before Eric. It never would be the same. She knew she couldn't encourage Connie. And besides, he wasn't really serious about her. He was womanizing, surely.

And then her thoughts drifted back to the night on Hollingsworth Drive when Eric Brown forced himself upon her. She shuddered and shook her head, trying to rid herself of the images of the assault. She jumped up out of the chair and hurried from the room, causing Arlie and Connie to wonder what was going on when she sped by the office.

When she returned a few minutes later, Arlie called out to her. "What's wrong, babe? Something botherin' ya?"

"No, no. I just felt a little sick. I'm alright. I think I ate too much today."

Connie stood and stretched. "I think I'll take a walk. Would you like to join me, Allegra? A little night air might settle your stomach."

"Ummm, all right."

"Do you mind, Arlie?" Connie asked.

"Not at all. I'm gonna turn in, anyway. Been a long day. I'm hopin' I'll stay awake long enough to get to my bed." He laughed and headed for the stairs. "Thanks for the talkin', Connie. I'm inclined to agree with you 'bout your Aberdeen Angus. We can talk some more tomorrow 'bout it. Good night now."

"Night, Arlie," Allegra said.

"I'll have some figures for you by morning," Connie said. "Sleep well."

Allegra and Connie turned and walked onto the patio through the open double doors. It was a clear, moonlit night. Millions of stars spread across the skies, proving Montana's big sky reputation.

"Exquisite!" Connie said, looking up into the sky's vast greatness.

"You won't find that view anywhere else. It's as if we're on top of the world, isn't it?" Allegra's face and eyes glowed in the moonlight.

Connie moved closer to her and put his arm across her back, resting his hand on her shoulder. He lightly gripped it, noticing how tiny it felt in his hand. A thrill ran through him, from his hand, up his arm, zapping his entire body. He wanted to hold onto this miniature woman. He wanted to hold her close forever.

Allegra awkwardly stepped aside and went to the edge of the flagstone patio. She turned and looked back at him. "Connie, I— I—"

"No, no, wait." He took her hands. "I didn't mean to—, I hope you know that I admire you very much, Allegra. I don't want to lose our friendship. Please don't shut me out."

She pulled away again and walked towards the house. "I have to go to bed, Connie. I'm just not feeling well. I'm so sorry." She almost ran through the open doorway and up the stairs.

Connie stared after her, chiding himself for overstepping his boundaries. He needed to control his feelings. It was time to go to Zurich.

Chapter 14

The next morning Allegra surprised Connie by asking him to ride up to the old Eureka ranch with her, so he put off his return to civilization for another day.

She wanted to take a look at the original ranch house, she said, which was hardly more than a mountain cabin. As she drove the Cherokee, she told Connie the history of the original McAdams homestead built just a few miles from the Canadian border in between Eureka and Rexford. She also told him about Allan, the problematic brother, and how he'd recently been to the ranch without telling anybody. Arlie didn't even know he'd been there. She found that strange, coming all the way from New York without telling anybody and not seeing his brother Arlie.

So she wanted to check things out, she said, and see if he had stayed at the cabin, if there was any evidence of it. She recalled how he would spend days at a time up in Eureka to get away from their dad and his criticism.

Connie thought of Eric as Allegra was telling him about Allan and his dad. It seemed to ring a familiar tone. Although he didn't believe Eric was gay, he seemed to display resentment towards women, which had puzzled Connie.

"Here we are. My favorite hideaway on the ranch." Allegra pulled to a stop, got out and unlocked the gate, then climbed back into the Jeep. They rode up the drive to the cabin that was nestled in the pines.

Wildflowers and berries grew in abundance all around the house and spread into the forest. Some had climbed up onto the old-fashioned porch and up the wooden supports of the tin roof. The place was in dire need of paint and repair, but it wasn't totally uninhabitable.

"I need to get someone up here to do some work on this place," she said as they went up the wooden steps to the porch and unlocked the door. "Whew! Something sure stinks in here. What the hell is that?"

She cautiously looked through the first floor rooms and then went upstairs, coming back holding a dead possum by its tail. "Poor thing. I don't like to see anything die like this. He must have been locked up in here when Allan left. Poor baby."

She went outside and dropped him in the incinerator, which was nothing more than a big barrel with a lid on it used to burn trash. Then she returned to the cabin and opened all the windows to air out the cabin.

"Connie, would you mind getting that cooler out of the Jeep? I brought us some drinks and lunch."

"Terrific! I was just thinking how I'd like to have a drink about now. Great!" He bounded down the steps as she continued airing out the house.

After an early lunch on the porch, they sat on the sofa swing together, drinking Coca Colas from cans. The only sounds were those of birds chirping and bees buzzing in and about the foliage, and every once in a while a rustle or two, probably rabbits and other rodents gathering food or chasing each other. It was a peaceful time. They both felt it.

"I could do this for hours. Could you?" Connie asked, looking at Allegra with her head leaning back against the cushion.

She turned and glanced at him before sighing. "Yes, and I have. I used to come up here and do just what we're doing, by myself. Listening to nature's sounds, breathing in pure, unpolluted air. Sometimes I'd close my eyes and try to visualize the life that lay ahead of me. Wondering what I'd be doing when I was all grown up. Wondering where I'd go to college and what I'd do after that."

"Has it turned out as you expected?"

Allegra thought for a moment while sipping her Coke. "Well, mostly. In some cases more than I'd ever dreamed, but not completely."

She had dreamed of a Prince Charming in those days, while sitting on that porch. A young girl's dreams of an idyllic romance, nurtured by fairy tales and movie fantasies. She never in her wildest dreams thought she would be a screenwriter, living in a mansion in Malibu, though. And alone. It never entered her mind. But here she was, not getting any younger, not married, and no one on the horizon. She'd always seen herself as a wife and mother.

"Why didn't you come back here to live after college? Connie asked. "You can write anywhere."

"Oh, my life here was over at the time. Plus, I needed to be where the people and the work were. The people who mattered in my business. You really have to be there to network and pitch and scratch and beg." She laughed.

"I don't see you scratching and begging. I've not seen you do either, even when you could have. But now you don't have to, right? You are through that door? You are in like Flynn?" he grinned widely. "I saw your last movie, you know. And I recognized myself. You really did a number on me. Am I really like that?"

"Oh, no. I didn't think you saw it. You never said anything." She blushed and quickly got up to throw her empty can in the incinerator.

"You needn't run off, I won't chide you," he laughed heartily at that point. "I found it quite amusing, actually."

She stood with her hands on her hips at the incinerator, looking back at him, wondering how he'd react if she told him what his son did to her. Would he blame her?

61

Connie got up and dropped his can in the barrel too. He noticed the toe of a burnt shoe sticking up through the ashes. "That's interesting."

"What is?" Allegra said.

He reached in and pulled the shoe from the incinerator, brushing the ashes from what was left of it. "This. It's a designer shoe. I know the maker in London. Makes his shoes from molds of his clients' feet. Strange it would be here, don't you agree?"

Allegra took it from him. She turned it over and over, wondering how it got there. "How do you know it's from that maker? There isn't a label."

"The intricate design on the toe. No one else does that, to my knowledge. See the swirls, the dots, how they meet and form a diamond shape in the middle? That's his trademark design. It could be a knockoff, but I don't think so. What's left of the leather looks like it's good quality material. Looks like it might be from a size ten shoe, or ten and a half. Could it belong to your younger brother?"

"I suppose it could. He's been to London. Quite a few times, as a matter of fact."

"Why would he burn his shoes?"

"Who knows. He's an odd one. One never knows what he's going to do next. It probably does belong to him. So he has been up here. That shoe proves it. You see anything else in there?"

Connie picked up a stick and rummaged around in the barrel, avoiding the opossum, not finding anything recognizable, but there were a few pieces of charred cloth. "Looks like some burned clothing, too."

Allegra smirked. "I can just see him, burning his clothes just because he was tired of them, or angry at someone. Or maybe because he didn't want reminders of where he'd been, who he'd been with, or just because. He is a strange one." She laughed as she walked up the steps with the remainder of the shoe swinging in her hand by her side, and went into the house.

"Allegra, why did you leave Malibu so abruptly to come to Montana?" Connie closed the door after he entered the cabin behind her. "When I walked you home from the party the night before, you didn't say anything about leaving. And your explanation over the phone doesn't seem to have been applicable, as far as I can determine. What was the real reason?"

"Uh, well, I had my reasons." She panicked. "I— I can't go into it right now, if you don't mind. But I had my reasons. Nothing to concern you, it's personal. It's something I have to deal with." She kept her back towards Connie as she spoke so he couldn't see the tears that had welled up in her eyes. *Damn him,* she thought, *why did he have to bring it up? I don't want to think about it.*

Connie knew she wasn't telling the truth. He felt it *did* concern him, and he was going to find out what it was. But he knew he had to go slow and be gentle with her. She was much more fragile than she wanted anyone to know.

That evening was quiet and peaceful around the glowing embers of the fire pit. Arlie had gone to bed early, leaving Allegra and Connie gazing at the stars and the burning coals alternately, while sipping their drinks and conversing about whatever came to mind.

Connie had tried once again to get the truth from Allegra, but she was steadfast in her answer that it didn't concern him and that she'd rather not discuss it.

She turned the conversation around rather adeptly, asking him about his life in England, about his first wife, and his mother.

He was free with the information, having nothing to hide from Allegra.

In turn she divulged more about her family life on the ranch before L.A. Talked about how her brothers were so opposite. Arlie was the strong one, the aggressive one, and Allan the gentler of the two, more artistic, passive. She told him how her mother protected Allan as long as she could, but it became impossible for him on the ranch as he grew older. Her father and Arlie were formidable; Allan didn't have a chance. Finally her mother sent him away to an art school in New York City to place him with others similar to him. Allegra told Connie it broke her mother's heart to see him go, but she felt there was no other alternative. And Allegra had agreed.

63

"Mother said she would make it up to him in her will. I always wondered about that, because there was nothing extra or out of the ordinary in the will for him. His portion was left in a trust to be dispensed by Arlie. I thought she meant that she was going to give Allan something extra special, like maybe the original ranch that he loved so much. I asked Arlie about it at the time, but he said he didn't know anything about it."

"Do you get along with your brother Allan?" Connie asked.

"Oh yes. I love both my brothers. And although Arlie doesn't like me to help Allan, I do it anyway. I have the money. It doesn't hurt me financially to share with him."

"No, but it might hurt him to know he can depend on you rather than make his own way. Lately I'm having those thoughts about Eric."

Hearing Eric's name was like a cannon ball blasting through her. She stood and turned in a circle, rubbing her temples, her eyes clinched shut.

"Are you alright?" Connie was at her side in an instant. "Allegra, what is it?'

She shook her head and opened her eyes. "I'm fine, I'm okay. Really, I am. Just had a sharp pain shoot through my head. I'm okay now. But I think I better go to bed. Too many late nights, I think. Too much to drink." She was embarrassed that she hadn't been able to control her reaction in front of Connie. She had to learn to do that, for he must never know what had happened.

"Come, I'll walk you to your room, then I'll come back and close up the house. Here, you need your wrap." He reached for the shawl that had fallen from her shoulders and was now in a heap on the Spanish tiles. "You must get a good night's rest. And you needn't see me off in the morning; I'll be leaving very early."

"What time are you leaving?"

"I must be at the airport at seven-thirty, so I'll leave here around six."

"I'll be up by then to see you off."

They walked in silence up the stairs to her bedroom door.

"I've enjoyed having you here, Connie. Truly." She turned and looked up at him, his arms holding her.

Their eyes met, he drew her closer, and before she knew it, he pressed his lips to hers, gently.

She pulled away reluctantly, wanting more but knowing she shouldn't. She acted as if it hadn't fazed her, even though she was dizzy with passion. She reached for her door and said, "When will you be back in Malibu?" as if a kiss from Connie was the most natural thing in the world.

"As soon as I can manage, but there's business to attend in Europe and England, as well as Australia and New Zealand. So I'm not certain when I'll return to the States. When will you go back to California?"

"I'm not sure. But we can email to keep track of each other. Right?"

"Yes, we can." He started to reach for her again, but she stepped backwards into her room, out of reach.

"Good night, Connie. I'll see you in the morning."

She shut the door.

He stood facing the closed door for a few seconds, sighed and then turned to head back down the hallway. He was feeling the aftermath of the most thrilling kiss he'd ever experienced, mixed with the heavy sadness of having to leave her.

The next morning Connie Brown left for the airport at six. Allegra hadn't awakened. He and Arlie shared breakfast with business talk about Angus cattle, and then off he went, on his way to Zurich.

PART TWO

Rachel O'Neill

Chapter 15

It was a cold, dismal day in Cornwall and the airport terminal was nearly empty, only a few evening travelers waiting to depart on the last flight of the day.

Rachel O'Neill was brimming with excitement in anticipation of the arrival of her dearest friend, Della Ballenchine, from Moscow. Rachel moved closer to the window pane as the passengers disembarked the plane. Her black-clad figure was more like a shadowy silhouette than that of a real person.

Direct flights to and from Manchester, the Scilly Isles, and London Gatwick were the basic flights on the year-round commercial schedule at Newquay Airport in Cornwall, while other destinations would open up during the summer. Newquay's small airport serving England's southwestern region, was just a hop, skip, and a jump from the seacoast village of Newlyn where Rachel lived.

As she stood there, eyes searching for the familiar face of her friend as the passengers climbed down the airstairs of the plane, Rachel thought of what a tiring journey it would have been for Della, the layovers and connections she had experienced in order to get to the west coast of England from Russia.

Rachel's first preference was traveling by train to and from London, the only exception being when she was in a hurry to connect with a flight in London to leave the country. So, there were times she would end up flying from Newquay to London, arriving at Gatwick Airport, then taking a train or cab to Heathrow Airport to catch the right plane. In fact, several times she'd made the same trip Della was making that very day.

Through Rachel's fiancé, Maxim Ballenchine, she had first met Della in Moscow. At the time, Della was in Russia on hiatus from New York City, taking a much-needed holiday from a stressful publishing career in Manhattan. Right off the bat the two women had something in common, Della being a publisher, Rachel being a novelist.

The happenstance had begun on a train from St. Petersburg to Moscow where Della met Anastasia Ballenchine, Maxim's sister. The two became instant friends and Anastasia convinced Della to hop off the train with her to meet her brother, Valentin, and see the village near the railway and have a meal with them before traveling on to Moscow. Valentin still lived in the Ballenchine family cottage where they were raised, had been there all his life.

It was love at first sight for Della and Valentin, and now they were married, which made Della a sister-in-law to both Maxim and Anastasia.

There she is! Omigod, look at the weight she's lost! She looks fabulous! Rachel waved through the terminal's massive glass panes.

Della shot her arm up, waving her hand high in the air while jumping up and down. She quickly made her way across the tarmac to the terminal door. Her abundant Irish red hair was whipping in every direction in the strong coastal wind. Before Della married Valentin Ballenchine, she was a Doheny, Irish through and through, freckled face, pale skin, and a hint of a brogue to go with it. Both of her parents were born in Ireland, and had settled in Oklahoma before Della was born. So Della's accent included a unique combination of a true Irish brogue, a mid-western twang, and a New Yorker inflection.

When Della came through the door, Rachel met her with outstretched arms and a huge grin. They embraced as if they hadn't seen each other in years instead of a few months. Their fondness for one another was evident to anyone who watched. They behaved more like loving sisters than not.

"I'm so glad you're here! I am, I am, I am!" Rachel repeated for the umpteenth time as they left the terminal heading for the car, arm in arm. "I think I need company," she added.

"Me too. You changed your hair color?"

Rachel laughed. "Not on purpose. I did it myself this time, and the color came out darker than the usual auburn. But I don't care, what does it matter?"

"Well, I like it. I'm so happy to see you, girl. Those two Ballenchine brothers are drivin' me stark-ravin' mad. I love Valentin to bits, but it's so good to get away from him. And Maxim's supposed to be retired, right? But he acts like he's still in the business, you know? And he and Valentin go at it all the time. Did Maxim call you? He said he would."

Rachel laughed. Della's non-stop fast-talking always amused her. She could say more and cover more in one breath than anyone she knew. "Yes, he called last night and twice this morning."

"He misses you terribly, you know," Della said and hugged Rachel again, her arm around her waist. "So have you thought any more about the weddin', when and where? You can do it at our place, you know. We'd all like that. We could do it up the same as we did ours. We'll use the carriage again, and all of it. You'd like that, wouldn't you?" She gave Rachel a sideways glance. "Or would you? I'm talkin' too much, I know I am. What are you thinkin', Rachel?"

Rachel put her arm around Della's neck, in a wrestler's grip, and gave her a big kiss on the top of her wild, curly bird's nest, and kept walking. "I'm thinking I love you, Miss Della Doheny."

"Now it's Ballenchine, it is. Not Doheny. Well?" Della asked.

"Well what?" Rachel took the car keys from her pocket.

"Rachel, you're stallin'. You haven't answered my question. Are you gonna get married, or not?"

Rachel laughed again as she opened the trunk of the car and tossed in the luggage. "Come on, I have a bottle of champagne and some fish and chips waiting for us. Are you hungry?"

71

"Damn right I am! You know I am. I hope you have a lot of bubbly. I have so much to tell you, Rachel. And I can't wait to talk about the ideas for the articles we're writin' together. I've got some new ones I hope you'll like. Been diggin' around and stumbled onto a few scary bits that will set your hair on fire."

"Sounds exciting to me. Can't wait." Rachel was relieved they were off the subject of marriage.

Chapter 16

The last dish was loaded into the dishwasher and Rachel pushed the start button. "There we go, all done." She turned and sat at the kitchen table with Della, who was sipping champagne. "Now I'll have me another glass of that too."

"I'll pour." Della took the bottle from the ice bucket. She reached for Rachel's glass. "The meal was fabulous, so Cornwallish. Fish and chips and champagne, although I imagine the locals do beer, not champagne." She laughed. "I just love comin' here for a change of menu, ambiance, environment, all of it, you know? I mean, I love Russia and the food and all that, but just some simple fish and chips on the Cornwall coast always does the trick. And the cole slaw was delicious. You made it yourself, you say? You didn't buy it from the Inn?"

"No, I didn't buy it. I made it. It's my new thing - cooking. I do several different cole slaws. In fact, I like to experiment with both green and red cabbage, and I even use shredded broccoli, which was in that one. It's fun cooking for myself these days." Rachel took a gulp of her drink.

"Well, I think your cole slaw would give Valentin a run for his money. He takes great pride in his cabbage dishes, you know. And

73

they're good, don't get me wrong. But we won't tell him I like yours best."

"So how is the restaurant doing? Is he still loving it?"

Della sighed. "Well, he's findin' out how much hard work it takes to be successful in the food service business, quite a big difference from amber minin', you know. And diamond minin'. But yes, he still loves it. I hardly ever see him anymore, though. He sometimes stays in the city overnight."

"That's not good, is it? I mean . . . well . . . how do you feel about that?" Rachel frowned as she watched Della's reaction to her question. She knew that facial reactions sometimes revealed more than words, and Della's were always such tell-tale expressions.

Hesitations were revealing too.

After a long pause of grimacing, Della leaned back in her chair and closed her eyes for a few seconds. "Well, I think I'm okay with it. For now I am. I know he has to make it work. That I understand. But I'm thinkin' it might be a good idea for us to get a house in Moscow. It would be easier for him and we'd be together more. At least we'd sleep together. Too many single beautiful women roamin' around Moscow at night, you know. And although your Maxim is never a bother, it would be nice havin' our own place away from the family compound. I mean you wouldn't want us around all the time after you're married, right out your back door."

"It wouldn't bother me at all. In fact, I'd love to be able to run across the garden to you when I needed to. But it's probably a good idea for you to live in town right now. Have you suggested it to him?"

"Just in passin', but not seriously." She looked around Rachel's kitchen and informal dining nook as if seeing it for the first time. "I love this white-washed Country French stuff, Rachel. Those bookcases, the mirror, and especially this table. You didn't have these last time. Oh my gosh, it's rainin'! Look at that, will you?"

"Yes, isn't it great? I love our storms."

They both took their glasses and moved to the Bay window looking out at the stormy sea. Lightning flashed across the sky, thunder rumbled.

"It's soothing, actually, isn't it?" Rachel said as she sighed.

"I never thought of it as soothin'. Storms scare me. All the noise. But that's okay if you think it's soothin'. I guess as long as we're warm and cozy indoors we're okay. Some of the storms we had in Oklahoma when I was growin' up were downright deadly. We had tornadoes, you know. So I'm not too keen on storms. We had hail the size of softballs, and wind that would lay you out flat on the ground if it didn't whip you away. The rain would come in at you sideways. Nope, storms don't soothe me at all. They scare the shit out of me."

"Come on, now, this one won't hurt us. We're okay. No tornadoes here." Rachel put her arm around Della's shoulders and directed her back to the table and they both sat.

"So, in answer to your question, Pete built those bookcases for the cottage down at the bay. I finally moved them up here, that's why you didn't see them before. My tenant wanted to put some of her own antiques in the cottage. She's such a good renter and a real dear, so I moved the stuff here out of her way. Actually, Pete and I found the mirror and the table in an antique store when I first bought the cottage." Rachel stopped talking and stared into her glass thoughtfully.

"You still miss him, don't you?" Della reached across the table and touched Rachel's hand.

"All the time. I loved him, really loved him."

"How long has it been now?"

"Well," Rachel put her hand to her temple and rubbed. "I lose track. Uh . . . four years, is it? Something like that."

"That has to be hard to get through. If my Valentin were to die, it would do me in, I kid you not. Would absolutely do me in. I don't know how I would cope."

"You learn to accept it, and live with it. It's getting easier, though. It is." Rachel's voice was a bit too quiet and not very convincing.

"Okay, time to change the subject. Tell me about you and Maxim. You've been avoidin' the conversation since I got here. When are you goin' to tie the knot? You've missed one Christmas and another one is comin' up. You still want a Christmas weddin', right? Isn't that the plan?"

75

Rachel shook her head. "I don't know what I want anymore, Della. I just don't know."

"You don't know if you want a Christmas weddin' or you don't know if you want to get married?"

"I'm not sure if I'm ready to get married, and having a Christmas wedding doesn't seem to be all that important anymore." She reached for the bottle and poured more liquid into her glass. "You want some more?"

"I sure do. Keep pourin' till the cows come home. Moo, moo."

They both giggled.

Rachel had accepted Maxim's marriage proposal at the reception of Della and Valentin's wedding, a lavish affair held on the Ballenchine estate outside of Moscow. Neither Della nor Valentin had been married before. They were late bloomers, both in their forties. But from the very moment Della saw Valentin, a tall, rugged Tom Selleck look-alike, standing near the train at Klin waiting for Anastasia, her heart was stolen away and she was sunk. There was no turning back. New York was history, and so was her publishing business.

So at their wedding, as with most weddings, the mood of the day was perfect for a proposal. And Rachel fell right into the romance of it all and said yes, nearly two years after Pete's death.

"So, what's wrong, Rachel? What's so different now? You fall out of love with Maxim? Is that what it is? I mean, it's okay if you have. I'm on your side. Although I don't see how you could fall out of love with him. The man is an Adonis. An older one, but an Adonis just the same. Those Ballenchine brothers take the cake, don't they? And win all the prizes. He's okay in bed, isn't he? I mean, there isn't a problem there, is there? I wouldn't think so. He looks and behaves so virile. And if he's anything like his brother, *va va voom!*"

Rachel laughed heartily. "No, no, no. It isn't the sex, or lack thereof." She began laughing again. "You really crack me up sometimes. And it isn't that I've fallen out of love with him. Not at all. Tell me, do you ever have even an inkling of regret for marrying Valentin? Do you ever miss your life in New York?" Rachel got up from the chair and went to the refrigerator. She reached for the orange juice and took it to the table. "I mean, don't you ever miss your publishing company and your total independence?"

"Hell no! Not at all. I was ready for Valentin, believe me! I was wantin' out of New York, I was wantin' to live in Russia and learn the people and the culture. I'd been comin' there for several years, wantin' more each time. But when it came down to it, makin' a decision, oh, I questioned it at first, you know I did. I wasn't sure, remember? But after I first saw him and fell for him, and when I walked down that aisle with that great big cuddly teddy bear, I was more than damn sure I was doing the right thing. I love that hunk of stuff."

"And he loves you." Rachel leaned back in her chair as she sipped orange juice.

"Yep, but he drives me crazy at times, and that's because we're so different. He has his own ways of doin' things, you know? Because he's Russian and all. But we have enough basic similarities to work for us. And I'm noticin' that we're comin' together more and more as time goes by. I'm not sure if he's becomin' more like me, or me more like him, though." Della laughed as she gulped the last trace of liquid from her glass. "I'll have some of that, too, dearie, if you don't mind. A bit of OJ with champagne. Yay! A mimosa!"

"So has there been any more danger, any trouble with the Mafia?" Rachel asked as she made mimosas in both glasses.

"Not for Valentin or Maxim, as far as I know. I think that's all over for them. And I think I could tell if it wasn't, even though they wouldn't tell me. They'd try to keep it from me. But I would know the signs, they'd be off whisperin' to each other. Jeez! I still remember the narrow escape we had at the estate. My Lord! Can you believe what almost happened to us? We're lucky to be sittin' here!"

"It still gives me the shivers when I think about it. We could have been killed, you know," Rachel said.

"Yep, but we weren't. Hallelujah! We were spared to marry us some real sexy Russian heroes."

"Heroes?" Rachel quizzed, grinning.

"Hey, they saved us, didn't they? They shot the bad guys! Well, they didn't do the shootin'. Their men did it." Della's grin spread across her face.

Rachel laughed, and soon they both were giggling and cackling into their champagne and OJ, feeling a bit intoxicated.

Chapter 17

They both slept till noon the next day. It was five in the morning when they finally gave up the ghost and went to bed - Della in a first-floor guest suite, Rachel in her second-floor master bedroom.

Rachel awakened to the bright sunshiny day. The view of the blue Atlantic stretching as far as she could see in both directions was always the first thing she saw when she awoke in her house on the hill. White fluffy clouds were making their way across the sky above the ocean, a stark contrast to the dark storm of the day before.

She propped herself up on her pillows and watched a freighter traveling towards the southeast beyond Marazion and St. Michael's Mount, all the while close enough to the shore for Rachel to make out its stacks and wheelhouse. She thought of the time she had wanted to take a cruise on a freighter, had priced cabins and charted ports of call to visit. At that time it would have cost twelve thousand dollars for nine months at sea. A friend of hers had done the trip, and it sounded exciting. But Rachel's life took its own course as it always did and that idea never came to fruition. But every now and then she thought of it, even considered it.

As she lay in bed watching the seagulls flying and squawking, she listened to the other sounds of the neighborhood drifting through the open louvered windows across the top of the picture windows.

She wondered if Della was awake yet.

She wondered if Della had a headache from the excessive imbibing the night before. They both overdid it. If it hadn't been for the Advil that Rachel had swallowed before she went to bed, she'd really be hurting about now. But she wasn't. Not much, anyway, only a hint of a headache, nothing more. More like a sleeping-wrong-on-the-pillow or maybe a Midori-mixed-with-champagne sort of ache. They had switched to Midori sodas after they ran out of champagne.

At that thought, she threw back the covers and stretched her arms high above her head before dropping her feet to the floor. She got up and did some toe-touching exercises, followed by twenty-five jumping jacks. It was going to be a good day. She felt it in her bones.

"Rachel, are you awake?" Della knocked and called out softly from the corridor outside Rachel's bedroom.

"Yes, I'm up. Come in."

Della opened the door, wearing a pink chenille robe over her silk pajamas, her fiery curly locks pulled up in a ponytail. "I brought us some breakfast, girl." She was carrying a tray laden with two mugs, a carafe of coffee, and bagels.

"Great! Set it on the table over by the window, will you? I've got to go pee. Be back in a minute."

"Sure." Della set the tray on the table and placed the coffee on the placemat already sitting next to the pot of violets in the center. There was an ecru-colored antique lace topper draped over the pink satin table cloth that hung to the floor. The pink and purple violets added just the perfect touch to the setting. "You always make everythin' look so pretty and invitin', Rachel," she called out. "I'm tryin' to copy you at home, and I think I've almost got it. Wait till you see what I've done to the house. I think you'll love it. But now that I'm thinkin' about movin' into the city, you'll have to come and make it easier for me and help me organize and decorate. You seem to be able to throw things together in the blink of an eye." She grinned at Rachel coming through the archway. "When do you think you'll be comin' to Moscow?"

"Oh, I don't know. I've some other places I must go to first. Like California, for one, to see my son. I need to do that. I have to sell

80

some of my real estate. I've been putting it off too long." She sat at the table and poured coffee.

"I forget about you havin' a son. You don't seem old enough to have a grown boy. You sure don't look it." Della took a bagel and split it to apply butter.

"Oh, I'm old enough alright." Rachel laughed. "Sometimes I feel too old, like maybe I'm his grandmother instead of his mother."

"He doesn't have any kids, does he? No grandkids yet?"

"Well, he had two from a previous marriage, a bad marriage. A boy and a girl, but their mother turned them against Devin. It wasn't all her fault, though. He was an alcoholic when he was younger, and there were some pretty rough times. So regardless of the fact that he recovered from his addiction, they don't communicate with him at all. With me either. They've more or less written us off. Sad story, I'll tell you about it sometime. Guess I'll consider this grandchild as my first, starting all over looks like."

"Oh, that's sad. I bet you're lookin' forward to being a grandmother again, though. Right? Here, you want some butter?"

"Nope and nope. No butter, no grandmother. I don't know how to be one."

"But you're the perfect godmother. You are so good with Paul's boys. I've seen that firsthand. It couldn't be more difficult than that. You just buy 'em gifts, love on 'em, play with 'em, and then leave 'em with their parents and go home." She sipped the coffee Rachel had poured for her. "Easy enough, I would think."

"Do you ever wish you would have had children, Della?"

"Oh, I did want them at first, when I was in my twenties. But I couldn't have fit them into my life then. I was on a roll, a corporate roll. Not even time to find a husband to make a baby. And of course, now I'm glad of it, that I was on that roll, for I would never have met my Valentin and wouldn't be livin' in Russia today. Can you imagine? I would have missed my happiness altogether. So no, I have no regrets. I can always volunteer at a child care if I feel the urge."

"Have you ever done that?"

"No, and I probably never will."

They both giggled.

81

"I think we're both right where we're supposed to be in our lives. I can't remember which one said it, my mother or daddy, but one of them said 'you are where you're supposed to be or you wouldn't be there'."

Della lifted her cup as if to toast. "I'll buy them apples."

Chapter 18

The sky was cloudless and blue, the sea and air clear as glass. It was an early afternoon following lunch on Rachel's patio in Newlyn, one week into Della's stay.

Clearing the table, Della took the dishes inside to the kitchen and on her return carried her laptop computer. "So did you find anything?"

"Not yet," Rachel said while browsing the internet on her own laptop. "I Googled Russian firearms, though. Found some neat info on the types of guns available today. I didn't realize that gun manufacturing is as big as it is in Russia. They develop such exotic, dangerous weaponry, don't they?"

"Yes, I found that out too. Pretty scary. Okay, I'll Google present-day Russian criminals. We'll find something that will spark our creative juices. Do you think it's harder to write true crime than fiction, Rachel? You have to stick to what actually happens in the news of the day, can't veer off with your own opinion and take on it."

"In some ways it is more difficult, but it other ways, fiction is harder but more challenging. You have to come up with a fresh storyline and create believable characters, all from scratch. Whereas writing true crime is more about investigative journalism. You delve into what's actually happened, and you already have the characters

83

written for you. But then again, although it can be just as challenging, there is a certain element of creativity to it. This is the fun part, researching and finding facts," Rachel said. "I've always enjoyed the research."

They both continued working for about an hour, sipping coffee, making notes, and periodically chatting about what they were finding.

"Let's take a walk, okay?" Rachel said suddenly as she sighed and closed her computer. "Want to? Towards Penzance?"

"Sure, I'm game. Always ready to play."

They put their computers in the kitchen, grabbed sweaters, and took off down the hill towards the seafront walkway.

"I just love it here, Rachel. Will you look at this beauty? The fresh smell, the granite boulders, the sound of the sea rollin' in, the green hills covered with houses of all colors, the flowers. It's captivatin'."

"It's heaven. I don't want to live anywhere else."

"I'm beginnin' to see why you're having second thoughts about livin' in Moscow."

"Well, I definitely couldn't live there full-time, that's a given. Maxim and I agreed that we would split our time between there and here."

"That's good. At least you're in agreement on the subject."

"Yes, but still . . . there's more than that to consider. I'm having a hard time visualizing sharing my life with a man. I know it's crazy to be thinking that way. I mean, why couldn't I share my house, myself, and my time? What's wrong with me? But it's like I look around my house and I don't see where Maxim fits in."

"Give him a floor. You've got three of them. Surely you can do without one." Della laughed. "He could set up a studio to do his metal work and have his own office and study, whatever he wants, right? But I don't think space is the real problem, dearie, is it?"

"Well, something is making me nervous about it all. I don't know, maybe it's too soon to make a commitment. I feel bad about saying yes to Maxim's proposal when I did, but then, I sort of fell head over heels into it, didn't I? It just happened. It's all your fault, you know. Your wedding did it to me." She was looking at Della, who wasn't sure if she was serious or not. "I'm kidding, I'm kidding."

"Okay, you had me for a minute. I couldn't figure how it was my fault. And you know what? You've got time to figure it all out. At least he isn't pressurin' you."

"You're right, he isn't."

They walked on in silence until they reached the lawn bowling club. The bowlers were out in full force. The club was on the left of the boardwalk towards Penzance and across from the saltwater swimming pool to the right on the beach.

"Have you used the pool yet?"

Rachel shook her head. "No. I'm not much for getting into pools or oceans. I'm more of a spectator. But I love being near the water. I can breathe the air, listen to the ripples or the waves. Soothing."

Della laughed. "I'm the same way. I don't even own a bathin' suit."

"Me either."

"We're a fine pair, a couple of genuine stowaways."

They both giggled.

Rachel sat on a bench facing the lawn bowlers.

"Look at that, will ya, all the bowlers are skinny as sticks," Della said as she sat down beside Rachel, a little out of breath.

"And old," Rachel added with a grin.

"I wonder why they all wear white."

"I don't know. Probably has something to do with it being a lawn bowler uniform."

They both laughed.

"We may as well walk on into town," Rachel said. "What do you think?"

"Sure. I need to go to a drugstore anyway. Want to get some aspirin."

"I have some Advil at the house," Rachel said.

"No, has to be aspirin. Have to take one a day. Doctor's orders."

"What do you mean?" Rachel was alarmed. "What's wrong with you?"

"Oh, just a bit of high blood pressure and of course the high cholesterol that comes along with it. Have to keep the blood flowin' smoothly, you know, make sure there's no little blood clots and chunks of cholesterol breakin' off. I've been on a strict diet, been losing weight."

"I can see that. You look great!"

"Yep, doc said to lose some weight. It's all that rich food Valentin keeps cookin', his sauces. So now I'm eatin' mainly veggies and fruit, less carbs and fat. No sauces whatsoever! Less sweets. Of course the champagne and Midori I've been drinkin' here doesn't help any."

"Okay, we won't do that again. I don't need to drink that stuff either. We'll be good from here on out."

Rachel loved her friend and didn't want anything to happen to her. She'd already lost one good friend, Paul's Belinda. She couldn't bear to lose another.

Chapter 19

"Della? Della, where are you?" Rachel called out, bounding down the stairs to the ground floor of her three-story house.

"In here. I'm in the living room."

"Guess who's coming to dinner?" Rachel was out of breath and grinning from ear to ear.

"Maxim! I knew he couldn't stay away."

"No, Paul. Paul Newland. You remember him. Paul and the boys? Belinda?"

"Of course. When are they comin'?"

"Just him. He'll be here at six, driving down from London. We'll go to the Ship Inn for dinner." Rachel plopped down in an overstuffed chair.

"Terrific! I love that place. Yay! Fish and chips! We can't go there enough as far as I'm concerned." Della looked at her watch. "It's four now, what are you goin' to wear?"

"Jeans and a sweater. Nothing fancy."

"You haven't said . . . is he doing alright, I mean . . . after Belinda's passin' and all, livin' in London?"

"Yes, I think he is. The boys are growing up so fast. I visit them every couple months or so, go to London and stay a day or two. He comes here when he can to check out the house, to see what I've added or taken away. Says he misses Cornwall." Rachel laughed. "But I think he misses this house the most. He and Belinda were so happy here and I think he comes back to remember. I'm glad I bought it, to keep it in the family."

"Sounds like it was a good idea, and besides, I love comin' here too." Della couldn't help but notice how Rachel had brightened upon learning of Paul's impromptu visit. She seemed to be glowing.

"You know, I was thinking," Rachel said, "maybe we should tackle a different perspective on crime in Russia, come at it from another direction."

"From what direction?"

"Well, why don't we write it as fiction, a novel, instead of a series of magazine articles? Novels have just as much of an impact, if not more, than articles. And we can take liberties and swear it's all fiction. Plus, it might be safer for us that way. Don't you think?"

Della hesitated. "You know, you've got a point. In fact, that would make it a lot easier, actually. We wouldn't have to be so careful about treadin' on toes. Great idea! Let's do it! Absolutely!"

"Good. Now I feel better about it."

"Why didn't you say you were concerned?"

Rachel sat up. "I wasn't sure what I was feeling, just felt a bit off kilter about it, out of my element. It just came to me a few minutes ago before Paul called. I was on my way down to talk to you when the phone rang."

"Then we have two things to celebrate tonight. Paul's company and our new crime novel! Hooray!" Della stood up. "I need to change clothes."

Chapter 20

"Paul just called and said he's running late. He'll meet us at the Ship Inn. So let's get going, girl!" Rachel said as she came down the stairs with her purse hanging from her shoulder and carrying a light jacket. Normally she wouldn't need more than the black turtleneck she usually wore with her jeans, but she'd been having chills all day.

March weather on the Cornish coast would range from a high of 53 degrees Fahrenheit to a low of 41. Although there were days of sunshine, it was still a bit cool. Perfect weather for Rachel, though. She was averse to weather in the upper 70 degrees and beyond. One reason she loved England.

"I'm ready," Della said as she donned her fleece-lined vest and followed Rachel through the kitchen to the garage.

They hopped into Rachel's year-old Vauxhall Insignia, an impressive black four-door vehicle. She liked taking it out at night, but used the Land Rover for day outings.

It was only two miles to Mousehole from Newlyn, which took about five minutes if there was traffic and if they had to search for a parking space. There was parking right down in the village, but normally it was full, so it was wise to park out of the village and trek in.

As it turned out, they were lucky to find a space a couple streets up from the pub. The Inn was on the waterfront, with only a very narrow lane separating it from the stone wall that rose up from the tiny beach below.

Mousehole's harbor was protected by two breakwaters of stone that jutted out into the sea. The view of the boats was a favorite of the inhabitants of the yellow-lichened granite houses crowding the hill above its cove.

"I love this place," Della said as she walked along the lane leading down the hill to the pub. "I think if I lived in England, I'd buy a house in Mousehole. I could fit in quite nicely."

"Yes, I thought about it before I bought the cottage in Newlyn."

"You're going to keep renting it out? Not going to sell it?"

"Can't fathom selling it. Lots of good memories there. Okay, here we are."

They pushed open the heavy wooden door of the Ship Inn and found themselves in the middle of the din of a crowd. They'd forgotten it was Friday night, one of the pub's busiest nights.

"Omigosh! I should have called and asked them to save us a table," Rachel said as she pushed her way to the bar. "Hey, we're in luck. Stools at the end. Grab them!"

Della quickly made her way to the far end of the bar with Rachel following, working her way through the crowd. They claimed all three empty stools.

"I wonder where Gina is?" Della said as she looked around the pub and leaned to peek into the adjoining room.

The bartender heard her and replied in his deep, gruff voice: "She took the night off, darlin'. Something about her mother being sick. What can I do for you young ladies?" To him they were young, he was in his late sixties.

"A bottle of champagne, please, a medium priced one, and three glasses," Rachel said.

"You know, I think I'd like to have a red wine," Della said. "Doc says it's okay for me to drink that in moderation."

"Of course." Rachel looked at the ruddy complexioned barkeep. "Let's change that to two red wines. I'm not sure what Paul wants."

"Comin' right up!" he said.

"Do you think we might be able to get a table for three? We'd like to have dinner." Rachel asked the barman, speaking loudly over the noisy crowd as he brought their drinks and set them on the bar.

"Might be an hour wait, but I'll tell Julie. She'll keep an eye out for ya. You want anythin' else at the moment, ladies?"

"No, that'll be fine. Thank you." Rachel lifted her glass to make a toast.

Della's glass was raised as she awaited some words of wisdom from Rachel, grinning cheerfully. "Yes?"

Rachel laughed. "Why don't you make the toast this time? I've run out of my clever and not-so-clever gems."

"Okay. Let me see . . . I got it. May those who love us, love us, and those that don't love us, may God turn their hearts. And if he doesn't turn their hearts, may he turn their ankles, so we'll know them by their limpin'."

Rachel burst out laughing. "That is so funny!"

"Just a little Irish ditty. My father used to say it all the time. Here's another one: may you never lie, steal, cheat or drink. But if you must lie, lie in each other's arms. If you steal, steal kisses. If you must cheat, cheat death. And if you must drink, drink with me, your friend."

"Oh, I like that one," Rachel said as her eyes sparkled. "That fits the occasion. I'll drink to that one."

"My daddy had dozens of 'em. He loved to make people laugh and they all loved him. I miss him."

"It's hard to lose parents, isn't it? I miss mine, too. Think about them all the time."

Della nodded as she sipped and looked around the pub at the patrons.

"There he is!" Rachel waved above the crowd at Paul Newland coming through the doorway.

He stood at least six inches above everyone else. His blond shoulder-length hair gleamed in the light above the entry.

"Gawd, he's handsome, isn't he?" Della said as she watched him work his way towards them. "Look at how the women are oogling him."

"I know. It's always been like that."

"He looks like he just stepped off the cover of a damn romance novel."

Rachel grinned, remembering how that was exactly what she had thought when she first saw him on a New Year's Eve in London that now seemed so long ago . . . when Ethan was alive, before she knew Pete, and before Paul married Belinda.

Chapter 21

"So while the boys are spending the summer with their granny in Hastings, I'll be doing a gallery tour in California." Paul put the napkin on his plate and motioned for the waiter.

"Oh? When are you going to the States?" Rachel's eyes widened.

"Sometime in June or July. My reps want me there for some personal appearances. They're going to schedule a bunch of galleries."

"I'll be in Malibu this summer, Paul. We'll have to get together."

Paul leaned forward, touched Rachel's arm and grinned widely. "Absolutely. I'll email you as soon as I get the schedule. Where in Malibu will you be staying?"

"My son moved from my father's house in Brentwood to a house in Malibu. Said it was more convenient for him. His wife loves the beach and the movie stars, so I'm sure that's the real reason they moved there. She's star-struck. So my dad's house is empty again. I may put it on the market while I'm there. You remember that house."

"How could I ever forget it?" He turned towards Della. "Has she told you the story about the Senator in California, the one who attacked her?"

"Yes, and how you came to her rescue. The bloody bugger got what he deserved."

"No," Rachel said. "He should have been executed, but he made it past the 'no death penalty' law that came down while he was in prison on death row. Now he's just sitting in jail, probably watching TV, reading, writing. Living life while those he killed or maimed aren't. I believe that when a man is caught red-handed, and there is no doubt in the world that he's a killer or a sadistic rapist, he should die! No ifs, ands or buts!

"I'll never forget what that asshole did to me, and to top it off, it happened twice! If it hadn't been for my hero," she clasped Paul's hand and looked up into his eyes, "I wouldn't be sitting here, hanging out with my two best friends in all the world." Rachel wiped tears from her eyes. "I'm sorry. Let's not spoil our night by wasting our breath on that scum. Now where were we?"

Paul hugged her, holding her tight.

Della squeezed her arm.

"You were talking about going to Malibu," Della said, stroking Rachel's back.

"Yes, but first I'm going to Montana, want to check on Mother's cabin and maybe spend a week or two there. Something I've wanted to do. I told you my stepmother Lee passed away in December, didn't I, Paul?"

"Yes, I was sad to hear that. I know how much you loved her. So you won't be going to Cambria this time?"

"No. No reason to. She's gone. I have no other reason to go there."

The waiter arrived at their table.

"The check, please, but no rush," Paul said.

"It's already paid. The lady paid it." He nodded to Rachel.

"Rachel, it was my invitation—"

"Too late." She laughed as she stood up and reached for her jacket on the back of her chair. "Let's go home, shall we? Time for a nightcap."

Della clapped her hands. "I'm up for that."

"I owe you," Paul said.

"So do I," Della added as she looked up into Paul's clear blue eyes. She was beginning to miss her husband Valentin.

Chapter 22

They arrived at the house on the hill. Paul had followed Rachel and Della in his BMW. It felt good to him to be pulling into the driveway that was once his. Memories of living there with his beloved Belinda flooded his mind. Tears came to his eyes, but he wiped them away and attempted to pull himself together as he opened the car door and headed to the garage where Rachel and Della were just getting out of the Insignia.

"How do you like the Vauxhall?" he asked as he caught up with them. "Have you had it out on the road?"

"I love it," Rachel said. "And no, I haven't tested the speed, if that's what you mean." She laughed. "I trust that it'll do well, if I need it, when I need it. I bought it 'cause I like the looks of it, not the speed, Paul."

"I'd like to take it out tomorrow, if I may. You may not know it about me, but cars are my weakness now. I've a new addiction, and I've wondered how these are on the open road."

Rachel walked into the service porch area. "Sure. The keys are hanging here inside the door. Take it when you want."

"Great! I'll hang my BMW keys here, and if you want to use it, go ahead."

"Not a good idea. When I drive a BMW I can't keep it down to a reasonable speed." She laughed. "There's something about that rumbling roar that urges me on, faster and faster. Dangerous for me to get behind the wheel of a BMW, especially one like yours. So I'll use my Land Rover if I have to run any errands."

They entered the kitchen and Rachel plugged in the tea kettle. "Paul, will you please open a bottle of champagne for me? It's in the dining room bar fridge."

"I'll set out the glasses," Della followed him into the bar area as she removed her jacket. "I think I'll have one glass. How about you, Paul?"

"I'll have a St. Pauli, don't need to tempt fate any more than I do." He pulled a bottle of champagne and the non-alcoholic beer from the bar refrigerator.

"Do you need a glass for it?"

"No, I'll have it from the bottle."

"Okay, but I need to go to my room for a sec. Be right back." Della hurried off.

Rachel called out from the kitchen, "You two want a cup of tea, too? I'm going to have one before I have champagne."

"I will," Della yelled from down the hall.

"How about you, Paul? You want a cup of tea?"

He stuck his head into the kitchen. "Sure, why not? I'll put the beer on ice."

Rachel was impressed that Paul had stuck to his guns after all this time. When he did drink, the most he would have was no more than two. And he'd had that at the Inn.

It was eleven and all three were starting to yawn and get sleepy-eyed. They had been talking for two hours in the living room. Rachel was curled up on the sofa. Della reclined nearby, her head on one arm of an overstuffed chair and her legs draped over the other arm. Paul was taking up an entire loveseat, his feet stretched out on the ottoman in front of him.

"I think it was fabulous the way you two met at Trafalgar Square in London. I mean, what are the odds something like that would happen and what are the odds your lives would come together like they have? It's incredible." Della's tipsiness began to show. "I mean it's just not that common. And you're still in each other's lives. How about that? What are the odds? You know?"

Rachel smiled at Paul, then sat up, yawning. "What I do know is I have got to go to bed. I really do. I hope you two don't mind if I just leave you here. You know where your room is, Paul. It's all ready. Just make yourself at home, since it *was* your home," she laughed and walked over to him and gave him a light peck on the forehead. "Good night, you."

Della sat up. "I'm going to bed, too. I think I've had all I can drink and if I don't go now, I might pour myself another and really be sorry tomorrow." She stood and hugged Rachel and bent down to hug Paul. "Good night, you guys." She cleared the glasses and took them into the kitchen.

Paul stood and stretched. "Well, I may as well hit the hay, too, which suits me fine. I'm weary; it's been an exhausting week. So see you girls in the morning. And don't get up for me. Sleep in, for I'll be heading out pretty early to take care of some business. But I'll be back around noon. Is it alright if I take your car, Rachel?"

Rachel was already on the stairs. "Absolutely! We'll see you at noon. Good night, guys." She barely made it to her room before she collapsed. She couldn't remember ever being so tired, and she fell asleep the moment her head hit the pillow.

Downstairs, Paul carried his empty bottle into the kitchen and asked Della if she minded having one last cup of tea with him.

Della added water to the kettle. Paul sat at the kitchen table while she prepared the tea. "Would you like some lemon cake with this, Paul? We have some left over. Rachel made it a couple days ago."

"Her famous lemon cake? I most certainly would!"

"Good, I'm a little bit hungry myself."

"So, tell me about Rachel and Maxim," Paul said quietly.

"What do you want to know?" Della sliced two pieces of cake and put them on plates.

"Well, do you think it's the real thing? Does she really love him?"

Della wondered why he was asking. It surprised her. "To be honest, I don't know. And I don't think she is sure she wants to get married. She's so attached to Cornwall and everything here. I think that's what's getting in her way, mostly. And there's the memory of Pete, still."

Paul nodded. "Yes, I know how that is. I couldn't fathom thinking of anybody else after Belinda, even though it's been over two years. I'm surprised she fell so quickly for Maxim. But I can understand it happening. He was a solace. He came at a time when she needed someone, when she was the most vulnerable, and being who he was, he totally swept her off her feet. What about him, Della? I don't know him that well. Is he honorable? Does he really love her?"

Della poured their tea and sat across from Paul. "Yes, he does. More than she loves him, I suspect. He would do anything for Rachel, if she'd let him. But she's pretty damned independent. Loves her house, her cars, her surroundings, her life, traveling, loves being able to do what she wants when and where she wants. That's pretty hard for a man to compete with, you know. And she doesn't want or need his money, so that makes it even more difficult for her to need him. You have to need each other as well as love each other."

Paul sighed heavily and became silent as he ate his cake and sipped his tea.

Della wondered if he was relieved to hear that Rachel didn't want to get married. It certainly appeared that way. She finished her cake and sat back sipping her tea.

"How are things in London?" she asked him. "The boys doing okay? I loved meeting them when I was here last time."

"They're a handful, but thank God for their granny. I've just hired a nanny, though. She'll start when they return from Hastings in the fall."

"That's good. They should have a woman's touch all the time. I hope she's a good one. I remember a couple of my nannies when I was growing up. They were absolute witches. You checked her credentials thoroughly, I hope."

Paul nodded. "Yes, I did. And I checked all the references. She's in her thirties, and as it turns out, after several conversations with her, she had an unfortunate life herself. She's from the Lake District. Her mother was unmarried and put her up for adoption at birth, which didn't work out. She went through four foster homes and after the last one she begged to remain with the nuns. It's almost another Jane Eyre story. She managed three households and their children, one after the other, from the time she turned nineteen. Loves children. Like I say, excellent references."

"Okay, good. Sounds great. Have you told Rachel yet? I know she's their godmother."

"Not yet, will tomorrow. Want to invite Dudley, their godfather, and tell them both together."

Upstairs Rachel was dreaming . . .

. . . walking through a summery rose garden in the country somewhere, wearing a flowing white lace wedding gown, a lace veil over her face, and yards of lace-trimmed voile trailing behind over the lush green grass. In one hand she carried pink and yellow baby rosebuds tied with streaming ribbons. Her father was holding her other hand.

Now they were both floating towards two men waiting under a canopy of wisteria that suddenly turns into the stone wall covered with wisteria that she had seen in Switzerland the last time she was there. She couldn't make out the faces of the two grooms dressed in matching tuxedos. She reached up to touch their blank features, trying to figure out who they were.

One of them vanished, while the other turned towards another woman coming into view. Rachel couldn't see who the woman was. She turned to her father just as he too disappeared. When she looked back, no one was at the altar, and she was alone. She dropped to the ground that was now cold and damp.

She cried.

Chapter 23

The next morning Rachel woke up feeling like she'd been run over by a steamroller. Every muscle and every single joint ached. Her head throbbed and her throat hurt. It felt like there was a big, sore lump in it, making it difficult to swallow.

She sat up in bed only to fall back again, dizzy and nauseous. For a moment she lay still, but then a fresh wave of nausea sent her lunging for the bathroom.

While she was vomiting her guts out, sickening waves of diarrhea coursed through her lower intestines. She didn't know what to do: sit on the toilet or stick her head in it. It became a tradeoff between the two.

It all hit her so suddenly she didn't have time to think, but wondered what the hell was happening. She thought back to the day before. Yes, she had chills, but where could she have picked up a bug? Maybe at the airport. All sorts of people passed through those doors during a single day, even sick ones. She'd noticed a couple of the employees had the sniffles and were coughing.

The attack subsided after it felt like her body was empty of all fluids and matter. She stood up in front of the bathroom mirror gazing at her sunken, red, watery eyes. Her face was flushed and she felt hot, so she reached for the thermometer in the drawer.

A temperature of 103! Not good.

She went to the top of the stairs and called out: "I need some help up here. Della, would you come up, please?"

Rachel stayed in bed for the next three days. At her insistence, Paul went back to London as soon as he finished his business. She didn't want him to be exposed to the flu any longer than he had been already. He didn't like leaving her while she was sick, but Della assured him that Rachel would be all right, and that she would be there to take care of her.

Rachel wouldn't let Paul come into her room to say goodbye, but talked to him through the doorway.

"I hate leaving you like this, Rachel," he said.

"You can come back when I'm over this, okay?"

"I had some things I wanted to discuss with you and Dudley, but that can wait till you're feeling better. You call me if you need me, you understand?" He looked at Della standing next to him and whispered, "Will you please call me and let me know how she gets on?"

"Yes, I will. Don't worry."

Della plied herself with multi-doses of vitamin C and other herbs and supplements. She drank a lot of juices with Rachel and both had plenty of chicken soup, Della's remedy for whatever ailed.

On the fourth day, a doctor came to the house, for Rachel's cough had worsened and her temperature had flared again. He said she had a bacterial flu, so he gave them both shots to combat it, but he was concerned about Rachel's temperature and cough and her difficulty in breathing.

That afternoon, Della took Rachel to the hospital per doctor's orders. She was admitted and tests were run.

She had bacterial pneumonia.

Della's voice wavered when the doctor told her. "Wha— what is that? What caused it?" She grabbed Rachel's limp hand.

The doctor sat on a stool next to the bed and explained. "Bacteria and viruses are the primary causes of pneumonia. When a person breathes pneumonia-causing germs into his lungs and his body's immune system cannot otherwise prevent entry, the organisms settle into small air sacs called alveoli. They continue to multiply, and as the body sends white blood cells to attack the infection, the sacs become filed with fluid and pus, causing pneumonia. We aren't sure what the bacterium is at this point, but we do know it's not a virus."

"Is that good or bad?" Rachel whispered.

"It's good. We can treat it with antibiotics. Virals cannot be treated with antibiotics."

Nine hours later, Rachel was on a breathing machine in intensive care. She'd taken a turn for the worse; fluid had formed in her lungs and was being drained.

Della was frantic. Through her tears she asked the doctor if she should call Rachel's son in the States and tell him to come.

The doctor told her to wait another twenty-four hours, and if she didn't improve, then yes, she should call him.

The next morning, Rachel was resurrected and Della felt relief.

The doctor asked Rachel if she had many bouts of bronchitis in the past.

"Yes, I have," she said, while Della stood by, listening. "But I self medicate and it always goes away. I usually cough for a few weeks afterward, but cough drops and cough syrup finally take it away."

"I would suggest you not self-medicate, that you come in right away. You're very susceptible to pneumonia and that is very serious."

"Really?" Rachel frowned and glanced at Della.

"Yes. Respiratory diseases like flu, asthma, chronic bronchitis, etcetera, and immune depressed states, alcoholism, are other conditions which increase susceptibility to develop pneumonia. Exposure to cold weather also increases risk of acquiring pneumonia.

So you must take care of yourself. And if you run a temperature, or develop a cough, please give my office a call."

"Alright, I will. Thank you."

After he left, Rachel and Della stared wide-eyed at each other.

Della broke the silence. "My heart and your lungs, *now that's a fine how-do-you-do!*"

PART THREE

Blue Montana Skies

"Free as the eagle flies in blue Montana skies,
with him my spirit soars and will be free . . ."
Rose/Autry

Author's note:

Some dream of a secret place, a place that is peaceful, spiritual, bountiful, and beautiful. Where one can run free and be close to nature and self . . . where one can be soulful and true . . . where the outside world and all its turmoil is non-existent. Well, in my dream, one such place is depicted in this next section – it is Rachel's mountain cabin in northern Montana.

Chapter 24

Rachel O'Neill marveled at the view of forests and lakes below, spreading from Kalispell north into Canada. The sun hadn't set yet as the plane approached Glacier Park International Airport.

In the month of June the days would be nearly sixteen hours long, the shortest days being half that in December. The length of days was the same as it was in Cornwall, she'd learned, however, the winter weather was much colder in Montana than Cornwall. In the northern states of the U.S. it dipped below zero at times, so summer was the perfect time of the year for Rachel to make the trip, with temperatures running from 75 to 90 degrees Fahrenheit.

She'd taken a flight from Heathrow at eight a.m. and was due to arrive at Kalispell at eight p.m., even though it had been a twenty-hour trip, due to the time zone changes. She decided about halfway through the flight that next time she would definitely plan an overnight layover somewhere, rather than attempt all twenty hours at once. It was just too much for her. And it was impossible to sleep at any great length on a plane, scrunched up in such tight quarters. Even when she flew first class it wasn't much better. She just couldn't sleep on a plane.

After gathering her bags, she picked up a rental car and headed for the mountain town of Whitefish, where she had booked a hotel. It had been so long since she'd been to her mother's cabin, she didn't know in what condition it would be, or whether or not she would want to stay in it. So she booked the hotel in Whitefish, which was a charming little town a few miles north of Kalispell, on the western edge of Waterton-Glacier International Peace Park and the Blackfoot Indian Reservation. Whitefish had everything she would need if she decided to stay in town for more than a few days.

She was in Montana because she was considering selling the cabin since she had only used it once since her mother's death. She didn't know how long it would take to get the ball rolling, so her plans were indefinite.

This trip to the U.S. was all about selling property—her mother's cabin in Montana and her father's home in California. She found that being a partner in the building business with her son in California was taking up more of her time and money than she'd figured, and she still had part ownership of the house in Paris as well as the two houses in Cornwall. It was time to downsize to maintain peace of mind and pocketbook.

Now that her son and daughter-in-law had moved from her beloved father's estate into a house they chose for themselves in Malibu, there was no reason to hang onto the Brentwood house. The upkeep and taxes on the Tudor house were astronomical, and it wasn't something she wanted to take the risk of leasing to a rowdy and destructive tenant, which was more apt in that part of the world than not. It would be more trouble than it was worth. So she was going to L.A. after she finished business in Montana to take care of business in California. She was sad to sell the house in Brentwood, for it was all she had left to remind her of her dear father, but it was time. The past was past and her life was changing every single day, going in a different direction.

Traffic leaving the airport was light at that time of day, the population of Kalispell a little over 21,500, so most people were home by nine p.m. anyway. She'd driven the fourteen miles back and forth from Kalispell to Whitefish before, so she knew the way well enough.

Nightfall was just beginning, and she noticed a few houses were lit up across the meadows and in the foothills leading up into the mountains. She'd always felt there was a warm and down-homey feel about this part of the country.

She drove with the windows down, feeling the breeze whip through her hair. *God, the air is so pure up here!* She breathed it in while thoughts of Maxim surfaced. She wondered what he was doing right at that moment. It would be early morning in Moscow, around eight, she figured. *I should call him right now. Nah, I'll call him later after I've settled in.*

She visualized him reading the newspaper, preferring to hold a paper rather than hunch over his laptop like she did. He was computer literate, but he still liked his morning news on real paper. In many ways he was old-fashioned. *That comes along with age, most likely,* she thought offhandedly as she slowed down and entered the upscale ski resort town of Whitefish.

Yep! It feels great to be back in the good ol' U S of A!

Chapter 25

The next morning, after spending the night in the charming mountain ski lodge, Rachel set off for her mother's cabin that was just off Highway 2; a portion of the loop that circled through the national forests and the wilderness areas. The cabin was east of Whitefish and west of the Blackfoot Indian Reservation and the town of Browning, where she'd gone for her mother's memorial service several years before. The cabin was situated halfway between Whitefish and Browning, near Essex.

Her mother had taught school at the reservation for years, being Blackfoot Indian herself. Rachel's father was British, so that made Rachel an interesting biracial mix.

Fifteen years earlier, while she was on a soul-searching trip, Rachel had shockingly discovered her mother teaching at the Blackfoot reservation in Montana. Since she was three years old, Rachel thought her mother, Lily, was dead. It was indeed a traumatic event, stumbling upon Lily as she did, but a moment she forever treasured because she was given the opportunity to get to know her mother in her final years.

She and Lily forgave Neal O'Neill for the vicious lie he fabricated when Rachel was a little girl, and they all moved forward with renewed spirits. Lily was a spiritual guru of sorts, and very wise.

111

She had been acknowledged for her accomplishments and deeds by people from all over the world. Rachel didn't know what all that entailed until the all-day memorial service in Browning after her mother died.

Lily had portrayed herself to Rachel as a woman with simple tastes and a simple life, never giving a clue of the accolades and eminent renown she'd attained through her teachings and the inspirational books and poetry she'd written using a pseudonym. It came as a great surprise to Rachel at the memoriam when she met some of Lily's followers.

The entire process gave Rachel more insight into herself, her roots, feelings, and traits. It had helped to encourage her even more, and she continued on her own spiritual path even more after that experience, guided by her mother's teachings and memory.

As her attention returned to the dirt road that led to the cabin, she realized just how long it had been since she had visited the place, and although she'd locked it up and made provisions for its safety and protection from the elements, she worried that neglect might have caused some deterioration.

She was pleased to find that it was in great shape. No trees had fallen on it, no break-ins, the shuttered doors and windows were still tightly fastened, and the water pipes weren't damaged. It took no time at all for her to start up the generator in the attached shed and to open all the windows to air out the place.

It saddened her to think about selling the place her mother had so artfully created and where she had spent all her years alone. Rachel began to have second thoughts about it.

Why couldn't she keep it? Why couldn't she spend more time there? It was easy enough to reach from Kalispell airport. She could drive directly from the airport to the cabin in a little over an hour. She didn't need to rent a hotel room in Whitefish.

She spent the rest of the morning cleaning: sweeping the wooden floors, shaking and beating the rugs, dusting the furniture, washing the windows, changing the bed linens, and tidying the bathroom. It was basically a huge one-room cabin, the ceiling being the underside of the high-pitched roof. The bathroom, storage, and closet ran along the north side of the cabin. The kitchen was a corner cleverly sectioned off in the great room. It was obvious how her mother had lovingly designed her home.

Through the open windows, the combined scent of pine trees and wildflowers rode the breeze into the house. Periodically Rachel would pause, standing up straight and stretching, then she would close her eyes and take in deep breaths of the mountain freshness.

It was a clear, brilliant day; cool, but not cold. Rachel wore a turtleneck sweater, her usual, and jeans. Suddenly she remembered a recurring dream she'd had a few years back . . . living in a mountain cabin, wearing black turtleneck and jeans, a flower garden, cats and dogs . . .

She dragged a chair made out of tree branches onto the wide front porch, then fetched a cup of coffee and sat with her feet resting on the porch railing.

This is the life! She sipped her coffee while gazing across grassy subalpine meadows graced with wildflowers that stretched to a small lake on the property that was busy with birds and other critters. She wondered how the fishing was.

The sounds of the forest, the rustling of foliage, crickets chirping, bees buzzing among the huckleberry blossoms and pink heather, lulled her senses.

A few of the herbs her mother had tended at one time still thrived wildly at the edge of the meadow: avalanche lily, queen's cup, beargrass, alpine paintbrush, and others with names Rachel couldn't remember. She had also forgotten how lovely it all was.

White rhododendron shrubs were in abundance. Her mother had loved their blossoms growing on the bushes at the base of the trees to the right of the cabin.

I can't sell this!

Chapter 26

Rachel moved her belongings from the hotel to the cabin. It felt right to be there. Over the next couple of days she settled in and didn't want to leave.

She decided to telephone her son. After dialing, she grabbed her glass of champagne and sat on the porch gazing at the stars that were beginning to appear.

"Devin?"

"Mom! It's about time you called. I was worried."

"Nothing to worry about, I'm still in Montana."

"I thought you would be here by now." Devin reached for a cigarette on the kitchen counter. It was six p.m. in Malibu. The sunset was going to be a beautiful one, he noted, looking through the expansive window that stretched from one side of the house to the other facing the ocean. "Wait a minute, Mom. Kellie!"

Kellie was standing at the glass railing on the veranda. She turned and Devin signaled for her to come indoors.

"So when are you coming?" he asked his mother.

"Well, I think I'll stay here another week or two. I'm really enjoying it. And I don't think I'll sell the place after all. It's such a neat cabin, Devin. You and Kellie have got to come up and use it whenever you want."

"So you're keeping it?" Devin looked at Kellie, putting his hand over the mouthpiece. "Mom's keeping the cabin."

"Yes, I believe so. It feels good. I'll just have to start coming here more often. I can use it to get away to another place to write. I had figured to do that at the beginning after your grandmother died, but for one reason or another I didn't. But I think now I will."

"Sounds good to me. I can use it to hunt and fish. Lots of that going on up there."

Kellie frowned. "What about me? What will I do while you're out doing your man thing?"

Rachel heard Kellie and laughed. "Tell her—"

"Wait." Devin put the speaker on. "Okay, she can hear you now."

"Hi, Kellie."

"Hi! Can't wait to see you!"

"Kellie, there're some really neat boutiques in Whitefish. It's a ski resort. You'll love it. They're trying to be another Vail, I think. Busy all the time. So you'll have plenty to do while Devin's being sportsy. And Kalispell isn't far away, either, has the big box stores and chains. So you can shop 'till you drop. And I've just installed a satellite service too, so no problem with computers and TVs. You can let the dogs run wild."

Kellie leaned in towards the phone. "Uh, what about the bears? Don't think I want my babies to be bear bait."

Rachel laughed. "They'll keep out of the way of the bears, I'm sure. And I don't believe there are many around. I haven't seen any yet, but we can find out about that before you come up."

"That's part of the draw of the north," Devin chimed in. "Bears and other big game."

"Oh yeah? Well, it isn't part of my draw," Kellie said. "You can go by yourself. Just leave me the credit cards and I'll be happy. A beach and a credit card is all I need."

They laughed.

"Well, there's a little beach of sorts down by the lake, Kellie," Rachel told her. "Not as warm here as you might like, but it's pleasant enough. So, guys, I'll be in Malibu in a couple of weeks or so. Want to take care of a few things here first before I leave, spruce the place up a bit. I am going to sell the Brentwood house, though. So if you'll make sure it's ready to list, Devin, that'll be great."

"Already is, Mom. I took care of that this week. Took care of a few repairs, so we're all set to go. All you have to do is set the price."

"Terrific! Okay, in a few days I'll let you know exactly when I'm coming. Bye. Love you."

"See you when you get here!" Kellie said.

"Bye, Mom," said Devin. "Love you too."

Chapter 27

A week had passed since Rachel had settled into the cabin, and she had made several trips back and forth to Kalispell, one to exchange her rental car for a pickup truck with 4-wheel drive to haul her purchases.

She bought a couple of picnic tables, the old-fashioned kind - redwood with benches attached - one for the lakeside and one for her front yard. She had always loved those tables. They reminded her of when she was a little girl growing up in Bakersfield, California. Those, along with clotheslines, fishponds, fruit trees, and flower gardens were all fond memories and gave her cozy feelings. Here at the cabin on the edge of the woods was a perfect place to recreate those childhood feelings. She had needed it, obviously.

She even installed a clothesline in the backyard for old time's sake. Finding clothespins wasn't easy though. The stores didn't carry them anymore. There evidently wasn't a market for them since most people used dryers. But she finally found some in a crafts store – wooden pins used to make clothespin dolls. Rachel also bought a top of the line washer and dryer in addition to the clothesline for the warm, fuzzy memories.

Now she was on her way to Kalispell for the third time that week. This time she was going to pick up sand and gravel to add to the beach at the lake, and to create footpaths around her flower beds and the cabin, leading down to the lake.

Her cell phone rang. She saw who it was on the led screen. "Hello, Maxim! You aren't going to believe what I'm doing."

"I could never guess, I am sure. What is it, my darling?"

"I'm driving a pickup truck to Kalispell to buy gravel and sand for the cabin. No writing for me today." She laughed.

"I wish I were there to help you. You may not know it, but I am a good hand in the garden."

"Oh, I do know that about you. I've watched you tend your grounds with your gardeners in Moscow. I know you love doing it. That's one of the things that attracted me to you."

"Is that so? And what else attracts you? Please tell me. I need to know," he said with a quiet, sad note in his voice.

Rachel heard it. "Are you alright, Maxim?"

"Oh, it's the adjustments I'm going through, I'm sure. Retiring has been such a life change. I find myself napping throughout the day. I've never done that before. I seem to get tired so easily. And I'm sad that you are so far away, my love. I'm missing you. This doesn't seem right for two people who are going to be married."

"As soon as I get to California we'll figure it all out. Maybe you would like to come there and meet my son. Would you like that? He lives in Malibu, a beautiful spot on the Pacific beach. Might be good for you . . . and me."

An SUV coming towards Rachel swerved off the road and toppled over on its side in the ditch.

"Oh, my god! Maxim, I'll call you back. A car just swerved and rolled into a ditch. I need to call for help. Bye!"

Before he could respond she had clicked off and called 911.

She pulled up a few yards from the vehicle and ran to see if the driver was alright.

A young woman was climbing out through the driver's window as the passenger side was in the mud. "Dammit!" she exclaimed. "Son of a bitch!" She was dusting off her jeans and re-tucking her shirttail when Rachel arrived.

"Are you alright?" Rachel touched her arm with one hand, and with the other searched her face and head to see if there were any cuts.

"I'm okay. Just a little shaken. Damn! I don't know what happened."

"You swerved into the left lane then cut to the right and rolled over. It's a wonder you're not injured or even worse. I've called 911."

"Can I use your phone?" the young woman asked. "Mine's somewhere in that mess. I need to call my brother at the ranch. He'll come get me."

"Sure. Here." Rachel handed her the phone.

The young woman punched in the numbers. "Arlie? I rolled the SUV. Can you come get me?"

"I can take you home," Rachel interrupted. "I'd like to. Please, let me."

The young woman looked at her. "Are you sure?"

"Of course. I'm not on a schedule, so it works for me. We can go as soon as the emergency people get here and we know for sure you're alright."

The young woman appeared to think it over for a moment, then acquiesced with a smile. "Okay. Arlie? I'll have this woman bring me. She saw the whole thing. No, just my car. I don't know how it happened. Swerved off the road and rolled into the ditch, I guess. I'm fine. No cuts, no bumps. I'm fine. Bye."

Rachel waited for her to hang up before introducing herself with a smile. "I'm Rachel O'Neill, and I have a cabin up on Highway Two near Essex."

The younger woman smiled back. "Do you? I'm Allegra McAdams. Nice to meet you."

They shook hands.

"That's beautiful country up there by Glacier Park," Allegra said. We have a cabin a bit to the east and further up by the Canadian border, as well as our main ranch just west of here. We're not far. I was on my way home from Kalispell, from a doctor's appointment." Her face seemed to cloud over. She turned and put her hands in her pockets, kicking at the gravel alongside the road. "What next? Jeez!

What is going to happen next?" She covered her face with her hands and began to cry.

"Allegra!" Rachel reached for her and put her arms around her. "Hold on, the paramedics will be here soon. I hear them now. Here, let's sit in my truck. You're in shock." She guided her to the passenger side and helped her into the seat.

Rachel stood by the open door, stroking Allegra's arm as the ambulance arrived, the state police right behind them. She waved to the paramedics, letting them know the driver was in her truck.

After a few minutes of checking her over, it was determined that she wasn't hurt, just shaken up, and could be taken home by Rachel.

The police made a report and the tow truck arrived. They emptied out the personals from the SUV and gave them to Rachel in a plastic bag, with a business card telling where the vehicle would be held for insurance purposes.

Rachel got into the truck and turned it around, heading north again, following Allegra's directions.

"I'm sorry I cried," Allegra said. "It's just that so much has happened to me in the past few weeks, and this is just the last damn straw!"

"Well, one thing about it, you're not hurt and your car can be fixed. So there's nothing to worry about."

Allegra shook her head. "It isn't that." She looked over at Rachel with tearful eyes, wondering, hesitating, then blurting out: "I just found out I'm pregnant!"

"That's great!" Rachel replied. "Congratulations!"

Allegra looked out the side window at the majestic mountains rising from the foothills. "No, it isn't great. I was raped a few weeks ago, and this is the baby. I'm not married, don't even have a boyfriend." She looked back at Rachel with tears in her eyes. "I'm sorry. It's just that I haven't told anybody about the rape, other than my doctor and brother." She began sobbing.

Rachel pulled to the side of the road. She reached over and held Allegra's hands. "I was the victim of a brutal date rape, so I know exactly how you're feeling."

"You were?" Allegra's eyes widened as she looked at Rachel.

"Yes, in fact the bastard went for me twice. Almost killed me the second time. And those memories will always be with me. But I'm alive, and I've created a lovely life for myself. Sure there have been bumps along the way, other tragedies, but somehow I always survive. That survival instinct is in all of us. Even in you."

Allegra thought for a moment as Rachel pulled onto the road. "You know, I thought I had it all under control. I'm good at that. Keeping everything under control. Hiding my feelings. And now there's this . . . this little, live being . . . forming in my body. A tiny being who doesn't belong to anyone, anywhere." Her voice broke again.

Rachel handed her a tissue from the compartment between the seats. "Not true. He belongs to you and doesn't know how he got here. Just knows he's in a soft, warm place and he's yours." Rachel grinned through tears of her own. She felt such empathy and motherly feelings for the young woman sitting beside her. It had been an instant attraction, as it had been with her dear friend Amanda in Brussels.

"Turn left by that bunch of mailboxes," Allegra instructed. "How do you know it's a he? You called it a he." She blew her nose and blotted her eyes.

"Oh, just a feeling." Rachel grinned back at Allegra. "So tell me what happened. It might do you good to talk about it. One of my best friends was brutally gang-raped and had a lovely baby. I'll have to tell you about it another time."

Rachel hadn't thought of Belinda lately, or the circumstances surrounding Baby Jake's birth. That's what they called him, Baby Jake, like *baby* was part of his name. She knew all too well that out of that tragedy nearly nine years earlier in London, a brief fairytale romance emerged, and the birth of two beautiful children.

"Stay at the ranch for dinner tonight," Allegra insisted. "Oh, turn right, just past the sign. Stay and we'll barbecue some steaks. Then we can have a nice, long talk. You tell me about you and your friend, and I'll tell you about me if you're interested. How's that?"

"Works for me," Rachel said with a grin as she drove through the open gates of the impressive McAdams Ranch.

Chapter 28

When they arrived, Rachel met the ranch foreman and his sidekick in the front yard. The two of them had just been inside the ranch house with Arlie.

Arlie must have heard them talking, for he came out the front door with a worried look on his face. "Leggie, are you alright? I talked with Jeb and he said it's going to take a lot of work to get the SUV up and running again, so I called the Dodge dealer and got you another one. They'll deliver it tomorrow." He hugged her gently. "Anything hurt on you? No bones broken, no bruises?" Holding her back from him he looked her over from head to toe. "How did it happen?"

"Well, if you'll stop talking for a minute I can answer your questions one at a time!" Allegra exclaimed. "But first I want to introduce you to the lady who saw it happen and came to my rescue. This is Rachel O'Neill," she said, gesturing toward the older woman. "She lives up on Highway Two on the south end of Glacier. Has a cabin up there, was on her way to Kalispell to do some shopping. And this is Arlie, Rachel. My big brother in more ways than one." She grinned mischievously.

Arlie shook hands with Rachel. "So nice to meetcha, ma'am. We're glad you came along just in time to pick up our little Leggie here. Come on in. This calls for a drink! I'm buyin'."

The two ranch hands said their goodbyes and headed for their pickup truck.

"Here we go, ladies, in here." Arlie beckoned them into his study. "This is my drinkin' room, Rachel. My library, study, or office, whatever you want to call it. Your choice. I'll pour the drinks and then we can go out on the patio if you want. Leggie, you want us to do that? Actually, y'all go on out there and I'll have Juan bring the drinks out to us. What's your medicine, Rachel?"

"You wouldn't by any chance have some champagne, would you? That's always my choice of medicine. Of course I know it might not be a staple in a ranch bar."

"I most certainly do have champagne," Arlie replied with a grin. "Some of the best around, as a matter of fact. Would some Moët and Chandon fit the bill? Brut, okay? Just got a couple cases from Billings."

"For goodness sakes, yes! Of course! I am so surprised." Rachel laughed.

"Well, you go on outside, the two of you. I'll follow along as soon as I find Juan. Go on, now. Skedaddle!"

Rachel followed Allegra down the long hallway to the Great Room and then out to the barbecue area.

"This is a beautiful ranch house, Allegra."

"Yes, it's a combination of my mother and father; they designed and decorated it together. When I'm here I feel like they're still around. Nothing's been touched since my mother was killed."

"Killed?" Rachel sat across from Allegra in one of the oversized cushioned patio chairs.

"She was murdered a little over two years ago. We don't know who did it. My father died before that, though. Had cancer."

"So the murder hasn't been solved?"

"No. It's a mystery to all of us, my brothers and me."

"You have more brothers?"

Allegra nodded. "Yes, a younger brother in New York. Allan. He wasn't living here when it happened, and Arlie was in Billings for a cattle auction. So Mother was here by herself that night. Except for

123

the ranch hands and the house help. No one heard anything, though. Not even the gunshots. She was killed with her own gun."

Arlie came through the double doors with Juan in tow. "Here we are, young ladies. Just what the doctor ordered. Champagne for you, Rachel," he handed her a glass, "and single malt for you, my dear Leggie. And a double whiskey for me." He lifted his glass. "To your safe return, sis."

"And to our newfound friend," Allegra added, grinning at Rachel.

Chapter 29

It was another meat-and-potatoes meal at the McAdams ranch that night. Arlie invited a couple of neighboring ranchers and their wives over to join them and meet their new neighbor. His waitress friend Tammy Sue was helping out in the kitchen.

Rachel was flattered that Arlie would go to all that trouble, and felt a bit ill at ease that he did. She wasn't among their 'rancher' ranks, being merely a visitor to Montana. A part-time resident at best, she explained, but they wouldn't have it. To them she was a neighbor, and that warranted the attention and the welcome they were giving her.

After dinner they all moved outdoors to the fire pit. Tammy Sue sat next to Arlie, as if she were attached to him in some way, other than being the waitress from the local diner helping out in the kitchen. In fact, it was obvious they were more than just friends as they would occasionally touch each other, and the way they looked in each other's eyes gave them away. No one seemed to be surprised, however, except Allegra.

One of the wives had heard about Rachel's mother, Lily of the Blackfoot Nation, and was familiar with what she'd done for the Native American children and causes over the years. She said her own daughter had read her children's books, so that was thrilling for Rachel to hear.

"Like mother, like daughter," Allegra said. "Both writers."

"And Leggie is a writer, too," Arlie piped up. "We're surrounded by 'em tonight." He lifted his drink towards them both, then gulped it down. "Well, I guess I better roust out our man. We're running a bit low in the liquid department. 'Scuse me, folks, I'll be right back." He went into the house. The men followed him.

The women stayed seated by the fire. After a few moments, Tammy Sue went inside to help out in the kitchen, not feeling comfortable among the ranchers' wives.

Joyce, the one who knew about Rachel's mother, reached for another stick of wood and placed it in the pit. "Leggie, what do you hear from Allan these days?"

Allegra shrugged. "He's okay, last I heard. You know how it is . . . no news is good news." She winked at Rachel.

"I've thought about him quite a lot lately," Joyce said. "He and our Les used to be inseparable. Allan was over at our place more than he was here, I suppose. While he was growing up. It was a shame he couldn't get along with your dad. I'm surprised he didn't come back here to live after your dad died. I would think he'd want to come back after that. He was more of a mama's boy, wasn't he?"

Allegra nodded. "Yes, you're probably right." She looked directly at Rachel. "Rachel, could you help me for a minute?" She stood and started for the house.

"Sure," Rachel said and followed.

Inside the Great Room, she grabbed Rachel's arm, giggling, and quickly took her up the stairs to her bedroom. They could hear the men laughing and talking in Arlie's office.

"I couldn't take another minute of that horrible, nosy, woman. She drives me nuts. It's like she's always trying to find out things, you know?" Allegra plopped down on the bed. "I am so tired."

"Why don't I go back down and tell Arlie you're feeling exhausted from all that's happened today, and that you want to call it a night?"

"And then come back up here so we can talk. Okay?"

"That I can do. I'll be right back. Can I bring you something?" Rachel stood at the door awaiting her reply.

"Yes, would you bring me some of that cake? I'm dying for another piece," Allegra said with a wide grin and then closed her eyes.

"I will. Be right back."

Within twenty minutes Rachel had returned to Allegra's room carrying a tray of tea and cake. She knocked on the door and waited. No answer. She gently turned the knob and saw that Allegra was sound asleep on the bed. She looked like a little girl lying there.

Rachel set the tray on a table flanked by two chairs near the window, then picked up what looked like a handmade quilt from the foot of the bed and spread it over the young woman.

After writing a note with pen and paper from Allegra's desk, she quietly turned off the lights and left the room.

She bade farewell to Arlie and the guests and left.

It had been a long day for her, too, full of unexpected happenings. Time for her to call it a night as well.

The drive back to her cabin was quick and easy.

The sky was darkening, stars were beginning to sparkle. Rachel marveled at the big, navy blue Montana sky as she lay in her bed gazing out the window that night at the moon.

She thought of her mother and the many moons she had watched from that same window. She felt Lily's presence and was at peace.

Thoughts of Allegra's mother disturbed that peace.

Thoughts of Allegra disturbed her peace. All Rachel could think of was how the girl had first lost her father to cancer, then her mother was murdered, and now she had been raped in her own home in Malibu. The poor girl had been through a lot, and it weighed heavily on Rachel's heart and mind.

127

Chapter 30

Allegra couldn't believe she'd fallen asleep and didn't wake up until morning. She had to focus to get her bearings, unable to figure why she was lying on top of her bedspread in her clothing with a quilt over her.

When she saw the tray of cake with a note propped up on it, she remembered.

"For heaven's sakes. How could I be that tired? How rude of me." She reached for the note from Rachel and after reading it picked up the phone. It was ten a.m. She'd slept at least twelve hours.

When the person on the other end picked up, Allegra blurted her words out in one long breath. "Rachel? Hi, it's Allegra. I'm so sorry I was such a party pooper last night. I wanted so much to hear more about your writing and life in the UK. Can we do lunch tomorrow?"

"Of course!" Rachel replied. "I'd love to. Why don't you come up here for lunch? It's easy to find. Call me when you leave and I'll direct you."

"Okay, I'll leave here tomorrow at noon. How's that?"

"Perfect! See you then."

Just as she ended the call, Allegra's cell rang. "Hello?"

"Hi, Leggie!"

"Allan! For heaven's sake, you must be reading my mind. We were just talking about you last night."

"Oh, my dear. Who was doing the talking? Don't tell me you were talking on the phone with my sweet big brother Arlie?'

Allegra laughed. "No, silly. It was that cow from down the road from the ranch. You know the one. She was getting pretty nosy so I just cut off the conversation. That's one way of stopping her probing questions."

"The only way. I do that quite often myself. Must be a family trait. I've become quite adroit at it. Uh, Allegra . . . I was wondering if you could send me some money, dear one. I'm really in dire straits and I know Arlie isn't going to go for it. He told me to piss off last time I talked to him. What's his problem, anyway? I'm still his brother whether he likes it or not. You know, dearie, I've never said anything, but I was at the ranch the week Mother was murdered, left the day before, and she told me she was going to leave me the little ranch and a thousand acres north of it. I could have sold the extra acreage, which is what she suggested, and not have the problems I'm having today. It's just humiliating to live in New York City without any money to speak of."

"I didn't know you were at the ranch that week!" Allegra exclaimed. "Arlie never said anything about it."

"Are you kidding? He didn't know. I stayed at the cabin, out of sight. Mother called me when he left for Billings to go to a cattle auction that week. I must have blocked it out of my mind after all was said and done. I thought I told you. It was just too painful to think of, after seeing her before . . . before that horrible thing happened to her. That's why I couldn't come to the funeral. Just couldn't do it. If only I had stayed a little longer. I feel so guilty, Allegra. That's why I don't talk about it."

Still a bit groggy, Allegra reached for the cold tea from the night before and gulped it down. "So have you spent all your trust money?"

"Almost. This condo costs me a fortune. And of course I had to furnish it top notch. I mean, I have visitors from all over the world. I've met some pretty high-up jetsetters, love. And it costs money to entertain them and to travel back and forth to Europe as much as I do. I have to keep up the front, right?"

"Well, if you're running out of money, I would think you would slow down a bit, don't you think? Live within your means? What about your art? Have you been able to do some painting? You're so talented, Allan. You shouldn't give up on that. You could be making a decent living from it."

"I know, I know. But it's so time-consuming, Leggie. I have so much I'd rather be doing. Now, I've been thinking about Mother's will. Why wasn't the little ranch left to me? Could you find out about that? She said she had an appointment scheduled with the attorney to change the will to reflect that, when I was there that week before she died. Seems odd to me that it wasn't done. Do you know anything about it? I've tried to call the attorney several times and he won't talk to me. Arlie's got a hand in it, I suppose. Why didn't I have all sisters? Life would be so much easier."

Allegra smiled as she visualized Allan, probably nude, in a white terry robe, sipping a mimosa on his balcony. She could hear the background music as well as the city noises.

"How much do you need?" she asked, heaving a huge sigh. If Arlie knew she was going to give Allan money again, he'd croak.

"Twenty-five thousand would tide me over for now, my sweet. The HOA expenses are paid for a year, so I just need it for incidentals and other living expenses. And I try so hard to keep within my budget. I do. But everything is so expensive. You know how it is; it must be the same in Malibu. God, it has to be expensive out there. Is the sun shining for you on the beach, dear?"

"I'm not in Malibu," Allegra replied. "I'm at the ranch. Came up for a few days and I'm still here, weeks later. Look, I'll wire the money to you this afternoon. Same bank account, right?"

"Oh my dearest, most dear, sweet sister! Yes, yes. Same bank. You have saved my hopeless little life. How can I ever repay you? I love you, Leggie-poo-poo. Thank you, thank you, thank you ever so much. Bye bye now. Hate to rush, girl, but I have to get dressed. Lots to do. Talk to you soon, love."

Allegra smiled and shook her head as she listened to the silence on her cell after he had hung up. She never could resist Allan's childlike behavior, any more than her mother could.

Why weren't the little ranch and the extra acreage left to Allan in her mother's will? Allan wouldn't lie about something like that. He wouldn't lie about anything. It wasn't in his nature.

Oh! She forgot to ask him about the shoe in the incinerator. Damn!

She made a mental note to call the attorney later about Allan's claim in the will, but first she needed to shower and go to the bank in Kalispell.

Funny how she'd not only forgotten about the shoe, but she forgot all about being pregnant.

Rachel spent the afternoon in Kalispell loading up with garden tools, new plants and shrubs, a fountain and a bird bath. She also bought several redwood planters as well as some decorative pots. It didn't matter where she lived; she had to have her gardens. It was the same with her houses in Cornwall and in Paris. She loved flower gardens.

Then she stopped by the drugstore to pick up a prescription she'd called in.

At Walmart she ran into Joyce from the barbecue the night before.

"Hiya, Rachel. I see you've found our Walmart."

"Joyce, is it? Good to see you again. Yes, I always am able to find a Walmart wherever I go in the States."

"What do they have in England? Do you have stores like Walmart?"

"As a matter of fact, Walmart owns ASDA in the UK, another big box chain," Rachel said as she placed a couple of blankets in her basket.

"They're all over the world, I guess," Joyce replied. "It's Woolco up in Canada that they own. Amazing, isn't it? Old man Walton knew what he was doing, didn't he? Now his kids have it all.

Are your novels here in Walmart, do you think? Would they be at Costco?"

"Don't know, might be. Haven't looked." Rachel inched away from Joyce as she spoke. "Well, it's been good seeing you again, got to get going, have an appointment with a carpenter. Bye now." And off she went before Joyce could say another word. She rushed to the opposite end of the store and peered back around a corner to see where she had gone.

She was at a check stand.

Hallelujah!

Rachel continued shopping and stocked up on enough food to last the duration of her stay. She figured two more weeks at the most would do it. She figured she should probably leave before the end of July.

Chapter 31

The picnic table and benches were perfect. A red-checkered tablecloth was spread over it and a potted yellow chrysanthemum was placed in the middle with ivy spread around it. Two red plates sat on yellow-and-pale-blue plaid place mats, and Lily's silverware lay neatly beside them on dark blue napkins.

Rachel had made a potato salad and pastrami sandwiches, all ready and waiting for her guest to arrive. It was nearly half past noon.

She heard the honks before she saw the SUV coming up the drive.

Through the screened door she flew and stood on the porch, grinning with excitement. Allegra was her first guest at the cabin. She had always liked the feeling that entertaining guests gave her. It was fulfilling in some strange way.

"I'm here! Sorry I'm late!" Allegra called out as she emerged from the SUV with two plastic bags. "Brought you some peaches and some tomatoes from our garden. Look at that, will you? You've already set the table. Wow!"

Rachel took the bags of fruit from her and set them on the table on the porch. Then she hugged Allegra. "How are you feeling, hon? Everything all right?"

"I guess so. I keep forgetting I'm pregnant. I don't feel anything, you know? I can't believe there's a baby growing inside me. When do I start feeling something?" She followed Rachel into the cabin.

"About four or five months you'll start feeling it. Trust me."

"Oh." Allegra figured she was around three months along.

"Have you had morning sickness?"

"No, nothing."

"Well, that's good. I was sick every morning for the first six months, and it was not fun. I ate more crackers and oranges during that time than I had in my entire life." Rachel laughed. "Hopefully you'll escape that part of it. So are you acclimating to it? Feeling a little bit happy about having a baby?"

Allegra sighed. "I don't know how I feel, actually. I mean, how am I going to face Connie when I go back to Malibu? I can't tell him it's Eric's. What's he going to think of me? That I've been out screwing around? That bothers me more than anything else."

"Time will fix everything," Rachel replied. "You'll see. Trust me on that one." She began coughing. "Dammit!" She quickly poured a glass of water and drank it.

"Are you alright?" Allegra asked.

"I'm fine. Had a bout with pneumonia before I left home, still have a nagging cough. Nothing serious." She picked up the tray of salad and sandwiches and headed back outside. "Come on, let's eat. I'm starving."

After lunch and washing the dishes, Rachel and Allegra sat on the front porch drinking lemonade. Birds and bees were going about their business, adding to the music of the forest. The thrumming of hummingbirds' wings was louder than usual since Rachel had hung feeders across the length of the porch.

"I just love it out here, don't you?" Rachel said.

"Yes. I need to come back to Montana more. I forget how it is." Allegra sipped her drink. "Allan called yesterday morning. He wanted money and I sent it to him." She looked at Rachel. "Arlie will kick my butt when he finds out, *if* he finds out. I'm not going to tell him and the banker better not."

"He won't, will he?"

Allegra shrugged. "I don't know. Seems to me it's a matter of confidentiality. He could get into trouble if he did. You know, Allan told me something I didn't know, said that Mother was going to leave the little ranch and some additional acreage to him. Said she had an appointment with the attorney to revise the will that week before she died."

"It wasn't in the will?"

"No, not a word about it. So I dropped by the attorney's office yesterday and he said he knew nothing about it. When I got home I looked in her diary. Nothing's been moved from her room since she died, and there it was. She'd scheduled the appointment for the day *after* her death." Allegra swirled her drink, staring into the glass. She looked up at Rachel. "That's odd, isn't it? Murdered the night before?"

Rachel nodded. "That proves she was going to do it, like he said."

"Yes. I found her file cabinet keys and started looking through her files when Arlie came in. So I just closed the drawer and put the keys in my pocket. I told him I was looking for my birth certificate, needed it to renew my passport. I didn't want to have to explain anything to him. He'd kill me if he knew I was helping Allan."

"That's wise. You don't need the aggravation right now. You need to concentrate on that baby now."

"Rachel, tell me about your friend, about her being raped and having a baby, will you? When did that happen?"

"Almost nine years ago. I remember exactly when it was because that was the year after I spent New Year's Eve in London's Trafalgar Square. That's when and where I first ran into Paul, who married Belinda later that summer. We all actually met when I was making the move to Newlyn, in Cornwall. Belinda was recovering from the rape and she and Paul were there to rent a place for her. They weren't married then. She couldn't bear to live in London after the rape. Too many reminders, and she was terrified anyway because the rapists were still out there. So she moved to Mousehole, lived above her studio, and shortly after, Paul followed. Mousehole is a tiny village a couple miles north of Newlyn Bay, as far west as you can get from London. In fact, as it turns out, I'm the godmother of both of her children. Two boys. They're adorable."

"So the first one was the result of the rape in London?" Allegra asked.

"Yes. A horrible gang rape that almost killed her. They meant to kill her. Stabbed her. Left her to die on a parking garage floor."

"God! That makes me shudder. Eric was brutal as it was, but to be attacked by several men . . . I don't think I would have been able to get past that at all. I probably would have died. Would have *wanted* to die." Allegra hugged her legs to her chest and rested her chin on her knees.

"What does that tell you about Belinda?" Rachel said. "She was amazing, and turned out to be an amazing mother. I still can't believe she's gone."

"Lymphoma, you said?"

"Yes. Nothing could be done when she reached the final stages. I miss her so much. I'm living in her house now, bought it from Paul. It's a lovely home on the hill by the sea. Suits me perfectly and I can feel her presence still."

"And the baby?"

"Baby Jake. Flaming red hair and a bundle of energy to match. He is precious, and so adorable. I can't imagine him not being born. It was her choice. She could have aborted. So you see, the baby can be a blessing, regardless of who the father is and what the circumstances are. Nothing is the baby's fault. They are born innocent. You have to remember that and deal with it as it unfolds." Rachel stood up. "You want some more lemonade?"

Chapter 32

Rachel woke up early one morning in the first week of July and put on the coffee. She wanted to watch the sun come up again before she tackled the novel she and Della were writing together. It had become a habit of late, up before sunrise. After she dressed in jeans and a black turtle neck sweater, she put on her boots and took a mug of coffee onto the front porch.

She breathed deeply and took a sip before she stepped down to the yard and walked to the redwood table. From the table she could see the first rays glowing in the east over the mountain. She sat, thinking as she waited, surveying her surroundings.

The garden blossomed, the wild herbs flourished, and the birds chirped uproariously as the skies began to lighten. It was a beautiful moment and Rachel felt humbled by it.

She cherished the quiet and the naturalness of it all. She felt her mother's presence that morning. No doubt about it.

When the sun's rays finally cleared the mountains, even before its fiery heart appeared, Rachel stood and walked back into the cabin to fix an egg and toast.

She felt her time in Montana was nearing an end, for she needed to get to California to take care of business. She'd put it off long enough.

But she was happy she'd come and happy she'd met so many people, from the ranch hands and salespeople in the town's stores to the neighboring residents, although far and few between. But there had been a few who'd stopped by from time to time, and a few who'd invited her to supper in the two fleeting months she'd been there.

One such neighbor was Sam Willis, a man whose property across the road ran up into the mountains to his log cabin. He'd seen her turn onto the main road from her driveway one day and flagged her down. He'd been fixing the fence along his property line.

"You livin' in Lily's cabin now?" he asked her when he got to the passenger window she'd rolled down.

"Yes. I'm Rachel, her daughter. Am fixin' it up a bit. You live on that side of the road?"

The man nodded. "I was born and raised here. In fact, I went to the Indian school and your mama was one of my teachers in high school. I'm part Blackfoot on my daddy's side. Your mama was my favorite teacher back then. She helped me go away to college and I did all that, did a stint in the Air Force, and decided after I got out that I didn't want to go anywhere but back home. I'd had enough of the big, wide world. So I came home and have been here ever since. Fifty years and this is a far as I've gotten," he laughed.

"Do you have a family?"

He shook his head. "No, never married, no kids, just me and my dogs and cats. And some cattle and horses. Oh, and some goats and mules. Rabbits, chickens." He laughed again, his eyes sparkling as bright as his teeth. "And you?"

"A son in California. I think it's neat that you knew my mother your whole life. I wish I had. Come over for supper one night and tell me some more about it. Would you do that?"

"I have a better idea. You come over to *my* place and I'll show you some pictures of her and our class way back then. And you can meet my family. The pets, of course. My family."

Rachel smiled. "I'd love to."

So she met Sam's pets and listened to his stories, and was surprised by his superb paintings: watercolor and oil landscapes of the northwest. He said her mother had taught him to listen to his inner self, and his inner self told him to paint. He gave her one of each.

Sam became a regular visitor. He would drop by, bearing fruit and vegetables from his garden, with or without warning and the two of them had some great laughs together. On occasion, Allegra would join them, sometimes Arlie.

It was easy making friends in Montana. Rachel had never been a neighborly sort before, and she had to admit she was going to miss them all.

Chapter 33

It was a brilliant morning, the sky a pale blue with a few billowing white clouds in the distance over the Teton Mountain Range. The sun blazed hotter than usual, causing Allegra to take off her leather jacket and place it over her suitcase.

"When did she say she'd be here? It's five after already," Arlie said as he removed his hat and wiped his brow with a neck scarf.

"She'll be here. We've plenty of time. Plane doesn't leave till eleven."

"A coincidence she's going to Malibu too, isn't it? And her son living on the same street you do. How many times does that happen? It's a damn omen, I would say."

Allegra shaded her eyes and looked towards the gate at the end of the road. "Yes, I believe it is. I was shocked that her son lives in the Colony too. Malibu's quite a drive from the airport, so this really comes in handy, him picking us up. You know, I think I met him at one of the parties. He and his wife. Nice couple."

"There she is now," Arlie said, pointing. "To the left by the sign on the road."

They both watched Rachel approach, turning towards them through the gates and coming down the long driveway to the house.

Rachel saw them waving as she got closer. She was still in awe of the serendipity of it all. What were the chances of meeting someone in Montana who was a neighbor to her son in Malibu, actually living on the same street? What were the chances of that someone being a writer? Rachel had been flabbergasted, and still was.

It was as if her belief in past life experiences were proven once again. Here was a prime example of traveling through one life to another with the same people, with those you've known before, in whatever capacity. She believed that Allegra had to have been in one or more past lives with her, for the two of them had immediately bonded. There were too many coincidences that had unfolded in the short time they'd gotten to know each other in Montana, way too many for them not to have been acquainted before in a past life.

As she lay awake most of the previous night, for she never slept the night before going on a trip, her thoughts had shifted between the possibilities of those past lives, to thoughts of Maxim, then just as quickly to thoughts of Allegra's mother. Such a tragic way to lose a mother. Rachel was grateful her own mother had died peacefully on the Indian reservation with all of her admirers gathering to honor her life.

Allegra's mother had to have known her killer, since it wasn't a break-in. And the killer had to have known her gun was in the drawer next to her bed. Unless, on the other hand, if she had heard someone coming in, she would have grabbed the gun herself and was holding it when he came into her bedroom. Yes, that's probably what happened. She heard someone and had the gun in her hand. But then how did her assailant manage to get it from her *and* shoot her with it? She had to have known him to put the gun down. She thought about the burned shoes and clothing that Allegra and Connie had found in the incinerator. Allegra had told her all about Connie's visit and the day they went to the cabin. Most of all, it was heartbreaking and frightening that the killer was still on the loose.

Rachel wished she had more time to spend in Montana. She felt she'd only scratched the surface of its offerings. The two weeks she had planned on staying had become two months, and now she had no choice. She had to get to L.A. to take care of business.

141

Living in her mother's cabin while refurbishing it had been both satisfying and healing, and it was difficult to leave it and her new friends.

At least Allegra would be going with her. She felt a kinship with the young woman, same as she did with the other important people in her life. Yes, Allegra was certainly part of the 'spiritual group' that was traveling with her from one lifetime to another. She was sure of it.

Chapter 34

July 15

Devin and Kellie O'Neill were waiting in the baggage area of Alaska Airlines at LAX. They spotted Rachel and Allegra coming down the escalator and waved at them with wide grins.

Devin took their bags, only one each, and led them to the parking garage where his SUV was waiting.

Kellie was talking non-stop, wanting to know all about Montana, how they met, and so on. She was a speed talker; no one could get a word in edgewise even though she asked a question every other sentence.

Rachel had learned at the get-go to wait for a break in her one-way conversation, then quickly jump in with the information that had been requested. It wasn't a bad thing as far as Rachel was concerned. That way she didn't have to do a lot of talking. And she had warned Allegra already. They both looked at each other and winked.

"So are you keeping the cabin? What all have you done to it? I've never seen it, Allegra, so I don't know anything about it. What do you think? Is it adorable enough to eat? Probably like a big fat cupcake sitting in the woods, knowing Rachel. She makes everything so beautiful and feminine. Did you paint the shutters pink, Rachel? She likes pink."

"Kellie, let Mom talk. You're shooting too many questions at them." Devin laughed as he put the luggage in the vehicle. "Mom, you get in the front with me. She can talk Allegra's ear off in the back seat."

"It's okay," Rachel said. "No, Kellie, I didn't paint anything pink this time, although it's a good idea. I'm sure I'll add pink somewhere before it's over and done with." Rachel was never slighted by Kellie's comments. She understood her daughter-in-law's childlike inquisitiveness and her humor, knowing she never meant harm.

When they were on Pacific Coast Highway leading from the airport to Santa Monica and heading north to Malibu, Kellie asked Allegra about her house in the Colony, if they'd found the burglars yet. She told her she'd heard about it from Connie Brown's housekeeper, who was a friend of her cook.

It seemed that most of the help in the area was either related or friendly with each other. News traveled fast in Malibu via the domestic chain of communications. Kellie was always on top of what was happening in all the other households on Hollingsworth Drive. Especially the stars, since she was starstruck. She had an uncanny knack for finding things out, for she was truly interested in the goings-on in her neighborhood and she loved people. Her personality reflected it.

"I think you'll love our house, Mom," Devin said. "You're sure you don't mind that we didn't want to live in Grandpa's house?"

"Of course not, Devin. Other than the den, I knew it wasn't you. Besides, I'm sure Kellie is much happier on the beach instead of in Brentwood. Especially in the Malibu Colony. Can't beat that. And you know Daddy's house is getting old, needs to be modernized. Someone will buy it and do what they want with it."

"So you definitely are going to sell?"

Rachel looked at Devin. He reminded her of her father more and more as he got older. "Yes. No point in holding onto it. I can stay with you when I'm in L.A. doing business with my agent. So I don't really need a home here. My heart's in England, you know. That's my home base and always will be."

Devin reached over and massaged his mother's neck and shoulders, knowing she loved him doing that. "Yes, I know. And how are you doing in Cornwall? I still haven't seen your new house. Well, I saw it when Paul and Belinda owned it, but not since you've lived in it. I can imagine it's changed quite a bit." He grinned at her.

"It's a total change. And what fun that was, redecorating it. Della came and helped me."

"So how is the Russian faction?" Kellie asked.

"Russian faction? Now that's funny." She chuckled. "Well, Della and Valentin are happy as can be. They make a good match. She came to visit in Cornwall before I went to Montana. We're writing a crime novel together, and you might say we've become the best of friends."

"And Maxim? What about him? Are you still in love? When are you getting married?" Kellie shot off the questions one after the other.

"Maxim . . . ummm . . . Maxim. Well, I'm still working on that one. It's a hard call."

"Mom, you either love the guy or you don't. Simple as that," Devin said.

Rachel shook her head. "Nope, not that simple. I wish it were."

"Devin, we're having a party tomorrow night," Kellie interrupted from the back seat. "I just decided. I'll invite some of the neighbors to meet your mom. You can come, right, Allegra? It'll be fun. A happy-hour party, cocktails and munchies. I'm good at munchies. Well, my Dolores is. I just watch her throw it all together. So what do you say, Rachel? Okay with you?"

"Sure. Sounds good to me. We'll unwind tonight and be ready to meet the neighborhood tomorrow. Sure." Rachel smiled. She was happy with her son's choice of wife this time around. The last one hadn't been so good for him. He said Kellie made him laugh, and that was good.

"And tomorrow we'll have lunch at the Colony mall, Rachel. Wait till you see the cupcake place. I mean, those suckers are gigantic! You can come too, Allegra. Want to?"

"No, not tomorrow. I'm afraid I'll be busy putting things together at the house since I've been away for so long, and I have a new staff waiting for me. Need to get to know them. And I've some calls to return to my agent and the studios. Back to work, you see. Lots to do. But happy hour sounds doable."

Chapter 35

"Oh, my goodness! This is a mansion, Devin!" Rachel was astounded at what she saw as they drove up the gated driveway.

"What did I tell you? I knew you'd like it."

Kellie moved closer to the division between the two front bucket seats. "And I've got a pool and a beach on the ocean. What more could I ever want? I'm happy." She was grinning from ear to ear. "And you'll have your own set of rooms, plus an office to work in. So you can come and stay anytime you want, and as long as you want. The house is so big, you'll never know we're here and vice versa."

"Oh, I think she'll be able to hear where you are," Devin said with a chuckle. "If it's quiet then that means you're either outside or asleep."

Kellie hit his shoulder. "That's not nice, Devin. And it isn't true, I'm not that loud. You're just not used to anyone talking to you, jerko!"

Devin laughed, always amused by his wife's unabated remarks. "Okay, I'll let you out here and I'll bring your bag, Mom. You go ahead with Kellie."

They got out of the vehicle and Devin drove around to the garages.

Rachel looked up at the stained glass panel surrounding the huge light oak double doors. "Oh, Kellie! This is beautiful! Wow! No wonder you wanted to move from the Brentwood house. No comparison."

"I was hoping it wouldn't hurt your feelings that we didn't want to live there, Rachel. It was just too dark and gloomy for me."

"No, no. I totally understand. I mean, look at this!"

The expansive entryway was constructed of white marble floors, walls and columns. A staircase wound up to the first and second floors from the right, and a huge contemporary chandelier hung from the stained glass rotunda ceiling.

As they stood in the entryway, they could see all the way through the house and out the glass wall dividing it from the beach and the sea.

"My God! What a view from here! Wow! I can't stop saying wow!" Rachel laughed. "And your choice of colors is perfect, Kellie. Light blue, pale yellow, and white. And the red. Just the right amount. Perfect. I'll say it again . . . *wow*!"

Two shiatsus dogs came yelping and running from the hallway on the left.

"Oh, here they are! My little babies. Say hello to gramdma Rachel." Kellie scooped them up and hugged them. "This is Dolly and Donnie."

"They're so cute," Rachel said as they petted them.

"Okay, that's enough. Come on, I want you to see the patio." Kellie set the dogs on the floor and pulled Rachel down the spacious corridor, through the open living area that stretched across the back of the house, towards the glass wall and the giant glass doors that slid apart to create an opening to the outdoors. "Here's where I spend most of my time."

She held the dogs back while she slid open the door enough for her and Rachel to go through, and then closed it behind her. "We'll be back in a minute, sit, sit!" she said to the dogs through the glass pane.

They walked across the verandas of flagstone and polished granite, where potted palms and peonies flanked them in abundance.

The lawn stretched the width of the house to each side of the stone steps in the center, leading several levels down to the beach.

"Come see how close we are to the beach." Kellie's excitement was contagious as Rachel followed her. "Aren't we lucky it's such a pretty day today? No fog. Just beautiful!"

Rachel took deep breaths at the top of the steps, filling her lungs with clear, clean, filtered ocean air.

Kellie stood with her hands on her hips. Her tanned legs were gleaming in the sun. "Can you believe this?"

"Where's the pool?" Rachel asked.

"Inside. You aren't going to believe it. Come on, I'll show you the rest of the house."

Devin was waiting near the patio doors, smoking a cigarette. He loved seeing his mother and his wife laughing together. They posed quite a contrast: Rachel with her dark auburn hair, black tank top and matching jeans, Kellie with her bright blonde hair, canary yellow tank top and white shorts.

At the beginning of Devin's marriage it had been rather touch-and-go, mother and daughter-in-law getting to know each other, learning to accept one another.

Trust is the key, Rachel had explained to Devin. Trusting the son to choose the right mate, and trusting him to know how to separate his love for his wife from his love for his mother without slighting either, a tricky age-old dilemma. Rachel had discussed it with him after a misunderstanding during his first year of marriage.

In turn he helped her understand that Kellie was his choice. And regardless of the type his mother thought he should have, the choice was his. It wasn't that Rachel wasn't happy with Kellie; it was that she felt he needed a more domestic wife. Someone who openly adored him, would cook for him, pamper him, cater to him and take care of him. But then, she reminded herself, that sounded more like a mother's role. It would be too boring for Devin and for Kellie.

So Rachel knew he was right. Kellie was fun. He didn't care if she didn't cook or pamper, as long as he enjoyed her sense of humor, her energy, and the lifestyle they had together.

And if it didn't work out . . . well, he'd just join the ranks of all the other divorced men in the world. And that would be his choice, too.

But it appeared their marriage was working, and Rachel was proud of them.

Chapter 36

Two weeks had passed since Rachel arrived in Malibu. The month of August was upon them and soon the Southern California fall season would emerge, later than in most states.

Rachel was thinking about her home in Cornwall that morning, missing it, comparing it to Malibu. Although the California beach weather was perfection with its glorious dawns and sunsets, sunshine most every day, she was torn between the Malibu Pacific and her dramatic Cornwall Atlantic coast where one day it could be storming bloody murder, the next day clear as crystal. It seemed to reflect her own ever-changing moods, hence the comfort of it.

As she sipped her coffee on the balcony extending from her bedroom in her son's Malibu home, she gazed out at the early morning view of the beach and the glistening calm waters of the sea. She couldn't help but marvel at the strolling couples passing by at the water's edge, bare feet in the wet sand. Morning couples, surprisingly enough, not unlike the sunset lovers one expects on a beach. Either hand in hand, arm in arm, or periodically stopping to embrace. In Malibu it didn't matter what time of day it was. Love was all around.

The visual stirred up a warm and fuzzy feeling within Rachel; a happy, warm glow. It made her feel good to see love and intimacy

151

happening right before her eyes. In a world of so much fear and hatred, the daily scene on Malibu Beach was in stark contrast. Why couldn't everyone experience this side of life? But she knew the answer. She knew she sometimes fell victim to the Pollyanna Principle because she wished life could be good for everybody. Regardless, she closed her eyes and wished happiness and love for all, knowing it wasn't practical. Just around the corner, mayhem and murder were happening along with countless other atrocities in the world. But at that very moment she felt a radiance engulf her that surpassed anything she'd ever felt before. It was one of those moments when she was in awe and at peace with herself, overwhelmed with gratitude and gratefulness.

She opened her eyes as the gentle sound of the waves was interrupted by a group of teenagers jogging by with dogs on leashes. Laughter and shouts obliterated the precious sounds of nature. But it was still nature in a sense. People nature.

Rachel sighed and picked up the Philippa Gregory novel she had been reading earlier, took her coffee mug and went into the house. She liked kids, but this wasn't the morning for it. She also liked peace and daydreaming.

Usually that part of the beach was pretty isolated, not much noise or children. The wealthy residents were either past child-bearing age or their offspring were adults and lived elsewhere with small children of their own. Malibu Colony was almost considered an adult community.

She reflected as she entered the corridor from her bedroom leading to the stairs. Although her son had been married before, he hadn't made Rachel a grandmother yet. His previous marriages had been short-lived, pretty much like his mother's. She smiled at the thought, wondering if Devin and Kellie would even want children.

"Hey, Mom!" Devin was climbing the circular staircase. "I was just coming up to get you. We're going down to the Colony mall for breakfast. C'mon, time to get you out of here. You're becoming a recluse."

"I *am* a recluse," Rachel said with a laugh. "Didn't you know that? Most writers are recluses, at least part of the time. I am all of the time."

"Yes, I'm seeing that side of you now. But you didn't used to be that way." He waited and they walked down the stairs together.

"Devin, have you heard from your kids?"

"Nope. I don't figure that will happen in a million years. Their mother has totally brainwashed them against me. I don't even go there."

Rachel frowned. "I know one day when they're married, they'll realize how it is, how there's always two sides of the story."

"I think Flora is married now and Danny is getting up there. But it's alright, mom. I don't like to think about it. They've done alright without me."

Rachel knew Devin's heart was breaking. Maybe they were doing alright without him, but she knew her son wasn't doing alright without them. "Are you and Kellie going to have children?"

Devin stopped. "What makes you ask that?"

"Oh, I was just wondering, that's all. Do you want children?"

"We've talked about it." He was grinning while a flush spread over his face.

They continued down the stairs in silence.

Kellie was in the kitchen drinking a Pepsi, her morning drink of choice. Her purse and cardigan were on the countertop. "It's about time, Mom. We were wondering if you were still here or if you'd slipped out and gone back to England already."

Rachel laughed. "Oh, I've been up for a couple of hours, made coffee, had some toast, and have been enjoying the view from my balcony. Until a bunch of kids came by and ruined it for me. I was on my way down when Devin came up the stairs."

"Yeah, and she just asked if we're going to have any kids or not." Devin cocked his head at Kellie, still grinning, eyebrows raised.

"Did you tell her?" she asked.

"No, we agreed *you* would," he said as he reached for his wife's hand.

Kellie was blushing. "Mom, we're pregnant. We're having a baby in the springtime."

Devin held Kellie close, his arm around her shoulders. "We don't know what it is yet. But we're hoping for a boy first, then a girl.

Two oughta do it." He stared at his mom. "I couldn't believe you asked me that because we were going to tell you tonight at dinner. How did you know?"

"I didn't. But I am so happy to hear this!" Rachel said with a brilliant smile. "A new baby in the family! I love my godchildren, but it wouldn't compare to having my own grandchild. This is exciting, isn't it?"

Kellie broke from Devin and reached for Rachel, hugging her. "Whatever it is, boy or girl, we're going to name it after you."

"You can't call a boy Rachel. No way. And not even a girl. It's such an old name. I'm not so sure I like it myself. Don't do that to the baby, please."

"No, Mom, we'll use your middle name, and we're going to use Grandpa's too for the boy. Martin Neal O'Neill, and we'll call him Marty. And the girl will have yours and Kellie's middle names. Rose Martin O'Neill."

Rachel grinned. "Oh, I love the name Rose. Good Irish names you've chosen. I'm glad we changed your last name when I changed mine back," she said to Devin. We're all O'Neills in this family."

They laughed.

"Even me," Kellie added, giggling.

"But not for long, Mom, you'll be a Ballenchine," Devin added mischievously.

"I don't want to talk about that right now. Let's talk about Rosie and Marty. I love it! Maybe you'll have twins," Rachel said as she hugged them both. "I think this is the happiest day of my life." Tears filled her eyes.

"Mom, you're crying! Stop that."

"Yes, stop it." Kellie dabbed her own eyes. "C'mon, let's get out of here and go do our Saturday morning stargazing. I wonder who we'll see today."

Chapter 37

Sitting on one of the patios of the Malibu Colony Mall, and milling in the boutiques were the Saturday morning shoppers from the Colony as well as those from across the highway and up the hillside. Even the Pepperdine personnel and year-round students appeared on Saturdays.

Kellie loved gazing at film and television stars. Holding a giant milkshake, sipping through a straw, her eyes darted from the cars searching for parking spaces to the walkways and entrances of shops and stores. It was impossible to talk to her and make eye contact with her, for when she was star-gazing her concentration on everything else was nil.

"*Omigosh!* It's Pierce Brosnan! Over there, getting out of his car!" she said and then sucked on her straw even more ferociously. She drained the last of her drink and reached the bottom of the cup, making loud rattling sounds as she sucked in air.

"You want some more?" Devin asked as he stood and reached for her cup.

"I'm switching to Diet Coke." Kellie handed him the empty container, darting her head from one side of him to the other trying to see around him.

"How about you, Mom? Want some more coffee?"

155

"Sure, I'll have another. Thanks, Devin," Rachel said.

"Oh look, it's Allegra." Kellie stood and waved. "Over here, Allegra!"

Allegra saw them, waved and grinned. She locked her car and walked over to them. "So, time for donuts, huh?" she said.

"Rachel's having them, I just had a milkshake. For the baby," Kellie said.

For a moment Allegra was confused about what baby she was talking about. "Oh?" She'd managed to ignore the fact she was pregnant, not wanting to think of it at all. "What baby?' She glanced between Rachel and Kellie and pulled out a chair to sit.

Rachel picked up the conversation, knowing exactly what was going through Allegra's mind. "Kellie's pregnant. Baby's due in the spring."

"Oh. Well then, congratulations, Kellie. Is it a boy or girl?" She sighed and leaned back in her chair.

Devin arrived with the drinks. "Hi, Allegra. Would you like some coffee? Donuts? Milkshake?"

"Milkshake sounds nice to me," Allegra replied, winking at Rachel. "I think I'll have one too. But I can get it myself." She stood.

"No no, sit down. I'll get it for you. What flavor?"

"Vanilla, please." Her eyes met Rachel's and they both smiled. "Guess I should join the ranks and drink what's best for my baby too."

Kellie's eyes widened. Devin's mouth dropped open.

"Yep, I'm pregnant too. Five months."

"This is so cool!" Kellie exclaimed. "Our babies will have each other to play with on the beach. That's exciting, isn't it? We can walk them in their carriages. I want one of those old-fashioned prams, you know what I mean? Like in the movies." Kellie beamed. "Do you know what yours will be? I want to wait till the last minute to find out. But we've already picked out the names. Have you picked any names? Who's the father? I mean, I didn't know you were married." At that moment she realized she might have been out of line, and looked up at Devin with a doubtful look.

Allegra blushed, unsure how to answer or even where to start.

156

"That's our Kellie," Rachel said. "She speaks and then thinks."

"Oh, that's okay. We're all friends here, aren't we?" Kellie said.

"I'll go get your shake," Devin said and scurried away quickly and deliberately. He knew some serious girl talk was about to happen and he didn't need to hear it.

"Kellie, Allegra isn't married," Rachel said.

"I was raped," Allegra added nonchalantly. "But I don't want anybody else to know. I didn't report it for several reasons. It happened in my house, about a week after the break-in. That's why I went to Montana so suddenly. And I'm glad I did go, for now I have some new friends." She reached for their hands and squeezed them, tears in her eyes. "Thank you for being here, both of you. I'm so glad I met you, Rachel."

"You'll get through this with flying colors," Rachel told her. "I know you will. And I'm glad you told Kellie. She can be a solace as well as a friend, someone to talk to." Wanting to change the subject, she added, "You know, I was thinking about that shoe and the burned clothing you found in the incinerator at the cabin. Don't you think you should give those to the sheriff's department, just in case? I'm with you that it doesn't make sense that they were burned. Are they still at the cabin?"

"Yes, I put the shoe in a basket on one of the bookshelves. I was going to ask Allan about it, but I forgot to ask that day he called before I left."

Kellie's eyes widened. "Wait a minute! What shoe? Burned clothing? What's going on? Tell the sheriff what?"

"Allegra's mother was murdered a few years ago," Rachel explained, "and it hasn't been solved. The murderer didn't break into the house, didn't steal anything, but brutally beat and raped her, and then shot her with her own gun. I'm sorry, Allegra, I know you'd rather not talk about this, but Kellie's sort of a mystery buff, figures it all out before anybody else does. I use her as one of my readers before submitting my novels. She's good, tells me if I'm on track, whether it makes sense or not. Sees things I miss."

157

"No no, it's okay. And I think that's a good idea. I'll call the sheriff and tell him about the shoe, by the way. Maybe they'll find something else up there. Although I don't see how it would be connected."

Kellie moved closer to the table, squinting at the other two women. "Where is the cabin? Is it far from the main ranch?"

"Not really, about a half hour to forty-five minutes," Allegra told her. "And it's isolated, off the road a bit, up into the trees. Can't see it from the road. My brother Allan usually stays there when he visits from New York. He and my other brother Arlie don't get along. In fact, he and my father never got along either. He was a mama's boy."

"So does Allan live in New York?" Kellie asked.

"Yes," Rachel answered.

"What were the shoes like? Could they have been his shoes? Or would they be your other brother's?"

Rachel squeezed Allegra's hand. "Here we go, the sleuth is surfacing big time." She laughed. "She reads mysteries and crime novels like they're going out of style, and watches TV programs and movies of the same genre: *Criminal Minds, CSI, Law & Order* . . . all of them."

"I suppose they could have been Allan's shoes," Allegra said. "Although they looked a little big for him. As for Arlie, he would never be caught dead in anything other than a pair of cowboy boots. The shoe was charred except for the toe, but the basic form was still there. Connie said the design on the toe belongs to a shoemaker in London, is patented."

"Connie was there? Our Malibu Connie Brown?" Kellie sat up straight, staring at Allegra.

"Yes. He called a couple weeks after I got there. He has business in Montana and he was worried about my leaving Malibu so abruptly. He wanted to see me before he went to Zurich, then he was going on to Australia and New Zealand before coming back here."

"Ah, so that's where he is. I wondered. So . . . does Allan go to London?"

Allegra nodded. "Yes. He travels back and forth between London and New York all the time. A jetsetter I'm afraid. Has friends all over the world that he can't afford. So yes, it could be his shoe. Probably is. Who else could it belong to? We're the only ones who have access to the cabin, so I don't think it has anything to do with my mother's death. But I'll call the sheriff anyway."

"I think you should," Rachel said.

Kellie was frowning in deep thought when Devin returned with Allegra's milkshake.

"Here you go, just for you." He handed it to her. "And your baby," he added with a blush.

"Actually he could have purchased the shoes in New York," Kellie suggested. She was becoming more interested by the minute. "Allegra, could you remember enough to draw me a picture of the design on the toe of the shoe?"

Chapter 38

It was on a vibrant, sunny Monday morning that Rachel drove Kellie's red BMW convertible to a scheduled meeting with her agent in Brentwood. Highway 1, the beach drive, had always been a pleasant one to Rachel, even in past years when she lived in the area while her father was alive.

Driving to Malibu for breakfast, lunch, or dinner was a regular jaunt for most people, including her, from west L.A. and Santa Monica. Even those from points east of L.A. would drive it on the weekends. Santa Monica Beach was the favored for beachgoers, and Malibu was favored for eateries and moonlight dining. But now Santa Monica had surpassed Malibu for upscale restaurants and trendy watering holes.

With the palm trees, sand, boat harbors, and sparkling Pacific, from Malibu as far south as Newport Beach was the place to be, to live and to play. Santa Barbara up north and San Diego far south were ultra desirable as well, and a few other places in between. All of the southern California coastline, as a matter of fact. However, property values being sky high made it impossible for the average person to live in the beach communities. Another example of the 'money begets money' principle. On weekends the average and less fortunate bussed, biked, or drove – whatever it took – to get to the beaches and seaside towns for temporary recreation and fun.

On Monday mornings the beach was sparsely populated, almost deserted, and by nine the work traffic on the coastal highway dwindled to nearly non-existent. So Rachel took her time and perused the businesses and the beach houses as she drove on the two-lane road leading to Santa Monica Beach.

She was tempted to take Sunset Boulevard up to Brentwood, but opted not to, afraid she'd get lost in the maze of roads and congested neighborhoods. She had gotten lost before, so she thought maybe it wouldn't be a good thing this time. She needed to be at her appointment at nine-thirty sharp.

So she took the ramp that would get her to Wilshire Boulevard and was at her appointment at the World Savings Building near San Vincente just in time. Her agent had moved a few blocks east of the Bundy Building across from Max Factor a few months prior, so they were meeting in a new office this time.

"Rachel, come in!" Anita called out through her open office door.

Rachel had entered the sixth floor receptionist's office to find no one at the desk.

"What happened to Sally?" she asked as she hugged Anita who met her half-way across her office.

"Oh, she called last Monday, said she quit," Anita replied. "No explanation, just said she was through. So there you go. Was with me nine years. Go figure. Here, sit down. Want some coffee? I guess it's too early for champagne."

"You got that right." Rachel laughed. "Coffee's fine. So are you looking for another gal?"

"Oh, yeah. Have interviewed tons of them. They're all alike. Just out of college, raring to go, wanting to break into the publishing world, the agent's world. All with ladder-climbing motives. I want someone who doesn't want to go any further than that desk out there. You know what I mean? Just a damn good secretary/receptionist. And she doesn't have to be young, for God's sakes. Know anybody?"

161

Rachel took the mug of coffee offered to her. "Nope, not a soul. I've been pretty isolated out in Malibu."

"How about that, your son living in Malibu? How'd he manage that? And in the Colony, no less."

"Well, he's quite a builder. Has taken on some pretty big projects and makes a lot of money doing it. And when this house went on the market by a client of his, he worked out a fab deal. Got it for two mill, unheard of in the Colony. Anyway, we had sold some of my dad's properties, put that into it, and since I'll be staying with them when I come to the States, I figured I could invest some of my own money in the house for him."

"I'd love to see it," Anita said. "Next time we'll meet there, if that's okay with you."

Rachel nodded. "Absolutely. They'd love it, especially Kellie. And the next party Kellie throws, I'll make sure she adds you to the guest list. She's great with parties. This is good coffee."

"Thanks." Anita opened a file. "My special blend. Hawaiian and chicory. So! Surprise, surprise! We have a film offer for *Murder on the Seine*."

Rachel nearly choked on her coffee. "Are you kidding?"

"Nope, I'm not kidding." Anita laughed. "And is it a doozy! They're looking for a screenwriter now."

"I know somebody," Rachel said. "I haven't read her work, but she's a freelancer as well as a studio writer. Take a look at her. Allegra McAdams. Here's her phone number." Rachel took a small address book from her briefcase. "Ready?"

"Yep, what is it?"

"310-666-8989. Allegra McAdams. She's a USC grad and is quite successful here in Hollywood. She lives in the Colony too, if that tells you anything. Like I say, I haven't read any of her work, but I have a good feeling about her. And I'd love to work with her if she's good."

Anita put the number away. "Okay, I'll look her up, see what she's done, and then pass it along to the producer. So, you interested in hearing the figures?" She grinned widely, waggling her eyebrows Groucho Marx style. "It's a big one."

162

Rachel laughed. "How much?'

"Read this and sign on the dotted line." Anita handed her a sheet of paper.

"Oh my gosh! This is the highest yet, isn't it?"

"That's affirmative. I think we've hit on something with the murder mysteries. The romantic novels are good too, but I think we've got a leg up with the mysteries."

Rachel nodded. "I must admit, they're fun to write. More difficult, but fun. I'm working on a new one as we speak. Have a co-writer this time. Della Doheny. Actually, her last name is Ballenchine, but she's using her maiden name."

"Great!" Anita exclaimed. "So I'll work out the details on this one, just need you to sign that, where I've marked, giving me the authority to wheel and deal for you, and as soon as it's firmed up and drawn up in a contract, I'll bring it to you to look over. Should be sometime next week. That okay with you?"

Rachel grinned. "Perfect."

Anita put the signed paper in the file folder. "So let's go have a late breakfast or an early lunch, your choice."

Chapter 39

At the Pacific Dining Car, the newest of the fourth-generation family-owned restaurants, Wes Idol III welcomed the two women to his dining room. Breakfast was served anytime of the day and night, which was one of the reasons Rachel had always loved going there. Her favorite was eggs benedict with a hollandaise sauce to die for.

"Long time no see, Rachel," Wes said. He handed menus to them and signaled for a waiter.

"I'm here for a few weeks, business and pleasure this time," Rachel said as she opened the menu.

"My wife is waiting for your next novel. She keeps track of you on your website."

"Oh, you might tell her it's changed to Rachel Oneill 100 dot com. Here, I have a card." She pulled the card from her wallet and handed it to him. "Here's one for you, Anita. Forgot to tell you about it."

"May I get you something to drink, ladies?" the waiter asked.

"Just coffee for me," Rachel said.

Anita added, "Me too. No champagne today, Tony."

"I'll leave you in Tony's good hands, then. Bon appetite!" Wes returned to his office near the kitchen, reading Rachel's card as he went.

"Nice young man," Anita said. "I miss his dad, don't see him around here much anymore."

"With his son here, he probably stays more in the background and tends business at the downtown L.A. location."

"You're probably right."

"I don't know why I'm looking at the menu," Rachel murmured, setting it down. "I'll have my usual: eggs benedict." Her phone rang. "Oh, got to take this. It's Maxim calling from Russia." She flipped the phone open. "Hello, Maxim. Yes, so good to hear you." Rachel got up and began walking to the entrance to take the call outside. "Hold on a minute, will you? I'm in a restaurant, on my way outside. Hold on."

The doorman opened the door for her.

"Okay, I'll just sit on the bench out here and we can talk."

"Are you in Malibu?" Maxim asked.

"No, I'm in Santa Monica right now. Had a meeting with Anita, my agent, earlier. We're having a late breakfast. So how are you?"

"Missing you very much," he said. "Are you coming here as planned?"

"I think first I'll go back to Cornwall for a few days to get myself together, and then I'll come to Moscow. Is that all right?"

"You could fly direct to here from L.A., could you not?"

Rachel hesitated. True, she could fly direct, but she wanted to go home first, dammit! "Well, I suppose I could. I'll think about it and get back to you. Okay?"

"I would love you to do that, Rachel. There are some things I want to go over with you. Things that might involve you here."

"You know what would be fun, Maxim? Why don't we come here for a holiday during the Christmas season? To Malibu? You'd love it. Let's talk about that, too, okay? I'd love you to meet my son and his wife, and my new friends. Let's plan on it. And the weather is sunny here in December, no snow."

"That might be possible. Yes. It might be doable. But you will be coming to Moscow before you go to England? Yes?"

165

Rachel sighed. "I could do that, yes." She stood to go back into the restaurant.

"Rachel, you know how much I love you, do you not?"

"Yes, Maxim. And I love you, too. I know it doesn't seem like it at times, but I do. Truly. It's just that when we're apart I seem to get involved with what I'm doing at the moment and our relationship feels like it takes a back seat. But when I hear your voice, my heart beats faster, and I want you to hold me. I'm so sorry I must do the things I do, away from you. I wish it could be different, but my life takes me to other places. I sometimes think that maybe I'm not cut out to be married or to even have a relationship with anybody."

"No, no. Do not say that, please, my darling. I understand you more than you realize. We will do whatever we can do to be together whenever we can. And yes, I'll come to Malibu for the holidays. You know, my love, I still wish for a Christmas wedding as you do. We missed the last one. We could do it this Christmas, in Malibu. Your son is there, and my family could join us the week of the wedding. Yes?"

Rachel's mind spiraled. *Omigod! This Christmas? This year?* Yes, she had said she wanted a Christmas ceremony, wanted to marry on Christmas Day. And yes, they didn't get married last Christmas when they were supposed to. The timing hadn't been good. But now to do it in just a few months? She hadn't even considered it being so soon. How could she plan so quickly? More importantly, did she *want* to plan that quickly?

"I don't know, Maxim. That's just a few months away. I don't know . . ." she muttered as she walked into the restaurant.

"We can discuss it when you come to Moscow in September. Yes?"

"Yes. We can discuss it." Her pulse quickened. Get married? Was she really going to get married in December? Her pulse raced and her heart began to thump rapidly. She took a deep breath as she reached the table where her breakfast and Anita were waiting. "Look, I'll call you when I get back to Malibu after I talk to Devin and Kellie about it. Is that okay? My breakfast is getting cold and I'm starved."

She raised her eyebrows at Anita as she sat and began coughing, still holding the phone to her ear.

"I love you, my darling Rachel," Maxim told her over the phone. "Are you coughing? Is that you coughing?"

"Yes, hold on a minute," she said. She reached for the glass of water and drank a few gulps. "Okay, I'm fine now."

"Call me when you can, darling. I'll be waiting. *Dasvidaniya*."

"*Paka*. Love you too."

Rachel set her phone on the table and lifted her napkin. Without looking up at Anita, she said, "He wants to get married this Christmas, here in Malibu." She lifted her fork and stared at her food. "You know, I'm not so hungry anymore." She dropped her fork on her plate and fell back into the booth, still staring at the food.

Anita's mouth was agape as she watched Rachel's metamorphosis.

Chapter 40

Allegra sat alone in her library, almost stoic.

She had visited her doctor earlier that morning and the bare gospel truth had finally sunk in, whereas before, the pregnancy didn't seem real. But now, there was no getting around it. She definitely was pregnant. The baby wasn't something she could pretend she didn't have, or believe would go away. That morning she had seen it on the sonogram. It was alive! She had to face it now. And facing it she'd been doing for the past hour.

The doorbell rang.

Ben, in his new gray suit and black tie, answered the door. His new duties included that of doorman and butler, as well as chauffeur and guard.

"Why Miss Rachel, good morning!" Ben greeted her. "Nice to see you again so soon. Does Miss Allegra expect you?"

Ben, Callie and Talutha were Creole like Trudy and Carl at Connie Brown's estate. They were all from the same family, all from New Orleans, all victims of Hurricane Katrina, one of the deadliest and most destructive hurricanes in U.S. history. Here it was, four years later, and Ben had only just found a new home with Allegra.

"Good morning to you, too, Ben. Yes, she's expecting me." Rachel stepped into the foyer as Ben closed the door behind her.

"Right this way, please," he said as he led Rachel to the library. There he announced her to Allegra, an unexpected formality that brought a smile to Rachel's face.

Rachel loved old-fashioned manners and etiquette. Her smile widened when she saw Allegra. "There you are!"

"Oh Rachel, I'm so glad you're here. Ben, would you tell Talutha we'll have the coffee and muffins now, please?"

"Yes, Miss Allegra." He turned to walk across the foyer.

Allegra turned to Rachel. "When you called this morning, it was a godsend. I needed someone to talk to. I went to the doctor."

Ben stopped dead in his tracks when he heard Allegra mention a doctor. He eavesdropped for a moment.

"No problems, I hope?" Rachel questioned.

Then Ben felt guilty for listening and continued on to the kitchen where Callie and Talutha were baking.

He wasted no time informing his fellow staff. "Callie, somethin's wrong with our Miss Allegra. She's up and gone to the doctor and is telling Miss Rachel 'bout it right now. She said to bring her those muffins and coffee."

Callie picked up the tray that had already been prepared and hurried towards the library. As she neared the doorway, she stopped to listen.

"I just don't know what I'm going to do, Rachel. How can I keep hiding the fact that I'm pregnant? Connie will be returning soon and he'll see it. He'll ask questions. I can't tell him what Eric did to me. Connie would kill him. No matter how much I hate Eric, there's no way to undo that rape."

Callie almost dropped the tray. She had to set it on the console table in the foyer to steady herself.

"I still shudder—" a sob caught in Allegra's throat. With tears forming in her eyes, she said, "I'm going to have the baby, Rachel. I've decided."

Callie picked up the tray and went to the doorway, announcing herself as she entered. She acted as if she heard nothing. "Here I am, Miss Allegra. Got Talutha's famous ginger-raisin muffins to go with your coffee. And a good day to you, Miss Rachel. So nice to see you again. You ladies look mighty fine so early in the morning."

Chapter 41

Paul Newland telephoned Rachel early afternoon. He'd arrived from New York the night before and was staying in Brentwood at his mother's home.

He had been raised by his father during his teens after his parents divorced. His dad was a philanderer, not the best example for Paul. And when Paul went away to college, his dad left L.A. and traveled the world until he died of a heart attack the year after Paul graduated.

Paul's mother was a restaurateur. She owned twelve restaurants, all named *Charmaine,* after herself. When she first started out in the business, she used the typical French *Chez Charmaine*, but eventually dropped the *Chez.* Her first two restaurants were in Beverly Hills and downtown L.A.. Then she expanded to San Francisco, Reno, Phoenix, Las Vegas, Dallas, Chicago . . . all across the U.S. from Los Angeles to New York.

So when Paul came to the States for art shows in the galleries his distributor set up, he would stay with his mother for the West Coast shows. He was pleased that Rachel was in California too, this time around.

"I'm here," he said over the phone when Rachel answered.

"Paul! I was wondering where you were. So come out to Malibu for Happy Hour and we'll get caught up. Here at my son's house. I'll text you the address and directions. Okay?"

"Exactly what I need, a sunset on Malibu Beach with my most favorite person in all the world. What time?"

Rachel chuckled. "Four or five okay?"

"I'll be there. Shall I bring something?" he asked.

"Just yourself."

"Okay, see you in a few."

Paul drove up in his mother's sky blue Cadillac sports coupe, not his first choice of cars, but it was available and free. His mother had left for the East Coast that morning, so he had his choice of her cars to drive, and this one fared better than the sedans.

Rachel was waiting on the portico, waving as he drove down the tree-lined driveway. He pulled to a stop and she ran to him. They hugged as if they hadn't seen each other in years. Something about being in another country made the distances and time span seem greater.

"I thought you'd be in California long before now," Rachel said. "You aren't going to have much time before the kids are back and have to go to school. Right?" she said as they walked up the steps into the entryway.

"Joanie will be there to meet the boys when they return from their grandma. So they'll be fine."

"Joanie?" Rachel asked as they walked through the house towards the glass doors leading to the veranda. "Come this way."

"Yes, you remember. I told you. The nanny? She's been at the house for a few weeks now, reorganizing *everything*. Even me." He laughed. "She's fabulous."

Rachel raised a brow. "Oh, really? Do I detect something more than a nanny emerging?"

Paul grinned. "You are too smart, Rachel. With a keen sense of perception," he said as he pulled out a chair for her at a well-set table on the edge of the covered patio. "Look at this, will you?" The

172

table had several trays of hors d'oeuvres, pitcher of iced tea, and a bottle of champagne, all sitting on a lace tablecloth.

"The lace was my contribution," she said. "Devin and Kellie aren't into lace, but I just happened to find this at a shop in Malibu today and loved it, so *voila!*" She grinned at Paul, noticing the sparkle in his eyes. "You look great, Paul. Life is agreeing with you."

He sat down across from her while a servant appeared and poured tea for him, champagne for her. "And you've recovered well from your bout of pneumonia," Paul commented. "I was so worried about you."

"Della and the doctors fixed me right up. I'm in tip-top shape now. Only a little cough left, but no more worrying."

"Is your son going to join us?"

"Yes, they'll be here in a minute. They're upstairs freshening up a bit. Later they have a dinner engagement with one of his clients in Santa Monica. So they'll be off after they join us for a few. Now tell me more about this, this . . . Joanie."

Rachel wasn't sure how she felt about Paul's evolving connection to his nanny. Of course, she of all people realized he needed someone to fill the huge void Belinda had left behind. God only knew how tragic the loss had been for him and the children, but there was something inside Rachel that pained her when he spoke of Joanie. A stranger stepping in. Surely she wasn't jealous? She shoved that thought down as deep as she could. *No way, couldn't be jealousy. Why would it be?*

"She's Scandinavian, blonde, light-skinned, just like Belinda was. Although she's a bit taller than Belinda. And she loves children, is an accomplished pianist, and has attended cooking school. Perfect, wouldn't you say, for a man like me?" He held up his glass and tipped it to Rachel.

She lifted her own glass and clinked it against his. "Sounds perfect, yes. What else do you know about her? Was she recommended by an agency? You can't be too careful these days, you know."

"Came from the best agency in London. I wouldn't trust just anyone with my boys. You know that. And as it turns out, we're very

173

compatible. The time we've had alone, together, while the boys are with their grandmother, has been very special." He paused, looked down at his drink, then again at Rachel. "I've asked her to marry me."

A jolt shot through Rachel, jumbling her senses. She couldn't think of anything to say. Words escaped her, her breath escaped her, her brain stopped working.

"I wanted to tell you first. No one else knows." he said.

Rachel stared at him, no words coming forth.

"So? What do you think? I mean she meets all the criteria," he said, starting to feel a bit nervous. "Rachel, are you okay?"

Devin and Kellie came through the doors just then. Kellie was talking to Devin a mile a minute.

Rachel spoke quickly, forcing the words out. "Well, whatever you think, works for me. We'll talk about it later." She stood up. "Here they are."

Paul stood up to greet the pair.

Kellie stepped forward with a smile. "My goodness, I forgot what a drop-dead gorgeous hunk you are!" She reached her hand towards Paul. "Will you look at those big blue eyes? How tall are you, Paul? You could be a movie star, or a model. Have you ever modeled?"

Devin stepped up to Paul and shook his hand. "Glad to see you again. She'll run down in a minute, Paul. Goes on like that all the time. Welcome to our home. Mom has told us about your artwork. I'm eager to see it."

"There's a show tomorrow afternoon in Beverly Hills," Paul told him. "You're all invited. You'll come, won't you, Rachel?" He was still thinking about her odd response to Joanie.

Rachel blinked, shook her head, and took a swig of champagne. "Yes, yes, of course. I'll be there for sure."

"Me too, me too! We're going, aren't we, Devin?" Kellie said as she reached for a glass of champagne, then decided against it, remembering she was pregnant. She poured a glass of lemonade instead.

"Of course. I'd like to buy one of your pieces," Devin said to Paul. "We need some new art." He poured himself some iced tea and raised his glass to toast.

The others did the same. "To a successful art show!" echoed all around as everyone clinked glasses.

After Devin and Kellie left for their dinner engagement, Rachel and Paul walked down to the beach. They stood near the water's edge, gazing out at the setting sun.

"This is what I needed," Paul said as he stood beside Rachel with his arm around her. "You've always been a solace to me, Rachel. We've always been able to talk about things, and I appreciate that. I really do. Thank you." He leaned over and kissed her on the forehead.

"Are you in love with her?" Rachel asked quietly. She looked out across the water.

"She's a wonderful person, would be easy to love," he answered.

"But do you love her now? I mean you've asked her to marry you."

"I think I do. I have to admit, it's hard to know for sure because I don't think I'm completely over Belinda yet. I see her face sometimes when I'm talking to Joanie. They're so much alike."

Rachel didn't know what to say. She had no business advising him on his love life when she couldn't even sort out her own. "Just make sure, Paul, before you tie the knot. For the kids' sakes. There isn't a rush, is there?"

"No, but if we're going to live in the same house, I can't keep sneaking into her room. The boys will figure it out. We'll have to do something about it sooner than later."

Rachel turned towards him and stepped back. "Oh, so that's how it is?"

"Well, she's been living in the house since the boys left. It isn't easy to ignore her presence. She's a beautiful woman, Rachel." He wondered what was going through Rachel's mind as she walked into the water. "You haven't updated me on Maxim. Have you set a

175

date yet?" He thought it might be better to get the focus off his love life.

Rachel didn't answer. She turned and started walking back to the house.

Paul trailed behind her. By the time he reached the table where she was sitting, waiting, she had downed half a glass of champagne.

"So, have you?" He popped a canapé into his mouth.

Rachel looked at him. "Have I what?"

"Have you and Maxim set a date for the wedding? I was all prepared to go last year before you cancelled it. What's the matter? Don't you love him?"

"Ha! Listen to you!" She grinned as she reached for a cheese and cracker. "Since you ask . . . I have to say I don't know. Half the time I think I do, then when we're apart for any length of time, I start having second thoughts. I'm perfectly content when I'm by myself. Shouldn't that be a sign, I ask myself? A sign that maybe I'm not cut out for marriage? I love being with him when I am, but I also like being away from him. You're a man, what would you think of a wife who didn't want to be with you all the time? One who would continually want to take three or four months away from you? Could you handle that?"

Paul cocked his head, squinted his eyes, and looked steadily at her. "I don't think so. But you might find out it'll be different after you marry. Maybe you won't want to be away from him. You might adjust easily. But you're right, that isn't a marriage, it's a part-time relationship."

"He says he can handle it, but I don't think any man can. And as for me adjusting, I don't think so. I think this is me, this is who I am, and as a matter of fact, I like it this way." She reached for the bottle and poured another glass. "I think I'm a bit inebriated, and you know what? It feels good for a change. You want one?"

"No, I can't do it. I'll drink lemonade. Once in a while I'll have a beer, but not often. I've made a life-long commitment about that and I try to stick to it, although I do slip up at times."

Rachel smiled. "You're a good man, Paul. Joanie will be very, very, very lucky to be your wife."

He reached over and touched her arm. "You'll find your way. You will." He leaned back, sighed, and added, "At one time, I thought it was going to be me and you, remember?" He laughed.

Rachel chuckled too. "Yep. There certainly was a sizzling attraction going on."

"Do you ever wonder what would have happened if we'd responded to that sizzle?"

Rachel locked eyes with Paul. "I used to dream about it."

"Me too," he whispered.

During the next awkward moment, they both reached for their drinks in unison and sipped them as they looked straight ahead and watched the sun drop into the ocean.

Chapter 42

"Rachel, where are you?" Kellie jogged down the corridor towards Rachel's suite of rooms.

"In here, writing." Rachel sighed and leaned back from the library desk that faced the sea. She had arranged the antique desk and chair she'd found at an estate sale so that she could see the view to Santa Monica and points south along the beach every day as she wrote.

Kellie hurried through the doorway, breathless. "I hope I'm not interrupting anything. I've got to talk to you about those shoes."

"What shoes?"

"The shoes Allegra found in the incinerator. Or shoe. It was only one, wasn't it? I think I've found the maker in London, and it says he doesn't sell wholesale to any other stores. They can only be purchased in his shop by registered customers." She handed Rachel a paper. "Here's a printout telling all about it. I've even printed out some pictures of the shoes with his trademark designs on them. We need to show them to Allegra to see if any of them are like the ones she found. And you aren't going to believe this, but it says here that every pair that is sold is custom made and registered. He makes a mold of the foot and then a pattern. And he keeps a record of every purchase. Lots of famous people order their shoes from him. So it should be easy to find out who they belong to, don't you think?"

"You're kidding?" Rachel's eyes widened.

"I'm *not* kidding. We can find out if her brother purchased them or not on one of his trips to London. Then she can ask him why he burned them. Doesn't make sense he would do that, though. Why would he? Sounds weird to me."

"I know. The whole thing doesn't make any sense," Rachel agreed. "Her mother didn't have any enemies. Everybody loved her. There was animosity between the brothers over the trust their dad drew up, but they weren't angry with her. It's strange, though, that there wasn't a will saying Allan would inherit the little ranch and land above it. He told Allegra his mother was going to change the will to make that happen. But she died before it happened."

Kellie was silent for a moment, pondering. "Hummm . . . well, a person could be frantic and angry enough to kill over that, but if one of the brothers did it, the rape doesn't make any sense. A son wouldn't rape his own mother. I mean that is really sick! Unless . . ."

"Unless what?" Rachel asked as she poured another cup of coffee. "You want a cup?"

Kellie shook her head. "No, thanks, I've had too much already. I'm buzzed. I'm thinking . . . suppose the killer could have hired someone to murder her, someone who would also rape her. That would throw the trail off one of the sons. I mean, it would, wouldn't it? But I can't imagine a son even hiring someone to rape his own mother. It makes me sick thinking about it." Kellie sat down across from Rachel, deep in thought. "But then again, worse has happened. Family members commit grotesque crimes against each other. Nothing is impossible. I just read about a doctor in the nineteenth century giving his wife and eight family members shots of influenza to kill them, and then he cut them up and burned them in an incinerator. Said they'd died of the flu and he cremated them to keep the germs from spreading. His extended family was irritating him, even his in-laws, so he got rid of all of them. Wiped out the entire family. Some crazy people out there."

Rachel stretched in front of the window. "I think I'll take a walk on the beach to clear my head. Want to come?"

"Sure. I'll grab a sweater and meet you out there. Are we still on for dinner at Allegra's tonight?"

"Yes, sounds like fun."

Chapter 43

Allegra's day had been busy. She'd made all the dinner arrangements for her group of newfound friends. She had ordered flowers for the dining table, which had just been delivered.

She went to the kitchen where Callie and Talutha were busy baking and handling the food preparation. They had been working at it all afternoon.

"Callie, I need two crystal vases for these flowers. Got any idea where they might be?" Allegra asked.

"Yes'm, there are two nice ones in the cabinet at the far end of the dining room. Would you like me to get them for you?"

"No, that's okay. You're busy, I can do it. Just didn't know where to look. The cabinet at the far end?"

"Yes'm. That be the one. In the bottom half, in the middle."

"Thanks." Allegra cheerfully headed for the dining room.

Once she found the vases, she set them on the bar along with the flowers and filled them with water from the bar sink. Then she snipped the ends of the stems and arranged them, taller ones in the middle, shorter ones graduating outward to the fluted edges. She stood back and admired her creations for a few moments and decided the arrangements were too tall for the dining table. It would be difficult to talk to her guests, looking over and around the flowers. So she decided she'd place them on the buffet table instead. Now to find something for the table.

Candelabras would do the trick. In the cabinet she found some medium-height crystal candle holders, with five arms on each. Three of them.

"Perfect!" she said aloud.

She placed them on the table, spaced equally. Then the search for the right candles took all of five minutes. There were different lengths in several boxes, but she found fifteen that would do the trick, in various sizes. Then she grabbed the scissors and went into the garden and cut jasmine branches, with their white, star-like flowers still blooming. She placed them down the center of the table around the base of the candelabras. The effect was exactly what she wanted.

She decided to set the table herself, which she loved to do. She selected the Lady Carlyle china: lacy pink border with yellow and red roses. After adding the crystal wine glasses and water goblets, she decided on the gold utensils.

"Napkins! Where are the napkins? Callie!" she called out.

Callie came into the dining room. "Oh, that is lovely, missus. So lovely. Look what you did with the jasmine vines."

"Where are the napkins, Callie? The cloth ones. I can't find them."

"Oh, they're all in the laundry room, ma'am. We just did 'em all, washed and ironed 'em. A late spring cleaning. I'll get them for you." She hurried out of the room and was back in a flash pushing a laundry cart. "Here they are. Which ones you want? The pink ones?"

"Oh, yes. Those are beautiful. The pink lace ones. Thank you, Callie." She started placing the napkins on the table, thinking of Rachel. She knew she loved lace.

"You want me to help you, ma'am?"

"No, no. You go on with the food. This is the easy part." She stopped and looked at Callie. "I am so happy you're here, Callie. You, Talutha and Ben. I don't know what I'd do without you." She went to her and gave her a hug. "Thank you so much."

Callie blushed. "We's happy to be here, ma'am. You've given us a home. We didn't know what we would do back in Louisiana. If it weren't for Trudy and Carl, and that Mister Brown, we'd still be homeless and living in the streets. It's me should be thanking you." She looked at Allegra with tears in her eyes. "Thank you."

"Now don't you make me cry, Callie. Go on, skedaddle. No crying today. It's a happy day." She beamed with the delight of the moment.

After placing everything she wanted on the table and selecting the serving dishes, she went into the study to collect her thoughts. She had a spare thirty minutes before going upstairs to dress for her guests.

She sat on the loveseat and put up her feet, leaning against one of the fluffy pillows that rose above the top of the carved-wood-framed settee.

She closed her eyes and thoughts of her mother and father came to mind. What would they think of her being pregnant without being married? Of course it wasn't her fault she was pregnant, but still, she'd decided to keep the baby. On one hand, she was glad they weren't there so they wouldn't have to endure the horror of knowing that she was raped. She believed her mother would have figured it out, she was sure of it. Her mother could read her like a book, just like Arlie had known something was wrong, but she and her mother were two peas in a pod. Her father wouldn't have guessed. He believed anything Allegra told him. Tears came to her eyes. She missed them both so much.

And now her baby wouldn't have a grandmother or a grandfather. It wouldn't have any grandparents. What kind of life could it have without grandparents? She remembered hers. They were so important in her life. She hadn't seen her mother's parents in years; they'd gone back to Belgium to live after her mother was killed, their only child. It had devastated them. Maybe she would reach out to them after her own child was born. Yes, that might be a good idea. Her father's parents were dead. Early cancer deaths, both of them.

As the thoughts trailed through her mind, she fell asleep.

* * * * *

"Miss Allegra? Miss Allegra . . ." Callie gently shook her shoulder, trying to wake her. "You must get dressed, Miss Allegra. It's five o'clock. They be here in fifteen minutes."

Allegra jumped up, wide awake. "You're kidding me! It's that late? *Omigosh!* Okay, okay. I can do this. Is everything else ready, Callie?"

"Yes'm, all ready. When you all are seated, we'll start serving. All you have to do is tell me when. And Ben is dressed and has got the bar all ready. He'll be serving the drinks before dinner. I'll set out the hors d'oeuvres in here while they be waitin'. So you jes go upstairs and make yourself pretty now, miss. G'wan! And if'n they get here early, Ben'll see to them till you come down. Don't you worry none."

Allegra moved towards the stairs. "Okay, it's all up to you and Ben, Callie. But I'll hurry." She ran up the first few stairs, then stopped suddenly halfway up. "Ohh! Ouch!" She bent over, clutching her abdomen.

"What is it, Miss Allegra?" Callie ran towards her as Allegra sat down on one of the steps. "What's wrong?"

"It's okay, I'm okay. Really. It was just a sharp pain. Took my breath away. I'm alright." She carefully stood up, waiting to see if it would happen again. "See, it's gone."

"I'll help you up the stairs."

"No, no. You have things to do. I'll be okay. It's gone. Probably just a twisted intestine. That happens once in a while. No problem."

"You need to start taking better care of yourself, Miss Allegra," Callie said. "Now that there's two of you to take care of."

Allegra stopped and stared at her. "How did you know about the baby?"

Callie realized the mistake she'd made. She didn't want Allegra to know that she would even think of eavesdropping. It wasn't proper for a servant to do so. "I jes know about these things, Miss Allegra. I can see it on you. Nothin' mysterious about it. And now you jes need to start plannin' to take it more easy than you have been. Me, Ben and Talutha will take care of you and the baby. Yes, we will. Now don't you worry 'bout it none."

Allegra frowned. "Callie, I'd rather you not tell anyone about the baby just yet. Okay? Promise me you'll keep it a secret?"

"No problem, ma'am. No problem at all."

Chapter 44

When Allegra came down the stairs to join her guests on their first round of drinks, she was radiant in a red silk blouse and a long black pencil skirt with black velvet slippers embroidered in red. Her long, rust-colored hair was brushed up and back into a pouf styling, very elegant and chic.

Paul was taken aback by her beauty. Rachel had told him about her, that she was a script writer and was from Montana, but he had no idea she was such a petite, adorable woman.

"Allegra, you look ravishing!" Rachel said as she reached for her hand. "I want you to meet a dear friend of mine. Paul, this is Allegra McAdams. Allegra, this is Paul Newland, my godchildren's father."

"The artist," Allegra said as she shook Paul's hand.

"Yes, and you are a writer, I'm told," Paul said.

Kellie clasped her hands in front of her. "You are all so creative! I feel like odd man out. Allegra, you look like you stepped out of a page in *Vogue*. How do you do that? And how do you get your hair to pouf out like that? It doesn't look stiff with hairspray." She reached to touch Allegra's hair. "It isn't stiff. How do you do that?"

Allegra laughed. "Blow-drying with a mousse. It's easy." She signaled Ben to bring her a drink. "And how are you, Devin? Building any new mansions in Malibu?"

Devin nodded. "Just contracted to build a sixty-thousand-square-foot house near Pepperdine, on the ocean side. Mediterranean style."

"A rich Iranian, of course," Kellie added. "I'm surprised it's so small."

They all laughed.

"I am amazed at the size of some of these houses. You can give me a cottage in lieu of a mansion any old day," Rachel said. "Except for this one, Allegra. It's terrific! I could stand one of these."

"But Mom, your cottage spans three floors and is pretty damn big, too, as I recall," Devin pointed out. "I saw it when we were there that Christmas. What a great house! When Paul and Belinda owned— oh, I'm sorry, Paul. I didn't mean to—"

"You needn't apologize, Devin. We enjoyed that house while it was ours, and Christmas with you and your mother made it even more festive. Belinda loved entertaining, especially on holidays. Fond memories, those, the house and all." Paul lifted his drink to his lips, paused, stared at it, then took a swallow. He walked over to Ben at the bar and asked for a refill.

Rachel wondered about the drinks. Paul usually didn't imbibe anything more than an occasional beer. Tonight he was drinking vodka tonics. He'd quit drinking before he and Belinda had married. At least he wasn't drinking straight shots. She supposed it could be worse. He must be stressed. Regardless, she wondered what had made the change in him. She would ask him later if she could corner him away from the others. He seemed to be quieter than usual too.

An hour after the to-die-for dinner, prepared as only Callie and Talutha could do, Allegra's guests left. First Devin and Kellie, then a few minutes later, Paul and Rachel decided to walk home via the beach.

187

Walking on the beach on a moonlit night was a favorite of the locals, and there were several others strolling arm and arm along the shore.

"What's on your mind, Paul? I sense something is bothering you." Rachel got right to the point.

Paul stopped and looked at her. "What makes you think that?"

"Well, you had four drinks tonight, for starters. That isn't like you."

They began walking again, eyes cast downward on the glistening sand as they talked.

"I'm just a bit confused, I think," he said.

"About what?"

"Oh, life in general." He looked out towards a sailboat, anchored in the moonlight. Laughter from the sailors wafted to the shore.

"What do you mean?"

"Well, I feel empty, lonely, not as happy as I should be, under the circumstances."

They both remained quiet for a few moments, but kept walking.

Paul stopped again and turned Rachel towards him. "I don't know what I want, Rachel. Something isn't right."

"But you have two beautiful little boys who love you to death," Rachel pointed out. "You're a successful painter, being shown all over the world, you've a wonderful house in London, and you have Joanie, who sounds like a terrific woman. It's a life most people dream of. What is it that is doing this to you?"

"I don't know." He dropped his hands and faced the sea.

Rachel caught a glimpse of glistening tears before he turned away from her. She wrapped her arms around him from behind and held him tightly.

"I hate to see you this way, Paul. But I know the feeling. I get it myself sometimes. I think it's just that we have a void that we've not learned how to fill. Or maybe it isn't supposed to be filled this time around. Maybe it's part of the process, our journey on this earth, to learn how to be happy, regardless of the emptiness we endure. Maybe we are supposed to learn how to deal with it without letting it overwhelm us. Like right now, being with you, consoling you has brought me out of my funk. Maybe that's how it's done, focusing on others' needs instead of our own."

Paul turned and held Rachel, both of them entwined in each other's arms. "I know, I know. I just feel so helpless at times. I love my babies, I do. I try to stay focused on them. I focus on my work, and I'm grateful for Belinda's mother being in our lives, for Joanie, but it isn't enough, Rachel. I miss this. This is what is missing." He stopped talking.

Their eyes met and their lips found each other. It was as if time hadn't passed beyond that New Year's Eve in Trafalgar Square many years before when they had first met and experienced that unforgettable kiss at the stroke of midnight. Before everything else had happened in their lives. It was as if nothing had happened to them since that night. They fell back in time for a moment, feeling only the kiss and their bodies pressed together.

"I . . . I . . ." Rachel spoke first, gaining her composure. "I think we should go. Kellie and Devin will be waiting up for us."

Paul nodded numbly. "Yes . . . of course . . . you're right."

They held hands as they walked silently up the beach towards the house and back to reality.

Once inside, Rachel stood facing Paul. "Looks like they've gone to bed. And I'm pretty tired myself. You can't be driving back to town tonight, so your room is up and to the left. The doors are open, you'll see it. Good night, Paul. Sleep tight." She turned to go.

"Rachel," he said, grabbing her hand. "I'm sorry, I didn't mean to do that. Neither of us have the right. Will you forgive me?"

She thought for a moment before replying. "Paul, I believe we are meant to feel the way we do about each other. We were together in a past life, that's why we are drawn together in this one. So, there is nothing to forgive, my love. I am happy you are as you are in my life, this life. Good night." She smiled, squeezed his hand, and walked away. "Coffee's on at eight, my eternal friend!" She looked back, grinning and happy.

Chapter 45

It was the middle of September, the day before Paul Newland was scheduled to return to England from L.A. His art shows had been successful, and his mother had finally returned in time for the two of them to spend a couple of days together, catching up on all the latest. Their relationship had always been strained and awkward, since he'd been primarily raised by his wayward father - raised in the sense that his father was his guardian, but Paul had more or less reared himself. His mother would pop into his life from time to time, but only as a visitor, not as a caring parent. So he had stumbled through puberty and his young adult years, among his other wealthy friends in L.A. who preferred to play rather than study and take responsibility.

Through it all, Paul graduated with honors from college, was on the UCLA football and track teams, earned awards for both, and landed a creative directorship with one of the leading international advertising firms, his office in London Headquarters. It was there he met Belinda, a graphic artist for the same company. She was British, born and raised in Hastings. Not someone he noticed beyond her work, and certainly not his type at the time.

But when his cocaine and Jack Daniels habits coupled with a sex addiction had almost killed him, and a heart attack landed him in

190

the hospital, it was Belinda who was there for him. No one else. Just Belinda.

Ever since Belinda had met him on her first day of work as a member of his creative staff, she had admired Paul and had a secret crush on him, but she knew he would never give her the time of day. She didn't hold a candle to the bevy of beauties that traipsed in and out of his office and life. His promiscuous lifestyle was obvious.

Then when Belinda was brutally gang-raped and left to die on the oily, dirty concrete floor of a garage in a high-rise, it was Paul who was there for her. No one else. Just Paul.

They were drawn together by circumstances and married, and were together until the day she died of lymphoma six years later.

Now he was on the brink of another life, this time with Joanie. He felt confused. All night he had lain in bed, unable to sleep, with thoughts of Rachel mixed with Belinda, morphing to those of Joanie. He wondered if he was doing the right thing, marrying Joanie. Maybe it was too soon. Maybe he should wait.

Yes, he had feelings for Rachel. Strong feelings. But maybe it was just as she'd said: the feelings were from a past life. Maybe that's why it felt so familiar and real. There had always been an undercurrent of feelings for Rachel, through everything that had happened, but it didn't mean that he was in love with her. Surely not.

"Damn it, damn it, damn it!" he said as he sat up and threw the covers back and ran his hands through his hair. It was almost noon. He'd finally fallen asleep after the sun rose. He looked out of the window of the seventeenth floor, a bedroom in a high-rise on Wilshire Boulevard, part of his mother's twelve-room condo occupying the full floor. The westerly view was of the Pacific, the easterly of downtown L.A. The location was well-situated in the middle of all that happened in Southern California, meeting his mother's proximity requirements.

He dreaded leaving Rachel behind, but why was it tearing at him so much? He was agitated and angry and couldn't seem to quell it.

He dialed Rachel's cell, but hung up before the second ring. Then he dialed Joanie's number in London.

"Hello?"

"Joanie? It's me. Are you sleeping?" He sat on the bed and leaned back on his pillow, relaxing at the sound of her voice.

"No, not yet. What time is it there?" Her voice was soft and gentle, lyrical.

"Eleven. Slept in this morning, had a night of tossing and turning. I miss you, love." He closed his eyes as he absorbed her voice; let it soak into every pore and fiber of his being.

"Oh, and I miss you too, my dear one. Can't wait to see you. I'll be there to pick you up."

She sounded like she meant it. It warmed his heart, soothed his soul.

Tears flooded his eyes. How could he have doubted his feelings for her? Joanie was the best thing to happen to him. She loved him, he knew it. She loved his boys, which was the most important of all. They needed a mother. He didn't want them to grow up as he had, never having a mother around to love them, to care for them, to be there for them. And Joanie wanted a family.

"I've decided to take an earlier flight, Joanie." Right at that moment, he had decided. "I'm thinking of leaving today at three. So I'll call and leave a message with the particulars. It should be the same flight number and the same arrival time on Virgin, but I'll find out for sure. Is that alright with you?"

"Oh, it's wonderful! I'm so glad you're coming home a day early. Yes, yes, yes. Please do. I love you, Paul. And I've so much to tell you about the wedding plans. I hope you're up for it."

Paul felt a jolt surge through his system. His chest tightened. Wedding plans? Anxiety engulfed him. He couldn't breathe. "I'll call you back. Got to go, love. Bye."

He dropped the phone on the bed and doubled over to his knees. He felt as if he was going to pass out. His heart was beating wildly.

"God, no! Please, not now!"

He got to his feet and grabbed a glass of water that was sitting on the table in front of the window. He gulped it on the way to the bathroom where he kept the nitroglycerin tablets he carried with him always. He swallowed two of them, followed by more water. After a few minutes, and some deep breaths, he felt better. He sat in the easy chair looking out towards Malibu and beyond.

He couldn't treat his body like he'd been doing while in L.A. He had been drinking too much, worrying too much, letting himself get agitated for no reason at all. He had to get back to London. He had to go home to Joanie, his new Belinda. His haven. At that moment, a feeling of calm engulfed him. Then he felt guilty for feeling that Joanie was his new Belinda. Joanie would be his wife, just Joanie.

He would call Rachel from the airport and cancel dinner.

Chapter 46

"Rachel! You've got mail!" Kellie called out as she hurried down the corridor towards Rachel's rooms. "A package from Maxim. Wonder what it is?" She entered the open doorway and made a beeline for her mother-in-law sitting at her desk.

Rachel had been diligently finishing up the latest edits she'd received from Della. Just three more chapters and the first draft would be complete. Then she would take a break for a couple of weeks before they began the rewrites and final edits.

"Were you expecting something from him?" Kellie set the package in front of her.

"No, not at all. We'll just have to take a look, shall we?" Rachel reached for the letter opener to break the tape seals on the medium-sized box, wrapped in brown paper. "I can't imagine what it could be."

There was a rectangular box inside, surrounded by tissue fluffing. This box was wrapped in pink and yellow rose-covered floral paper, with pink ribbons in abundance.

"Beautiful wrapping. He knows what I like." Rachel grinned and quickly removed the ribbons and paper, eager to see what was inside.

"Oh my gosh! Look at that, will you?" Kellie said. "A pink, pearl-studded cardigan! Wow!"

"Lovely, huh?" Rachel didn't know what to think. She was puzzled. She pressed the knitted softness to her cheek. "Cashmere, no less."

Kellie couldn't hide her excitement. "Are the pearls real, do you suppose? I just love the way they create the outline of baby roses on the front and the back. Usually sweaters are only beaded on the front. This is something else. Ex-pen-sive!"

"They could be real, knowing Maxim. I don't know. Regardless, it's fabulous, isn't it?" Rachel stood up and slipped her arms into the sleeves. "Fits perfect. How does it look?"

"Looks perfect too. I've not seen you in a color other than black."

"That's the only problem, I don't know if I can wear pink. It's more your color." She ran her hands down the sleeves, adjusting the fit on the shoulders as she looked into the mirror. "Tell you what, you can wear it anytime you want. I'll do the honors when I see Maxim, but I don't think I can comfortably wear pink. It just isn't me." Rachel laughed. "But the thought is what counts, right? He's a very thoughtful man. I guess I'm pretty lucky."

"You guess? I would say you *are* lucky! That man adores you. It's obvious."

"Yes, I think he does. I had a call from him last night. He still wants me to come to Moscow this month. I keep stalling."

"Why?" Kellie asked.

"I don't know. I need to reassess my feelings. And I need to poop or get off the pot," Rachel said, still grinning. "Or as Devin would say, 'shit or get off the pot'."

They both laughed.

"Says that to me all the time," Kellie remarked. "So when is Allegra going to be here? I want to run to the store and pick up some snacks and sandwiches to eat. Anything in particular you'd like?"

Rachel thought. "You know, I haven't had a tuna sandwich in ages. I've been craving one. In fact, that sounds good to me right now.

Tuna and cheese, with bread-and-butter pickles, onions and lettuce. Yum! I must be hungry. What time is it?"

"Eleven," Kellie replied. "Okay, I'll get stuff for tuna sandwiches."

"I think Allegra's coming over around three. So I'll just make myself a salad in the meantime."

"There's plenty of leftovers, too. Be sure you check that out first. Okay, I'm off to the village store." Kellie turned and started for the door.

"Here, wear the sweater," Rachel said as she handed it to her. "Don't button it up, let it hang open. It'll look good with the top you're wearing and the white shorts. Elegant, in fact. Frosting on the cake. A cupcake." They both laughed

Kellie stared at the sweater. "Are you sure?"

Rachel nodded. "Yes. Take it. Keep it. And if Maxim ever shows up, I'll borrow it from you. It'll be our secret." She smiled as she watched Kellie's eyes widen and glisten.

"I'll take care of it. I promise," Kellie vowed. "But I'll be so nervous wearing it, afraid I'll get something on it or lose a pearl."

Rachel waved a hand. "Don't worry about it."

Kellie left the room wearing the sweater as Rachel settled back into her chair to read the note Maxim had enclosed. That's when she saw another small white box stuffed into a corner of the large box, in the crumpled tissue paper. She removed its pink ribbon and lifted the lid. Her mouth dropped open with a squeal. It was a ring, a huge pink diamond in the center surrounded by pearls and smaller diamonds.

"Omigosh! What is this man doing to me?"

She put the ring on her right hand. It fit her third finger, and she held her hand up to see the sparkling stones from all angles. It fit perfectly.

"This, I'll wear myself," she said with a giggle.

The accompanying note was written in Maxim's beautiful handwriting, using one of his calligraphy pens. She recognized his favorite pen-and-ink flourish.

Rachel, my love, the garment is to warm your body while you dream on the Malibu seashore. The ring is to warm your heart and forever remind you how much I love and adore you.

She read the lines over and over, each time filling up with more love and gratefulness for Maxim. It wasn't the gifts that made the impression, for she was not a person who required elaborate gifts; it was what he said about them. How could she not love this man? How could she not believe that only happiness could ever come from their union?

She stood and looked out at the blue water that stretched to the horizon where the sea and azure sky merged. The smell of the ocean air was even more breathtaking that morning. It was crisp and cool, compelling one to take in deep breaths of refreshing rejuvenation.

In that instant Rachel realized that Maxim would never put constraints on her, on her time and space. She felt he loved her enough to let her be who she was and who she was to become.

It was a meaningful and gratifying moment as Rachel O'Neill stood at the open windows overlooking Malibu Beach, visualizing a future with Maxim. She felt she had come to a turning point and was happier than she had ever been. She felt at peace with the world and with herself.

Chapter 47

"What am I going to do, Rachel? Connie gets home today, Trudy told Callie this morning. He didn't mention it in his email yesterday. I think he wants to surprise me. What am I going to do?" Allegra was frantic, almost in tears.

"Nothing. You aren't going to do anything. You aren't showing yet, at least not enough for him to notice. Men don't see those things. And it's still easy to cover it up, you're so tiny. Not like me. I ballooned to one-sixty in no time flat. Looked like I was going to have a baby elephant."

Allegra laughed. "I can't believe that, you're not much bigger than I am."

"Oh yes, I am. Twenty-five pounds more. Anyway, when does he arrive? Did they say?"

"This afternoon. Three, I think."

"Well, I imagine he'll be jet-lagged, so you probably won't hear from him or see him 'till tomorrow at the earliest. So, let's go shopping. I'll pick you up in thirty minutes. Let's go to the Promenade in Santa Monica. Maybe we'll take in a movie while we're there. Okay? I need a break from this damn revision. It's driving me crazy."

"Okay, you're on."

"You can tell me how the screenplay is coming along while we're having lunch," Rachel said.

"I'll be ready in thirty. Bye."

Rachel turned and began looking for the shoes she was wearing earlier. She had a habit of kicking them off when and wherever the mood struck, making it difficult to relocate them when she wanted them later. This was one of those times. The patio. They were on the patio.

"The Broadway Deli is closed? Where did it go?" Rachel stared at where it used to be on the corner of Third and Broadway. "Damn! That's where I wanted to have lunch. I used to come here all the time on the weekends when I lived here. Loved it. Now what?"

Allegra shrugged. "Let's just walk along and choose one. Doesn't matter, does it? I'm just going to have a salad, so I can have that anyplace."

"You're right. There's a nice one down there, next to the theatre. Is that okay with you? We can sit outside if you want." Rachel glanced at a scantily-clad group of young girls strolling by. "God! Did you see that? They were as good as naked. I swear I saw some pubic hairs."

Allegra laughed as they walked to the bistro cafe. "I know. It's getting worse and worse every day. I don't get it. Whatever happened to modesty and leaving something to the imagination? They put it all out there now, so there's no mystery at all about any of their body parts. And sometimes it can be pretty disgusting."

After they were seated and perused the menu, they ordered.

Sipping champagne, Rachel did her share of people-watching. The sidewalk musicians and homeless were out in full force, same as always, she noticed. Shoppers filled the promenade, going from one boutique to the other, one cafe to the next, or straight on to the indoor mall that held three floors of the larger department and chain stores. The moviegoers were lining up for matinees.

The promenade was a favorite for film buffs because there was so much to choose from: four movie houses and a Cineplex. A one-stop shop-eat-and-be-entertained venue. People from all walks of life came to the Third Street Promenade in Santa Monica. Great for people-watching.

"So, I need to ask you . . . do you see Carla or Penelope as your protagonist in *Murder on the Seine*?" Allegra sipped her tea.

"Carla, definitely," Rachel answered. "Although the story is about both of them and they meet along the way in the middle. But Carla is the predominant one. She is the common thread. How far along are you?"

"Part Two," Allegra replied.

"Well, you'll see when you get to Part Three. That's how I write all my novels. Usually four parts, introducing the two female leads in Parts One and Two, then the main one emerges more than the other in Part Three. Although it's a pretty close run sometimes, I usually favor them both." Rachel laughed. "My editor tells me I need to sort that out, give more to the main character to pull her to the frontline."

"I like the way you write them side by side," Allegra said. "They both have stories, they both are important. I'm thinking that I'll write the screenplay that way too. Two stories, merging just before the point of resolve. What do you think?"

The French waiter set their plates in front of them. "Would you ladies care for anything else?" He gave them a toothpaste ad smile, his dark eyes glistening. Definitely a fledgling actor.

"That's it for me," Rachel answered.

"Me too," Allegra added.

"Bon appétit!" He walked away.

Rachel rolled her eyes. "I get so tired of hearing that. *Bon appétit.* And what's the other thing they always say? Oh, what is it?"

"I know what you mean. I can't think of it either." Allegra picked up her fork and tasted the dressing before pouring it on her salad. "Yum, perfect!"

"I'm glad I ordered the tuna sandwich. I've been craving them a lot lately. Wonder what that means?"

"Too many pregnant women around you, most likely, if you've got the craves."

They both laughed.

"How is Kellie coming along with her pregnancy?" Allegra asked.

"Perfect. I think she's made for it. She loves all the attention from Devin." Rachel took a second bite of her sandwich, followed by a sip of water. "Enjoy! That's it! The other thing the waiters say after they've served. Enjoy! That really annoys me."

Allegra laughed. "It's too canned, yes. They should individualize their comments. Make them their own." She took a bite of her salad. "Have you decided when you're going home, or are you going to Moscow first?"

"I'll go home to Cornwall for a while. I'm missing my own space and I need to spend some time alone before I'm tied to Maxim permanently." She smiled at Allegra. "So as soon as I finish the rewrite, by the end of next week, maybe sooner, I'm off."

"Oh, no! I'm going to miss you, Rachel."

"I'll be back. Maxim is coming out in December. So I'll be back here before that to plan the wedding."

Allegra sputtered the tea she was drinking. "You're actually going to do it? You've decided to marry him?"

"Yep. Gonna do it. He's the one. I've made up my mind." Rachel was grinning radiantly. "Oh, I almost forgot. Kellie wanted me to show you this. She found some more information about those shoes in London." She reached into her bag and pulled out folded pages that had been printed from the Internet. "Look who has accounts at the shoemaker. Both Arlie *and* Allan."

Allegra blinked. "Arlie? Why would he have one? He doesn't wear those shoes. I've never seen him in anything but boots or moccasins." She looked at the printouts. "This doesn't make any sense whatsoever."

"Has Arlie ever been to London?"

"Well, yes. He's been all over the world looking at cattle. Especially before Daddy died. They both went."

"Maybe your dad bought shoes in London on one of those trips," Rachel suggested. "Could those in the incinerator have been your father's? Could one of your brothers have dumped some of his clothing there for some reason?"

Allegra thought for a moment. "I don't know. Why would they? I could see Allan wanting to burn Dad's things just out of spite, but I don't think he'd really do it. There would be no reason Arlie would. I mean, he didn't want anything of Dad's to be touched or disposed of for the longest time. We had a hard time with that, both of us. Arlie finally boxed it all up and put it in storage, he said. He wouldn't have thrown any of it away."

"A mystery, that's for sure," Rachel said as she took another bite of her sandwich. "Do you think you should fax those to the sheriff up there? I think any bit of information might be worth something in the investigation. Might give them a lead. Kellie's all excited about it, says she believes the shoes have something to do with the murder. She's sure of it."

Allegra shrugged. "I guess it couldn't hurt. I told Arlie about what we found in the incinerator, so they do know about it. But I'll send this to them tonight."

Chapter 48

At eight in the morning, with his hat in his hand, the Flathead County sheriff knocked on Arlie McAdams's front door.

Arlie opened it after a few seconds. He'd been waiting for him. "Come in, Jake. Good to see you. How long has it been?"

"'Bout six months, I reckon. The last time was when we had a lead that fell deader than a doornail. I hope we've got something more substantial this time. How you been?" Jake Caruthers was a big man, bigger than Arlie, at 6' 7", 265 lbs.

"I've been busy buying and selling cattle. It's the season. Come on in, have a seat." He pointed to the leather club chair near the sofa in the Great Room. "Would you like a cup of coffee?"

Jake shook his head. "I'm about coffee-ed out, had more than my share already, so I'll just pass on the offer. Tell me what you got." The sheriff sat and looked across at Arlie, waiting.

"Well, you know my sister's in California, and a friend of hers was doing some searching on the Internet and came up with some information on those shoes they found up at the little ranch. Here's the printout." He reached for the sheets of paper on the giant timber table in front of the sofa and then handed them to Jake. "It says Allan and me both have accounts at that shoe store where those shoes are sold in London."

The sheriff read the information and pondered for a few moments. "I don't know," he murmured. "It might be something, but I don't know. Did you ever buy a pair like those that were burned?"

"No, I never did. But my dad might have, and Allan could have. It's more his style than mine. I have my boots made there, though. The guy made a mold of my feet and anytime I want a pair I call him, tell him what I want, and he gets right to work on them. I've never had such perfect-fitting boots from anybody. The guy is a genius."

"Do you mind if I keep these?" Jake asked.

"Sure, go ahead. I already made copies, and Allegra has copies too. I was wondering, Jake," Arlie paused, hesitant. "You know I stored Dad's clothing and a bunch of his stuff up at the little ranch. Some up in the attic and down in the basement, and out in the shed. Do you suppose someone could have gotten into it? I never thought to look when we were up there last. Nobody knows about it but Allan. I didn't tell Allegra we kept it. Some vagrant could've found the place and took some of it, then dumped the shoes in the incinerator when they didn't fit him. What do you think?" Arlie rubbed his temples. His head was beginning to ache.

Jake nodded. "I'll take a drive up there and check it out later this afternoon. I'll have one of my deputies meet me there. Do you mind?"

"Hell no. Anything you want, Sheriff. Anything. You just ask. If it helps to find out who murdered my mother, we'll do it. Do you need me to go with you?"

The sheriff stood up, straightened his pants and put on his hat. "No, don't need you to tag along this time, Arlie. I can handle it."

Arlie saw him out the door and stood watching him drive down the driveway to the main road, his vehicle kicking up dust on the way. He rubbed the back of his neck. The headache was getting worse. Stress did that to him. He turned and went to the kitchen cabinet where he kept some prescription pain pills and downed four of them with a glass of water.

He was worried about Allegra. When she called him the night before, she sounded different. Something was bothering her and when he questioned her, she began to cry. She'd done that her whole life. When his dad or his mother would press her about her problems, she'd always start crying. And that's what she did on the phone after she told him she had sent him a fax and what it was.

He knew she wasn't crying about the fax and its contents, no. He knew her crying didn't have anything to do with the murder. It was something else. He could feel it in his bones. When they were growing up, he was her protector, and he reveled in that fact. She was such a tiny little girl and needed protecting. In fact, the more he thought about it, the more he realized she hadn't acted normal when she came back to Montana. There was something bothering her then, too, more than the rape. He was feeling the pull. He needed to go to California and make her tell him what was wrong.

By noon, not able to stand it anymore because his thoughts were running wild, he picked up the phone and called his pilot. He told him to schedule a trip to California on Friday. He was going to take the Citation CJ3. His father bought the plane, had been a pilot himself, and so was Arlie, although he wouldn't be doing the flying by himself this time. Allegra never would fly with their dad or with him. She preferred commercial airlines; she felt safer, she said. His mother had been more daring; in fact she'd begun taking pilot lessons just before she was killed.

Arlie's thoughts went back to when they found his mother. He and his foreman discovered her two days after she was murdered. He had been in Billings at a cattle auction all that week, his foreman out on the range, camping with the herd. He still had nightmares about the bloody, grotesque scene he found in his mother's bedroom that morning when he returned. He could still see her, eyes open, a look of horror frozen on her face, hands tied behind her. Her nude body mutilated and violated. He was thankful Allegra hadn't been there to see it. It would have totally destroyed her. It almost destroyed him. Allan didn't even come home for the funeral. It took Arlie three days to contact Allan in New York. He'd been traveling, he said.

Arlie never could understand his brother, and never would. They were worlds apart.

Chapter 49

"Mind if I come over for coffee this morning?" Connie asked Allegra over the phone. He had been waiting an hour to make sure it wasn't too early to disturb her. Every time he woke up during the night, his first thoughts were of her, sleeping just across the lane. If he hadn't been so tired when he got home from the airport the previous evening, he would have made a beeline for her door.

"Sure. Coffee's on already, so come on over." Allegra's heart quickened. As much as she was afraid he might figure out that she was pregnant, she was eager to see him. She'd made the decision to just let go and let things unfold as they were meant to. Rachel had convinced her of that. Worrying didn't solve anything. And as much as she wanted to cry every time she thought of it, she was working on that too. Time to grow up. Time to accept challenges and go with the flow.

"I'm on my way," Connie replied.

Allegra heard the grin in his voice. It brought a smile to her face too. Okay, she could do this.

She hurried to the kitchen to tell Talutha to put together some muffins and breakfast rolls, said Connie was on his way over. Then she ran upstairs and ran a brush through her hair and put on some lip gloss.

The door bell rang.

Ben opened the door and welcomed Connie, ushering him into the library. "Miss Allegra will be right down, Mister Brown."

Talutha entered with a tray of goodies and coffee. She poured a cup for Connie and left the room.

Just as he took his first sip, Allegra came through the doorway looking early-morning bright. The adrenaline shot through his body at the sight of her. She looked even more ravishing than he'd remembered. She was literally glowing.

"Good morning, Connie," Allegra said as she stepped to the coffee pot to pour herself a cup. "You're looking alive and well. So tell me about your trip. How was Australia and New Zealand?"

Connie wanted to toss his cup aside and take her in his arms and kiss her, but he controlled himself, being the stately, reserved Brit that he was, and just acted nonchalant.

"It was a productive trip. Although Eric didn't cooperate, which didn't surprise me. I don't know what to do about him. He doesn't seem to fit in with any of the businesses. I try to help him find his niche, but there doesn't seem to be one. I guess I should give up, just give him a lump sum of money and let it go at that. I'm almost to that point. But let's not talk about that. I want to hear about you. What's this I hear about your writer friend from England? Rachel O'Neill, is it? Is she still here?"

Allegra nodded. "Yes, she is. But not for long." Glad to get off the subject of Eric, which was making her extremely uncomfortable and unsettled, Allegra moved to the sofa and sat. "She'll be going back to Cornwall any day now. Have one of those bran muffins, Connie. Talutha made them this morning."

"Don't mind if I do." He cut one in half. "Would you like the other half?"

"Sure, thanks."

He put it on a plate and handed it to her with a fork, then took his plate and sat next to her on the sofa.

"I'm adapting one of Rachel's novels to a film script," she told him. "The studio is making a movie of it. Quite a coincidence that we're both writers and now I'm working on a project with her. It just blows my mind that of all places, we met in Montana. And her son is Devin O'Neill, down the street. You know, the contractor and his wife Kellie? The blonde?"

"Oh? The builder? That's incredible. Some definite serendipity going on here, don't you think?" Connie put a forkful of muffin in his mouth. "Ummm, this is wonderful. The molasses just makes it. I wonder if she uses sorghum instead of dark molasses? It makes all the difference. She probably does, just like Trudy."

Allegra nodded. "I have to thank you again for their being here. Callie, Ben, and Talutha. Your Trudy and Carl are godsends too, I would imagine."

"My life would be asunder, if I didn't have them. How is your brother Arlie?" He sipped his coffee.

"Funny you should ask that. He called last night and said he's coming out Friday. Said he has business in L.A., which is a shock to me. He's never been here since I've lived here."

"That's wonderful!" Connie exclaimed. "You must bring him over to my house for dinner while he's here. Will you?"

"Well, I'm not sure what his plans are, but I'll let you know as soon as I find out."

"Good."

A few moments passed; quiet moments, awkward moments. It seemed they had run out of things to say.

Allegra's cell phone rang.

"Excuse me, I need to get this."

"No problem." Connie stood and went for the coffee pot to freshen their portions.

"Hello?" Allegra said. "Rachel. Yes, come on over. Connie's here, I want you to meet him. Okay, great. Bye." She lifted her cup after Connie filled it. "You'll like her. She loves England, comes from a long line of Brits, so you've a lot in common."

After an hour of conversation, laughter, and reminiscing about England, Rachel and Connie acted as if they were old friends. Allegra was right; they seemed to get along instantly.

"Oh, Arlie's coming Friday, Rachel. I forgot to tell you."

"That's great. Is there a special reason for his visit?" Rachel wondered if it had anything to do with the murder or with Allegra's condition. Maybe he'd guessed. She remembered Allegra telling her that he never came to L.A., so it must be a damn good reason he'd chosen now to come. It concerned her.

"He didn't say, just said it's business."

"I've invited the two of them over for dinner," Connie said. "You must join us when we decide what night it will be, Rachel."

Rachel grinned. "I'd love to."

"Which reminds me, I'm sorry you'll be returning to England so soon. I'm planning a New Year's Eve party this year." He turned to Allegra. "Would like to talk to you about it." Turning back to Rachel, "It would have been good to have you there too."

Allegra grinned. "You're in luck! Rachel will be here. She's getting married here in Malibu on New Year's Eve. Right, Rachel? It is New Year's Eve, isn't that what you said?"

"Yes, we'd planned to do it at Christmas, but I've changed my mind. Gives me an extra week to have it on New Year's Eve. My fiancé is coming in December from Moscow, Connie. We're having a small intimate ceremony late afternoon on the patio of my son's home."

"Wonderful! Then you can make it for the midnight celebration at my place? Or do you have other plans?"

"We won't be leaving for our honeymoon cruise until the next day, so that sounds fabulous! I love New Year's Eve celebrations." She squeezed Allegra's hand. "I think I'm finally getting excited about it all."

"Oh, which cruise?" Connie asked.

"I don't know yet. Maxim is putting that together. I'm in charge of the wedding." She grinned as she blushed, her eyes sparkling. "I can't believe it's finally happening."

"So this is your second marriage? Devin was by your first husband?" Connie asked.

"Actually, it's my third. After Devin's father, there was another bad choice, and it ended in divorce too. But it's been years since that one. I raised Devin by myself and have been a single woman all these years. And . . . I was engaged twice, but both died. The last was just a few years ago. Tragic death, shot and killed by poachers in Brazil. He worked for the Eden Project in Cornwall."

Connie nodded grimly. "I'm very familiar with the Eden Project. Was he a researcher?"

"He called himself a gatherer, but yes, he did research and went where they sent him to gather specimens for the domes. He loved his work more than life itself, as it turned out. I didn't think I'd ever survive his death, but then Maxim came along and swept me off my feet."

"Maxim is Russian, is he?" Connie took a sip of coffee.

Rachel nodded. "Yes, but we met in Brussels. A dear friend of mine lives there, and I happened to be there that New Year's Eve, and I met Maxim at the celebration in the main square. But it's been an on-again, off-again romance, until just recently."

Allegra leaned over and hugged Rachel. "And this time it's gonna stick. This is the one."

"Yes," Rachel whispered, hugging her back. "I do believe it is."

Chapter 50

Arlie telephoned Allegra from the rental car on the way from the airport to Malibu. His aircraft crew was at the Airport Hilton, settling in for the weekend.

When he pulled into the circular drive, he couldn't believe his eyes. The mansion was set back from the street, an iron fence across the front, all but the walkway and front portico shielded from view by lush landscaping, huge trees and flowering shrubbery, a few palm trees spaced strategically to remind one of the proximity to the beach. There was another drive branching off around the left of the house to a parking area in the back. He figured it was used primarily for delivery trucks and personal guests who knew of the parking area.

Allegra had told him to pull into the back and come in the French doors leading into the back sun porch, not through the blue door into the servants' quarters. Ben was waiting for him and opened the doors as soon as he parked and got out of his car.

"Hello, Mister McAdams. I'm Ben, your sister's help. A jack of all trades. Welcome. Come on in." Ben's bright face was beaming and his grin was sparkling. A more vibrant welcome could not have been had by anyone.

Arlie grinned back. "Ben. You can call me Arlie. No formalities needed here. It's nice to meet you." He extended his hand to shake Ben's.

From behind Ben came Allegra, squealing with delight that Arlie was finally in California to visit her. It was something she'd longed for since she'd moved to Malibu.

"Arlie!" she shouted, running toward him. He lifted her into the air like a rag doll.

"My little Leggie! Love you, girl." He set her feet down on the stoop and held her shoulders squarely, looking into her eyes. "I've come to have a heart to heart with you, girl. But first, show me your house. It's a beauty!" He gazed to the left at the staircase leading to the upper two floors. "What is it, three or four floors you got here?"

"Three, and a basement. And a guest house out back. Come on, I'll give you a cook's tour." She laughed, but at the same time wondered what it was he wanted to discuss with her. Maybe the shoes. Yes, that was probably it. But why would he come all this way to talk to her about that?

"Okay, first we'll start with Callie and Talutha. You've already met Ben, right?"

"Yes, good choice."

"You'll love the girls, too."

Later in the day, as they sat in the library sipping drinks, Arlie a bourbon and Coke and Allegra an iced tea, the conversation worked around to Arlie's reason for being there.

"Leggie, the sheriff and his deputies went up to the cabin and snooped around. They picked up the shoe and when they went out back to take a look at the shed, they found clothing that didn't belong to any of us. You know I stored Dad's stuff out there, never did get rid of it. They found some of Allan's clothing and some that I'm sure didn't belong to him. It was bigger than he would wear. Designer stuff, yes, but not his. And that's not all. They found traces of cocaine inside the cabin and in the shed. Said it looked like maybe it had been stored there at some point."

Allegra stared at him in surprise. "How can that be? You don't think Allan had anything to do with drugs, do you?"

Arlie shrugged. "Well, I don't know. I called him and he hung up on me when I asked him about it. I need you to see if you can get anything out of him. And there is something else. They were able to lift some traces of blood off the shoe, and it's Mom's DNA."

"*What?*"

"I didn't want to tell you this, baby, but the shoe has Mom's blood on it."

"But— how can that be? There's no way it was Allan. No way. I won't believe that, Arlie. No!"

"We don't know that it was Allan, so relax. It's just a lead and we'll get to the bottom of it. This is the first clue that has surfaced, baby. We're getting closer, hon."

He hesitated a moment. "And Leggie, I know something else has been bothering you. It was going on when you were at the ranch, and I can see it in your eyes now, so I want you to tell me what it is. And I mean it. You can't pull the hood over my head on this one. I know my baby sister too well to have my chain jerked. So out with it. What's going on with you?" He leaned back in the club chair and took a sip of his drink, staring intently at her, waiting. Not about to give up.

The doorbell rang.

Allegra jumped up. "Oh, I think that's Rachel. I told her you were coming. Hold on a minute." She was grateful for Rachel's timing. It gave her a moment to collect her thoughts. What was she going to tell Arlie? She couldn't tell him the truth. She knew him; he would put two and two together. He might tell Connie. She panicked.

Her panic was obvious to Rachel when she opened the door.

Allegra whispered quickly, "Arlie suspects something. He wants to know what's wrong with me. I can't tell him, Rachel. He'll tell Connie and they'll figure it out."

Rachel put her arm around Allegra. "Let me handle it."

They went into the library and faced Arlie.

Arlie stood up and reached for Rachel's hand. "Hello there, girl. Glad to see you again. I see you haven't returned to England yet. You must love it here a bunch, and I sure as hell don't blame you if

213

you do." He continued grinning as he returned to the chair after the girls sat on the sofa.

Ben appeared and served Rachel a glass of champagne, her usual.

"I was just asking Allegra what's been bothering her lately, Rachel. I know something is and I need to know what it is. I'm not leaving till she spills the beans."

"Arlie—" Allegra began.

"I'll tell you what it is," Rachel interrupted. "She's . . . she's caught up in a lawsuit over a damn script. It's as simple as that." Rachel looked at Allegra, whose eyes widened to extreme proportions.

Allegra picked it up from there. "I . . . I didn't want to worry you about it, Arlie. It's being handled by the studio. I shouldn't be worrying about it either, but it's been weighing on my mind. Sorry I didn't tell you when I was home."

She and Rachel exchanged triumphant glances.

Rachel added, "I've been sticking my nose into it, too. Have my attorney and agent working on it, so she'll be okay. It'll be over soon and she'll come out smelling like a rose. You needn't worry. It's almost a done deal." She squeezed Allegra's hand.

"You sure you don't need the family attorney, Leggie? I'll put him on it, you just say the word."

Allegra frowned. "No, no. We have a rights attorney, someone who deals with this type of thing all the time. No problem. It's almost over, so you needn't worry. Truly."

"Would you like another drink, Mister McAdams?" Ben asked.

"Sure, but call me Arlie, like I said. Please."

"Okay, Mister Arlie." Ben took his glass and refilled it. He chuckled to himself at the cleverness of the two women in his presence. He knew there wasn't a lawsuit. He knew what the real problem was. And he knew the girls had handled it right. It wouldn't do any good for a big, rough, gun-toting cowboy to get into the middle of what was bothering Miss Allegra. No, it wouldn't do anybody any good at all.

214

Allegra's cell phone rang. It was Connie and he was on his way over to see Arlie.

"Connie's on his way," she said after she set the phone on the lamp table. "Ben, could you get the door, please, and then pour him a scotch?"

"Sure 'nuff, ma'am." He left the room.

"So how was his trip?" Arlie asked.

"I'm sure he'll want to tell you all about it. In fact, I think Rachel and I will bow out for a few minutes. We've got to go over a few things for a script. Do you mind?"

"Of course not. I know how talk about cattle can be downright boring to women. You girls go on about your business. Then I'll take us all out to dinner, how about that? I saw the Moon Shadows Restaurant on the way here. Can't go a day without my steak, you know."

They were standing as Ben ushered Connie into the room.

Chapter 51

Arlie returned to Montana on Monday morning.

Allegra drove to the studio.

Connie attended to pressing business from his office at home.

Rachel got up early to finish off the final rewrite before emailing her manuscript to Della that afternoon.

Maxim telephoned Rachel. "When are you coming to Moscow?" he asked after the initial greetings.

"I've decided to go home, Maxim. I hope you understand. I need to go home, it's already October. I've been away too long. Then I'll come back to Malibu to plan our wedding. We can be together then, here. There isn't much time left to do everything, so I don't see how I can take time to come to Moscow now, before we're married on New Year's Eve. Please understand."

Maxim hesitated a moment before answering. Rachel wondered what he was thinking. "Have you decided about the honeymoon?" she asked.

"Yes, I'll tell you all about it when I see you. And yes, I do understand, Rachel. I'm just eager to hold you in my arms. It's been too long since we've been together. I need you."

"I'm missing you, too, my love. But now that the novel is done, I just want to go home first and collect my thoughts and take care of a few things before I come back here and devote all my time to the upcoming wedding and to our life together. We can be together as much as we want to be from December on."

"And it will be wonderful, my love," Maxim replied. "You needn't worry about where we'll spend our time, for I am perfectly happy with being wherever you want to be, whether it's here, or Cornwall, or Paris, wherever. I'm at your disposal. You don't have to worry about me at all. I will not put constraints on you as you have feared. I won't do that. And there will be times we are separate, doing our separate business. But I do hope you will spend some time with me in our Moscow home."

"Of course, Maxim. I love it there. You know I do. And with Della and Valentin close by, I'll look forward to our time in Moscow. Truly. I want that as much as you do. In fact I would hope we go there straight from the honeymoon. I need my Russian fix, you know. I really do. Yes. And I feel the same as you, darling; I want to please you too. I know I've been distant at times, but I'm sure it will all work out perfectly for both of us."

"I feel so much better now that we've talked about this. It has been heavy on my mind. I have felt you drifting away from me."

"Oh no! Never! Don't even think that. Please, Maxim."

"Then I will see you the first week of December in Malibu."

"Yes, perfect!"

"I love you, Rachel."

"I love you too. Very much."

Part Four

Big Skies of Cornwall

"And is it like this in the homeland, Mother?
Is the grass so green and the sky so big?
And is the sea so blue in the homeland, Mother,
The land where our fathers rest,
Resting in the grave 'neath the granite cross
Looking forever to the far horizon."

Clies Stevens

Chapter 52

Rachel arrived at London Heathrow Airport the morning of October 15. When she stepped off the commuter plane a couple of hours later at Newquay Airport in Cornwall, it felt as if a dead weight lifted from her shoulders, she was home. *She was home.*

During the cab ride to Newlyn, she took in every view along the way, every village, every cottage, the quaint pubs, people walking their dogs, children playing, cattle and sheep in the fields, the lush greenery, the sea. She saw swans floating on the roadside streams and ponds, ducks and geese. It all made her breathe easier and lighter.

Every time she returned from being in other parts of the world, she felt this way. She wondered why she would even think of abandoning her life in Cornwall. It was sufficient for her. She could do her research on the Internet and from her memory. She'd been to enough places on the planet to supply herself with a lifetime of writing material. She needed nothing else.

She forced herself to quit thinking as she was. She had to stop in order to keep from stressing out about what lay ahead of her in the near future, the changes she'd be making.

She meant it when she said she loved Maxim. She meant it when she told him that she was happy and looked forward to their life together, but something was still tugging at her, deep in her soul. Something kept her from being completely at ease about it, completely sure of the decision to marry him.

She shook her head as the cab entered Penzance. Just two more miles to her beautiful hillside home.

She loved her home so much. All she wanted to do was hibernate for the next few weeks. No interruptions, no people, no decisions. Just she and her house and her favorite place upon the earth: Cornwall.

Rachel leaned back in one of the Adirondack patio lounge chairs she had spent days searching for after she bought the house on the hill. The chairs were emerald green, same as the other chairs stretched across the lawn. Although she missed the little bluff above the bay at her original cottage in Newlyn, now being rented from her by a lovely older woman, here she had the panoramic view of the sea stretching from Marazion on the east of the bay to the curve of the road towards Mousehole on the west. She had the entire view of Mount's Bay, named after St. Michael's Mount, which perched on a rocky island two miles east of Penzance, a half mile across the channel from the medieval town of Marazion, one of the oldest towns in England, chartered in 1257.

It was in Marazion that Rachel had met Margaret Trimble, of the St. Aubyn lineage, the owners of St. Michael's Mount. Margaret owned the Godolphin Inn across the bay from the Mount. It was Pete Bell, Rachel's deceased fiancé, who had introduced her to Margaret, and together they had reinforced the possibility that Rachel had lived in Cornwall in a past life. Margaret was a believer too, as was Pete. Their friendship led to finding a connection between Rachel and a historic family in Port Charles. It came down to discovering a great possibility of her existence of a past life in Cornwall, and explained the extreme draw to that part of the world and explained her dreams even before she arrived there.

Memories of Pete surfaced as she lay with closed eyes in the Adirondack. It had been a beautiful and memorable short time with

Pete, a time of discovery in more ways than one. Discovery of her ability to love again, to open up to a sexual relationship after such a tragic date rape experience, discovery of a corner of the world where she thrived, and discovery that her dreams of another lifetime were real, proven beyond a shadow of a doubt. All of this because she'd listened to the beckoning of Cornwall.

Now, once again, she was listening.

After a couple of hours basking in the sun, then watching dark clouds gather in the sky just offshore while fishing boats and sailboats scurried back to port, Rachel decided to drive to Mousehole and have an early dinner of fish and chips.

Maybe she'd run into Dudley. She hoped he wasn't on hiatus again. Such an independent chap, he would close his rock shop for days whenever it pleased him on a moment's notice and take off for parts unknown. Pete had teased him on a regular basis about doing that, telling him he couldn't make money as a shopkeeper closing up all the time. Dudley's reply was always the same: "I'm not a shopkeeper. I'm a rock hound." And that would be the end of it.

Dudley was godfather to Paul and Belinda's children. He'd been such a good friend to both of them, sharing building space with them where their art studios were housed. They had cut an illegal door through the wall between their shops, so one could mind the other shop when either was out running errands. And Dudley took the children off Belinda's hands on a regular basis, to the park or to the beach. Now all that had changed with the death of Belinda.

She'd met Dudley at the Swordfish in Newlyn, at the same time she met Pete Bell, who was the manager of the pub. That was before Pete went to work for the Eden Project in St. Austell.

Dudley was such a loving soul and Rachel was as much attached to him as anyone else. Yes, she hoped he would be at the Ship Inn. She needed to see him. She decided to call the pub. Sure enough, he was there.

When she entered the heavy timber door of the Ship Inn, her eyes had to adjust to the dim light to make out the patrons. She heard Dudley's voice calling out to her from the far end of the bar.

"Over here, Rachel. Champagne's poured and waiting," he said.

Yes, she was happy now. This was her world and she loved it. Four more weeks of it were not enough.

One morning, Rachel, refreshed from a full night's sleep, decided to drive further up the west coast of Cornwall to Port Isaac and possibly beyond, if she felt the urge. It had been a while since she'd taken off like that, and she felt compelled to do it today.

The drive to Newquay was effortless, stopping there for a cup of coffee and a raisin scone in a cafe near the beach. People were already out in full force: children in their bathing suits with sand pails and shovels, mothers nearby on blankets and beach chairs, having morning confabs with each other while watching the wee ones, fathers walking back and forth from the beach pubs and food stands, sneaking glances at bikini-clad girls. Rachel grinned as she watched the scene before her. It was heartwarming to see families together, enjoying their Saturday at the beach.

An aging man in only a thong who should have been elsewhere in full dress came towards her as she sipped her coffee on the cafe patio. She averted her eyes, for he was staring at her. She turned away, looking back at the waiter at the food counter. She signaled him for the bill.

"Hello. Do you live here?" the nearly naked man asked Rachel, standing before her. His hair was combed over his crown in a futile attempt at covering the bald spot on top of his head.

There was a bulge in his loosely-fitting, dingy white thong, and it was pointing right at her. It grossed her out. If anything could drive her into seclusion forever, that ungodly sight could.

She couldn't believe he actually asked such a stupid, mundane question. "No, I don't live here, thank God. I'm just passing through. In fact, I'm just leaving." She stood up, gulped her coffee and walked to the counter to pay her tab. As much as she loved talking to people, especially strangers, this just wasn't hacking it this morning.

Yuck! she thought as she left the sidewalk cafe and hurried to her car, looking back to make sure the overly tanned dork wasn't following her.

"Ohhh," she groaned as she shook her head and shoulders, trying to rid herself of the vision of him standing before her, his hairy groin at her eye level. "Damn. I'll never get over it. I won't!"

She backed out of the parking lot and continued on towards her destination, Port Isaac for lunch. A few miles down the road she began laughing out loud. She laughed until she was hysterical and tears were running from her eyes. The look on his face when she said she didn't live there was priceless.

Padstow in north Cornwall was the next stop on her day trip, situated on the west side of the Camel estuary. *An area of outstanding natural beauty with wonderful bays and beautiful golden beaches*, the travel brochures said.

She drove a crooked street that sloped down to the harbor through medieval buildings to its popular fishing port. She and Pete had taken the evening river cruise on the Jubilee Queen from Padstow to Wadebridge several times on their weekend jaunts north. Memories of those times flooded her thoughts as she came to a stop and parked near the Jubilee Queen dock.

She got out of the car and walked to a seating area at sand's edge. A young couple were sitting there, obviously in lust. She grinned, remembering how she and Pete must have appeared to others when they sat there, same as the young couple.

The fresh smells of the beach, the cool breeze and the sun rays chasing the breeze caused Rachel to catch her breath at the sights around her. This could be enjoyed by anybody, didn't cost anything, and was always there. Places like this were all over the world, if only people would take advantage and breathe in its vapors to clear their minds and souls, maybe there would be less sadness, confusion, and pain.

She took off her shoes and walked down the beach near the water's edge for a short distance, then returned and went back to her car.

She drove to Wadebridge, and then on the winding narrow roads down to Port Isaac. She wasn't sure where she would be able to park when she got there, for it was basically a carless village. No cars, no garages. She didn't know where the people who lived and worked in the cove kept their cars, although the houses above the village had garages. The village itself was set down in a cove of narrow lanes leading up through the shops and houses to the bluffs above and beyond. But she did know of a hidden parking area up the steep lane to the left of the bay on the south side of the tiny fishing cove.

The grassy parking lot was just a short distance from the house where the British series *Doc Martin* was filmed. It was the title character's office and home. The lane in front of it led down to the village and the fish market where many scenes were filmed: the cove, the cafes, the candy store which was the pharmacy in the series.

Rachel had found out on a previous visit that there wasn't a pharmacy in Port Isaac, nor a doctor or dentist, so the film company rented the candy shop for a month during each filming session and would convert it to a pharmacy. In reality, those who needed medical attention had to go to Wadebridge, the nearest town. But lack of medical facilities and supplies didn't seem to matter, because Port Isaac was one of the quaintest and most picturesque spots on the Cornwall coast and the tourists loved it. They flocked there every season. Rachel loved it too.

This was the first time she'd been there since she and Pete had spent a few weekends at the White House Cottage, two doors down from the Doc Martin cottage. As she walked by both cottages she stopped and breathed deeply, remembering, before she continued on down the lane to the cove.

She hadn't decided if she wanted to have lunch at the Mote Restaurant, in the heart of the village right on the harbor front, or The Golden Lion, a popular old pub and restaurant further up the lane behind the Mote. The Lion had balcony seating with a view over the harbor. It was best for happy-hour sipping, so she decided to go to the Mote, a fifteenth-century building with two tables nestled outside its front door and seafood to die for. Her favorite meal at the Mote was the salmon, and that was what she would have. She was hoping she'd get there early enough to get one of the two tables outside, and she did. The interior of the restaurant's unique coziness, two floors of it, presented something for everyone. The charming ambience of wall hangings, old world art, cozy niches, candles, timber tables, friendly staff, and a special cave-like rock booth were available to fit all moods.

As Rachel's favorite Rastafarian waitress in her dreadlocks appeared with a menu, her grin widened. "Oh my gosh, you're still here?"

The woman grinned back. "Of course! Where else would I be? Oh, I remember you. The writer, right? So where is your handsome bloke? Will he be joining you?" She began to set two place settings.

Rachel shook her head sadly. "No, he died, honey. A few years ago."

"I am so sorry. I really am. I didn't realize it had been that long. So what would you like to drink? Let's change the subject before I cry."

"You know, I'm going to have a bottle of champagne," Rachel declared. "How's that for a starter? And I've just decided to spend the night in the village. Any suggestions where I could get a room at this late notice?"

The waitress thought for a moment. "You might try the Slipaway across the way. Or the Old Schoolhouse up the lane. I'm sure you can find something. If not, they'll be able to suggest something for you. But I'd try the Slipaway first. You want me to call them for you? I can do that."

"Do you mind? That would be great."

"Sure. But first, champagne coming right up."

Chapter 53

The short weeks spent in Cornwall flew by, and before she knew it, Rachel was reluctantly heading back to Malibu. Before flying out of London, she took a train *into* London to spend a few days shopping for a wedding dress and gifts for her friends. She'd opted out of having Maxim's sister Anastasia design her dress because Anastasia's styles were now a bit too avant-garde for her ever since she'd switched to designing high fashion for the runway. And Anastasia wouldn't be attending the ceremony anyway, so Rachel knew her decision wouldn't hurt her feelings.

And although Amanda, Rachel's designer friend in Brussels, would be coming to the wedding, her young designs didn't lend themselves to Rachel's taste either. That left a few of her favorite designer boutiques in London to choose from, so everybody was happy.

Rachel decided not to call on Paul while she was in London as she didn't want to impose upon his new situation. She didn't know how she felt about that yet. She wasn't sure he was making the right decision, that he had merely been looking for a Belinda replacement, and had selected a Belinda lookalike in Joanie.

So it was three days of simple freedom and shopping on her own. That's what she needed, and that's what she liked.

PART FIVE

Blue Malibu Moon

Blue Moon
Now I'm no longer alone
Without a dream in my heart
Without a love of my own

Rogers & Hart

Chapter 54

When Devin and Kellie picked up Rachel at LAX Airport, both couldn't help but notice her gloomy mood. She wasn't the lively, cheerful mom she usually was, especially now when she should be happy because of her impending wedding.

"What's the matter, Mom?" Devin asked as he stood in her bedroom doorway after she'd settled in. "You're too quiet."

Rachel flopped into the overstuffed chair. "I know."

Devin sat on the sofa next to the chair. "You thinking too much about nothing?" His loving grin always warmed Rachel's heart.

"Probably so." She laughed. "You know me, I can ruminate myself to death."

"So what are you ruminating about?"

"Oh, I don't know. I'm just wondering if I'm doing the right thing. One minute I think I am, the next I'm not so sure. I thought if I went home and had a chance to clear my head, it would be easier. But being home made me want to be there even more. By myself. I don't know what's wrong with me. I love Maxim, I do. But I can't seem to get it together when it comes to thinking about getting married and being with him the rest of my life. That's a serious commitment. I don't know if I can do it. I haven't been able to do it yet. I mean, look at my history. It's as if I'm not supposed to be married."

"Mom, your history is behind you. And besides, it wasn't because you grew tired of your husbands. Each time it was different. How were you to know they'd be losers?" Devin held up five fingers and counted them off. "One, you didn't know Dad would run off with another woman. Two, you didn't know the second asshole would be abusive. Hell, no! Those two happened to you, you didn't ask for what they did. Three, and then came the rape. Mom, that wasn't your fault. The guy was a criminal. Four, then came Ethan, who you really didn't want to marry, and you didn't. You made that decision and it was a good one, I'm sure. And you didn't know he would die in a car crash. And five, Pete. I do believe you loved Pete, and I think that would have been a good marriage. I would have liked to have met him. And I know you're still trying to get over him. But he's dead, Mom. I hate to be so blunt. You've got to move on." Devin placed his hand on his mother's shoulder and stroked it. "Just relax, Mom."

"I'm trying to do that, I am. I don't know what's getting in the way. I probably shouldn't think so much about it, should probably just let things happen and not get so uptight. So now I'm starting on the other hand." She held up five fingers, laughing.

"What a concept!" Devin raised his eyebrows, grinning even wider at his mother. "You're right." He held up his hand, five fingers spread apart. "Six—."

"Oh, you!" Rachel stood up, laughing, and bent to hug Devin. "You make it all seem so simple."

"It *is* simple. Hey, if it doesn't work out, you can get a divorce."

"Oh, shut up. Let's go have a cup of tea on the patio. I'm ready."

Devin snorted. "Tea? Are you kidding? I'm having a beer."

Rachel grinned "Okay, I'll have one with you. Do you have Corona Light, and limes?"

Devin smirked haughtily. "Hey, I have thirty kinds of beer. Corona is only one of them. Let's go."

Chapter 55

A few days later, they were back at LAX and Rachel was waiting for Maxim to come through customs. She was excited and nervous all at once. Devin and Kellie were standing on either side of her, showing their anticipation as well.

"So is he short, stocky, and bald, like Khrushchev?" Devin chuckled. "Or a wiry little runt like Putin?"

"Devin!" Kellie hit his shoulder. "Just wait and see. That isn't funny." She looked at Rachel. "So which is it?"

They all burst out laughing.

"There he is! See for yourselves." Rachel waved and actually jumped up and down when she saw Maxim. He outshone and stood a head taller than all of the other male travelers. He glowed.

"Oh my gosh!" Kellie squealed. "The silver-haired fox? The one in the gray slacks and black turtleneck, your favorite shirt?"

"That's the one." Rachel's heart quickened. How could she ever be doubtful about her feelings for Maxim? He filled her up, he made her feel alive.

"Jeez, Mom, you did good this time. I think the guy might even be better lookin' than me."

"You got that right, ponyboy," Kellie teased as she slapped his arm.

"Ponyboy? Where in the hell did that come from?" Devin laughed.

Giggling, Kellie watched Maxim walk towards them. "God, Rachel. He is *bee-yoo-tee-ful!*"

"He's beautiful inside, too," Rachel said as Maxim reached for her and lifted her off the floor, swinging her around in a tight hug.

"I've waited too long for this," he whispered in her ear. "I will never leave you again, my darling. Never!" He pressed his lips to hers, slowly letting her slip down his body to stand on her own two feet.

Kellie whispered to Devin, "God! Talk about goose bumps! Why don't you do that to me?"

"Later," Devin said, grinning.

Rachel finally caught her breath. "I want you to meet my son, Devin, and his wife, Kellie."

They broke from the embrace and Maxim reached out his hand to Devin.

"Devin, Maxim," said Rachel as they shook hands.

Maxim grinned. "So nice to meet you at last, Devin."

Devin grinned back. "Yes, me too. Glad to have you here. How was the flight?"

"Very long. Very, very long."

"I bet." Devin looked at Kellie. "My wife. Watch out for her, she'll talk your ears off whether you want it or not." He chuckled.

"Devin, that's not nice. I won't do that. Nice to meet you, Maxim."

Maxim took her hand and kissed it softly. "You are lovely, Kellie. And congratulations on the news of your baby. Rachel told me about it. Both of you, congratulations."

"Thanks," Devin said. "So shall we get the luggage and head out to Malibu?"

"Yes, yes. I am all yours. Lead on." He put his arm around Rachel and squeezed her as they headed for Baggage Claim downstairs in the terminal.

A week later, Devin and Maxim were sitting on the patio, on a beautiful December day, having a late-afternoon beer. In their conversation, Devin was impressed by Maxim's business acumen and his successful career in the diamond and amber trades.

"So your brother is out of it too? He's in the restaurant business now?"

Maxim nodded. "Yes. It was time for both of us to take other roads. The family mercantile was over for us. We had reached our apex, put in our time, as some would say, and we realized the dangers that were becoming more prevalent were not for us. Valentin has a new life with his Della, and I with your mother. This time I want to do it right."

Devin smiled. "I think you and my mom both agree on that. I know I had to make some drastic changes when I married Kellie, or we wouldn't be together today. Most people say it's up to the woman to make a relationship work, but I don't agree. It's as much up to the man. Maybe even more. If you begin with mutual love, then the man has to make sure he's on the mark and doing his best to make his woman happy." He stood up. "You want another beer?"

"Yes, I could drink one more. Yes. Thank you."

Rachel came through the doors as Devin went into the house.

"Everything okay out here?" she asked Devin as he passed.

"Perfect! Couldn't be better. Want a drink, Mom?"

"Sure, I'll have a glass."

Maxim stood up as she reached the covered seating area. "Did you have a restful nap, my dear?" He leaned over and kissed her on the lips.

"Yes, I slept soundly for about an hour, then heard the jets just a few minutes ago. They were pretty low, weren't they?"

"Extremely low. Amazing how they do that. The risk of a down draft is always there. Dangerous."

"So did you and Devin solve all the problems of the world?" Rachel grinned as she reached for Maxim's hand and squeezed it.

"Oh yes, we certainly have all the answers." He laughed heartily. "Your son is smart, Rachel. Seems to have it all together, as you say."

Rachel nodded. "I think he does. Considering all he was subjected to growing up, it's a wonder he's as cognitive as he is."

"I was hoping you'd come out soon, for I want to talk to you about what I've planned for our honeymoon."

"Oh boy! Can't wait to hear it. So what are the plans?" She leaned towards him and they kissed.

"Well, I've made an itinerary. It's here in this file." He reached for the manila folder on the table in front of them. "As you will see, we'll start in Barcelona, Spain. There is where we'll board the ship for the cruise. So on January third we'll fly out of LAX to Barcelona. Is that suitable for you?"

"Of course. Sounds perfect."

"Then we'll board the Seabourn Sun. Here's a photo of the ship."

Rachel's eyes widened. "It's huge!"

Maxim chuckled. "Yes, thirty-eight thousand tons. Holds four-hundred and eighty passengers. So we'll have lots of company on this cruise."

"I'm so excited! What ports will we be visiting?"

Maxim showed her a map. "Here we are. First, Cote d' Azur, Villefranche, France. Then Livorno, Civitavecchia and Rome, Italy. Corfu, Greece is next, then up to Venice. Around to Dubrovnik, Croatia and Kusadasi, Turkey. And at last we dock in Istanbul."

"Oh my gosh! That is some trip, Maxim. I hope I don't get seasick." Rachel laughed.

"The doctor onboard will give you a potent shot if that happens. It will take the sickness from you instantly, no problem."

"Works for me," Rachel said. "Then after Istanbul we fly to Moscow?"

"Yes, if that is all right with you? Is it?"

"Of course it is. I'm looking forward to being back in Russia. It's my home away from home now. England being my true home."

"And we will work that out, my love. I know how much you love your Cornwall. I will respect your feelings."

Rachel climbed onto Maxim's lap and hugged him tightly. "Too bad you didn't come in and take a nap with me." She giggled.

"Why didn't you say so?" He brightened. "I would have come to you in a second."

"What's going on out here?" Kellie said as she came through the doors carrying a file folder. "You two lovebirds at it again?"

"Yep!" Rachel said through a radiant grin. "Why not?"

Kellie grinned back. "You are so right. Now if I can only get Devin on the same page as you guys, I'll be happy." She laughed as she sat across from them. "Got something I want to show you, Rachel, and ask what you think." She opened the folder and took out a sheet of paper. "So, did you tell Maxim about Allegra's mother's murder?"

Rachel looked at her curiously. "Yes."

"It puzzles me that the criminal has not been found after all this time," Maxim added.

"Kellie's been playing the sleuth," Rachel explained. "And she's actually come up with some remarkable information. She found the maker of the shoes found in the incinerator, and now we know that those shoes are only sold from a shop in London," Rachel said.

"And both of Allegra's brothers have accounts there," Kellie said. "But it doesn't make any sense that either of them would have raped and killed their own mother. That's just disgusting, and I don't want to go there. But someone they knew had to be the one. There wasn't a break-in. Look what I found in the *New York Times*, Rachel. I did a search in the archives of both Arlie and Allan McAdams. Voila! Allan was arrested for possession of cocaine, quite a bit of it, as a matter of fact. Enough to suggest he was either a dealer or a smuggler. Evidently Allegra doesn't know about it. And look here. This name keeps popping up related to drug busts, one of the guys who was arrested with him. A Canadian. They suspect a drug ring smuggles it in from Canada over the border into Montana. That's where the cabin is, right? Near the border?"

"Yes, but I don't see how that relates to the shoes," Rachel said.

"What if Allan's druggie friends stayed at the cabin, what if Allan has been doing this all along? Look, it says here that suspicions led to the arrest of some Londoners too."

Maxim took the printout and began reading it.

"Did Allan go to jail?" Rachel asked. "It doesn't say."

"Here." Kellie handed her another printout. "He was in jail for ten days and was bailed out by some big lawyer in London, along with some of his pals. I've found nothing that says they did any time. Money talks, as usual."

"So, what are you saying, Kellie?" asked Maxim after reading the article. "You think his London connections, that he could have housed in Montana, killed his mother? How does that connect?"

"I don't know yet. I'm working on it. But I've got a feeling there *is* a connection. Allan, those shoes, and London. Drug smuggling and Canada. Allan didn't kill his mother, though. No, it wasn't him. It had to be one of those dopers. You know, he could have taken one of them up to the house and introduced his mother. He may have wanted to show off the ranch, maybe even barbecue or something. Who knows?"

"I think we need to ask Arlie if Allan ever brought anyone home with him before their mother was killed. Or ask Allan outright, which would be best. I need to tell Allegra about this and see if she'll call Allan and get some answers. She needs to know what he's been doing and the type of people he runs around with. You know, it would have to be a psychopath to have done what he did to their mother. I wonder if they tested those shoes for blood splatter?"

Rachel looked at her grimly. "I think you're right. We should show this to Allegra tomorrow morning. She'll probably want to fax it to Arlie to give to the sheriff. As for tonight, Maxim and I are going for an early dinner and then the theatre. We're going to do some shopping too. So we'll go to Allegra's for coffee in the morning and show her what you've found. Okay with you?"

Kellie nodded. "Sure."

Chapter 56

It was early evening and the more Kellie thought about it, the more she felt like she should go over to Allegra's right away to show her what she found, not to wait until morning. She couldn't stand waiting.

"Devin, I'm going over to Allegra's and give her this stuff," she said, holding up a file folder. "I'll be right back."

"Shouldn't you call first?" Devin suggested. "I mean, she might have company or might not be home. It's almost six-thirty, she could be out."

"Nah. I need to take a run on the beach anyway. Didn't do it today. Be right back," she said, heading toward the glass doors. She opened them and hurried across the patio, then down onto the beach.

Allegra's house was six properties down, set back from the beach.

The sun was setting, nearly half gone by now. Other joggers and strollers were out, as they always were at that time of night.

When Kellie got to Allegra's beach gate, she jogged up the winding path through the overgrown garden to the tall shrubberies that bordered the parking area in the back of the mansion.

She stopped dead in her tracks and quickly stepped behind a tall Italian spruce. She couldn't believe who she saw pull around to the left of the house and then get out of his sports car. It was Eric Brown. And he was heading for the French doors that led into the garden room. He walked right past her, close enough for her to peer around the spruce and see him wearing a pair of shoes identical to the ones in the photos she was carrying. It looked like he punched in a security code before he opened the French doors quietly, without knocking, and appeared to be sneaking in.

"Oh my God!" Kellie ran as fast as she could back to the beach.

Chapter 57

Connie hadn't heard from Allegra. It was after seven, and she had told him she'd call around six p.m. to talk about dinner. He was worried. The several calls he had made in the past fifteen minutes had gone unanswered. Something wasn't right.

He grabbed his keys, and for some reason, he reached for the hand gun in his desk drawer. He checked to make sure the clip was loaded and shoved it into the gun. With the safety on, he pocketed it and ran from his house.

Carl was standing to the side of the portico, smoking a cigarette. "Mister Brown, where you going in such a hurry?"

Connie stopped and looked at him. "Carl, do me a favor, will you? Get your gun and follow me over to Allegra's house. Something's not feeling right. I can't get her on the phone, and I know she's home. Hurry. I'm going on over. If it's those damn burglars again, I'll—I'll— I don't know what I'll do, but they won't be doing it again." He got into his Porsche and squealed tires on the pavement as he headed towards the gates that were already opening. Although it was a walkable distance to her house, he didn't want to waste any time getting there.

He was right: her lights were on upstairs. He headed around to the servants' quarters and saw the tail end of his son's car parked back under the trees on the opposite side of the house, almost hidden. That surprised him. What would Eric be doing there?

He knocked on the blue door.

Ben opened it. "Good evening, Mister Brown."

"Ben, is Miss McAdams at home?"

"Yes, she is, but I haven't seen nor heard from her since around six-thirty. She said you would be coming over, sir."

"Is my son Eric here? I see his car is parked over there in the trees."

"I don't believe so, Mister Brown. I don't know why his car would be here."

Connie wondered what the hell was going on. He didn't even know Eric was in town. And why would he be at Allegra's?

Carl rounded the corner, out of breath. "I'm here, Mister Brown. Hurried as fast as I could. You alright?"

Connie looked directly into Carl's eyes. "Carl, why would Eric come to see Allegra without telling me he is in town?"

"Eric, sir? You think he is here with Miss Allegra?"

"That's his car over there, isn't it?"

"Oh no, sir! This isn't good. He hurt Miss Allegra, sir! He hurt her bad. My Trudy told me so"

"What do you mean?" Connie's heart starting pumping harder and faster.

"When he was here for the big party, sir. Before Miss Allegra went home to Montana the next day. He hurt her bad. Trudy made me promise not to tell you."

Connie pushed past Ben and raced through the house to the staircase leading up to Allegra's bedroom. Carl was right behind him.

He tried her door, but it was locked. Then he remembered the adjoining room connected to her bathroom. He tried that door as well. It wasn't locked. He gently pushed it open and crept inside, motioning for Carl to wait. He could hear Eric's voice. Connie's anger rose almost to its limits as he got nearer and could hear Eric's sinister words.

"Clever of me, I must say, but stupid of you, don't you think? Leaving your security code lying on the desk downstairs. I found it last time I was here. Dumb, just plain dumb." He laughed. "You know, you do remind me of your mother. Are you aware she was much prettier than you naked? She was. Isn't this ironic? Your brother Allan and me, you and Connie, one big happy family. What are the chances of all of us knowing each other? Of course, Allan thinks I'm gay. He's into S and M, that's how we met in New York. He came in handy smuggling cocaine over the Canadian border through Montana. He doesn't even know how many times my friends and I used that old cabin of his. What an idiot! He didn't know I paid your mother a little visit before I went back to London that week. She wasn't very cooperative."

Connie barged into the room. He froze in place, unable to believe what he had heard and now what was before his eyes.

Allegra was huddled naked on the bed, shielding herself with a sheet clenched in her fists and drawn up under her chin. Her tear-stained face and eyes were contorted in shock and fear. Her lip was bleeding.

"You son of a bitch!" Connie leapt across the room, shoved Eric aside and helped Allegra from the bed, wrapping the sheet around her.

"Get out of here!" Eric yelled. "This is my party! Get out or I'll—" He reached for his coat thrown over a chair and pulled out a gun. "Yes! I can fix this to look like someone broke in and killed both of you. What a joke on you! No one knows I'm here."

"Put that gun down!" Connie ordered. "What is the matter with you? Everybody knows you're here. Are you going to shoot us all? Put that gun down, right this minute! This is insane!" He pushed Allegra behind him, stepping in front of her as he saw the evil increasing in Eric's eyes.

"Connie," Allegra whispered weakly, clinging to him with one hand and holding her belly with the other, "he killed my mother . . . and he tried to kill his baby . . . it hurts, Connie . . . it hurts . . ."

"Carl! Call the paramedics and the police!" Connie yelled out, as he turned to Allegra to lift her into his arms.

"Oh no, you don't," Eric growled as he aimed at his father and pulled the trigger.

242

Connie felt the bullet hit him in the shoulder, knocking him into the bedside table. He slid to the floor, but remained conscious. The sound of more gunshots came from the adjoining room.

"Carl! No!" he yelled as he struggled to get to his feet.

Eric reappeared. "Carl, yes!" A twisted grin spread across his face. "Now it's your turn, ol' man. Then hers. Then everybody else in this house!" He had the most insane, vile, and hateful look on his face as he raised his gun once again. "Say goodbye, my dear dada."

But before he could shoot, Connie shot him in the head.

Kellie and Devin ran through the open door below and saw Callie, Ben, and Talutha huddling together in fear.

"Somethin's happened, Mister Devin," Ben said. "Somethin' bad has happened. We heard gunshots. I called the police."

Devin took his own gun from his pocket. He told Kellie to stay with them and lock themselves inside the kitchen, then he rushed up the stairs.

Chapter 58

Allegra didn't lose the baby, although it was touch-and-go for the first few days. Her belly was badly bruised where Eric had beaten her, it was a miracle the baby was unharmed.

She spent two weeks in the hospital under close scrutiny of her physicians at St. John's in Santa Monica and the best therapists southern California had to offer. Not only the physical was being tended, the emotional was as well.

Connie and Rachel, one or the other, were at her bedside nearly every waking hour. Someone was with her 24/7.

Luckily, Carl's wounds weren't fatal. He survived.

Arlie flew in from Montana and was at the hospital the first week with Connie and Rachel, worried sick about his sister. As soon as he found out she would be all right, he returned to Montana. Before he left, he told Rachel and Connie that the sheriff had found evidence of drug trafficking at the little ranch and that the FBI had been called in. He said Allan had been arrested in New York City, and that although he was part of the drug trafficking ring with Eric, the FBI was convinced he had no knowledge of his mother's murder. And as much as Arlie disliked his brother, they were of the same bloodline, and Allegra had begged him to do what he could for their brother.

Hearing that Eric had murdered his mother and then raped Allegra shattered Allan, and he withdrew into a catatonic depression. No one could reach him. He was placed in Johns Hopkins Hospital in Baltimore for treatment and observance.

It had been a horrid experience, not only for Allegra and her family, but for Connie. Having to kill one's own son in self-defense would normally leave a parent in a very precarious emotional state. And not only because of that, but the fact that he was a murderer and a rapist almost destroyed Connie.

So the first week Connie, too, was in doctor's and psychiatrist's care. His mother-in-law Greta came from England to be by his side. His own mother was ill and couldn't come, but with Greta's help and the doctors' care, as well as the love of Rachel and her family, it didn't take long for Connie to realize that what he had done was all he could have done under the circumstances. Shooting Eric was the right thing to do; their lives had been in jeopardy. His heart ached nonetheless, much more than the bullet wound in his shoulder. His son's crimes weighed heavily on him.

He asked himself over and over why Eric would do such violent things. Was it something Connie did? Or didn't do? What could he have done differently?

At the beginning of the second week, when Greta could see improvement in Connie, she sat with him in the hospital chapel early one morning and told him a story. She told him that before her daughter, Sally, Eric's mother, had met Connie, she had a relationship with a man in London. The man was a criminal, the usual type that Sally fell for, and she became pregnant. Eric was his baby, not Connie's. Greta apologized over and over for keeping it from him, but she had only wanted what was best for her grandchild.

Regardless, it didn't relieve any of Connie's pain to know that Eric wasn't his biological son. He raised him. He was the one in his life.

They cried together in the chapel that morning, and Connie was devastated once again. He didn't know if he could ever recover from the tragic harm Eric had done, much less from killing Eric, and now finding out that Eric wasn't his son after all. There was nothing he could do about any of it.

There were no answers, and there never would be.

At the end of the third week, when Allegra was released from the hospital and seemed to be herself, smiling occasionally and talking more, Connie drove her home.

Callie, Ben, and Talutha were waiting at the door with tears in their eyes, eager to pamper their mistress and happy to see that she was alright. They loved Allegra. All three of them.

"My goodness! I'm alright, I really am," Allegra said as they each hugged her in turn.

"Now remember what the doctor said, you must have plenty of rest and stay off your feet till the baby is born," Connie said as he took her arm and guided her to the staircase. He stopped suddenly. "Maybe we should put you in a bedroom here on the ground floor. Is there such a thing?"

"Good idea," Ben said. He read Connie's eyes and saw his reasoning.

Callie added, "There's the room and bath on the other side of the garden room, Miss Allegra. What about that one? I can fix it up for you in no time flat."

Allegra nodded. "Yes, that would be fine. Thank you, Callie."

"So let's just wait in here, shall we?" Connie hadn't taken his hands off her.

They went into the library and sat on one of the sofas.

"Can I get you something to drink, Miss Allegra? Are you hungry?" Talutha asked. "I can fix you something before I go help Callie and Ben fix up your room."

"No, I'm alright. I'll be fine right here. Connie will be with me if I need anything." She looked up into Connie's eyes and saw the gentleness and concern.

"If you don't mind, I'll have a shot." Connie stood and went to the bar.

"I'll have a shot of milk then," she said with a laugh. "The baby's moving around, maybe it will appease him."

"Then you've found out it's a boy?" Connie's widened eyes were staring at Allegra.

"Yes, a boy." She rubbed her hands over her belly, talking to the unborn child. "You're going to be healthy, aren't you, baby? Mommy loves you. My gentle little boy."

Connie's eyes filled with tears as he stood holding the shot of scotch he'd just poured for himself. Watching her caress her baby, even before he was born, warmed his heart.

He remembered all those years before, when Eric's mother was pregnant, how she had hated every minute of it. She tried to abort twice during her pregnancy. Deliberate attempts. Later she was diagnosed with schizophrenia.

Seeing Allegra's loving kindness to her child moved him. He turned to the French doors and with his back to her, he pulled out his handkerchief and wiped his eyes.

"Connie, come sit by me," she said, for she realized what he was doing.

He downed the shot, then set the glass on the bar. "I most certainly will, my love."

"Are you alright?" she asked, looking at his face. She raised her hand to his cheek, wiping away a remnant of a tear.

Her touch radiated through him. Healed him. The love he was feeling for Allegra was too much to contain. He lifted her chin and pressed his lips to hers. "I love you, my angel. Will you marry me?"

Allegra pulled back and gasped. "What?"

"Don't say anything right now. Please. Just hear me out. I'm asking you because I've loved you from the first moment I saw you. And I'm not asking because of the present circumstances, although it has given me the motivation and guts I've lacked." He grinned and kissed her lips again. "Let's marry before the baby is born so he will come into this world to a loving, devoted father and mother. So his life can be as normal as it can be from the start."

"Connie, I—"

"No, no, no, please hear me out before you decide. Please. I need you. I promise to be a loving husband, a good father, and I will love our baby as much as you will. I'll protect you and him and love you both for the rest of my life. Please say yes." He pulled her to him, gently kissing and nuzzling her sweet-smelling tresses. "I love you with all my heart, Allegra, and I am so sorry for what my son did to you. He—" Connie broke down with thoughts of the pain his son inflicted and the pain of killing his own son.

"Connie . . . Connie, please don't. Please don't cry. It's okay. I love you, too, my darling," Allegra whispered as she clung to him. "And yes, I would love to be your wife and the mother of all our children. Yes, yes, *yes!*"

Chapter 59

Three days before Rachel's New Year's Eve wedding, Maxim's brother Valentin and his wife Della arrived in California. Maxim and Rachel picked them up at the airport and they returned to Malibu along the coast highway through El Segundo and Santa Monica, pointing out some of the sights along the way. It was Valentin's first trip to the West Coast.

The excitement in the air was evident from the moment they met at the airport and then through the next three days as the preparations were made for the late afternoon ceremony that was to be held on December 31.

Della and Allegra wouldn't let Rachel do anything. With Kellie's help, they took care of all the arrangements for flowers and food.

The men spent most of their time on the patio or in the library, either talking business or laughing and joking. In the evenings when the moods were quieter, they would join their women and either go to dinner at a five-star restaurant, or dine casually at home.

It was a perfect three days. Everyone got along flawlessly.

On the evening before the wedding at the O'Neills' and the New Year's Eve party at Connie's, the rest of the Ballenchine family arrived and were staying at the Loews Hotel at the beach in Santa Monica.

Maxim and Valentin drove to the hotel to have brunch with the rest of the family on the day of the wedding, and to catch up on family matters. Their sister Anastasia and her partner came after all, which was a total surprise, along with sister Irina and brother Leonid. So once again, all of the Ballenchine siblings were together for another wedding, two sisters and three brothers.

Rachel stood in front of the gigantic mirror in her bedroom. The strapless ecru silk charmeuse floor-length gown that Anastasia sent to her at the last minute seemed to flow over her body like cream, pooling on the floor in back, rising above her toes in front. The dress Rachel bought in London before she returned to Malibu would be worn to the New Year's Eve party later that evening. Even though she'd planned to wear it at her wedding, the magnificent dress Anastasia sent was perfect and had more meaning to her.

Unbeknownst to her, Amanda and Anastasia had put their heads together via phone – Anastasia in Moscow, Amanda in Brussels – and now Rachel wore a pearl-studded lace bolero with a keyhole back designed by Amanda, topping off Anastasia's silky creation with regal elegance.

Tears welled her eyes as she gazed into the mirror, happy tears, thinking of all the love and compassion that had gone into the designs.

Della and Allegra were speechless when they saw Rachel as they entered the room in their own special gowns of pink and blue silk. They'd gone shopping together in Beverly Hills to make sure their dresses wouldn't clash, since they would be standing beside the bride on her very special day.

"You look fabulous!" Della exclaimed.

"That is a perfect look for you," Allegra added. "Not too frilly, just simple and elegant. I love it!"

"And look at you two!" Rachel remarked. "My goodness. Wow!" She dabbed her eyes with a tissue. "So are people arriving yet?"

"They sure are," Kellie said as she entered the room. "In droves. I wonder how many we invited. It doesn't matter because we have the entire beach to spread out to." She wore a pale yellow, fitted satin suit with a skirt that fell to mid-thigh, and matching gloves and heels. A gardenia corsage was fastened to her wide lapel.

"Oh, Kellie, you're gorgeous!" Rachel exclaimed, reaching to feel the satin fabric. "I love this."

Kellie grinned. "So we're just about ready. Devin will be waiting for you near the patio doors to walk you down the aisle. Oh, I think I'm going to cry." She covered her mouth as her eyes watered. "He's so proud to be able to walk his mother down the aisle. All morning he's been tearing up out of nowhere, he's a cry-baby. Happy for his mommy. And I'm so happy for you, too, Rachel." She hugged her mother-in-law and then kissed her on the cheek. "Oh, your friend Amanda and her husband are here. They're in the front row with Paul and his girlfriend and two other couples. Your friends Shellie and Janet?"

Rachel's eyes widened. "Oh, my God! They made it! I didn't think they'd be able to come."

"Your brother's here, Allegra," Kellie said. "And all of Maxim's family. Plus some people I've never seen before. So it's a pretty good turnout for a New Year's Eve. All my neighbors are here. And they'll be at Connie's party later, too. What a day! Party, party, party! Okay, I'm going back out and I'll let you know when it's time. Relax. Champagne's on its way for you three ladies to have a toast before you go in. Okay?"

Della grinned. "Hallelujah! I'm a-needin' it pretty bad right now. I hope I don't trip and fall on my arse in front of all those people."

Rachel laughed. "You'll have Valentin to hold you up. And Allegra will have Connie. So we're all set, not to worry. We have some pretty darn good-looking, strong men to walk us down that aisle, thank God! So we should be all right."

251

Chapter 60

White, yellow and pink roses, white lilies, yellow and white gladiolas, baby's breath and palm fronds made up the lush floral arrangements in tall white baskets standing on both sides of the grassy aisle carpeted with rose petals. The aisle led from the patio to a rose-covered gazebo on the lawn, the beach and ocean stretching beyond.

Rachel stood with Devin, the bridesmaids and groomsmen already walking the aisle before her. "I'm nervous," she whispered.

"Don't be. I like Maxim. He's perfect for you."

"I know. Look at him. How did I ever get such a man? It doesn't make any sense."

Devin looked down at his mom. "Excuse me, how did *he* ever get *you*?" He grinned as he admired his beautiful mother, glowing and looking like a thirty-year-old. She didn't look like she was in her fifties. No way.

"Oh dear," Rachel murmured, slightly breathless. "Here we go. Oh my goodness. Oh, oh."

"Take it easy, Mom," Devin whispered. "Take it slow. Listen to the music. It's your favorite, or did you notice? Kellie had them play it instead of 'Here Comes the Bride'."

They walked down the aisle to a live combo playing "When I Fall in Love".

The three-hundred guests rose from their seats and stood as the bride walked by with her son. Not a dry eye in sight. Something about a wedding did it every time.

When Rachel saw her friends on the front row lined up and waiting for her, she almost lost it. Devin heard her breath catch and knew what was coming next.

"Mom, look at Maxim. Look at him. He's grinning like a Cheshire cat. Look at him," he chuckled. "But he is a handsome devil, isn't he? You did good, Mom." He placed his arm across her shoulders, leaned and whispered, "I love you, Mom."

She looked up at him and smiled through her tears. "I love you, too."

Devin gave his mother's hand to Maxim in front of the gazebo and stepped to the left where Valentin and Connie stood.

It had been decided to mix up the ceremony, combining both Russian Orthodox and American contemporary.

The bride and groom stood together, hand in hand, waiting for the priest to descend the Gazebo steps as rehearsed. Della and Amanda were standing to the right of the bride.

Two tall candelabras were positioned on each side of the aisle, one candle burning in each. When the Russian priest stepped down, he took a lighted candle from one candelabra and handed it to Maxim. Then he took the other candle and handed it to Rachel. The music stopped.

The priest faced Maxim and said "The servant of God, Maxim, is betrothed to the servant of God, Rachel, in the name of the father and the son and holy spirit, amen." Then he stepped in front of Rachel and repeated the same to her: "The servant of God, Rachel, is betrothed to the servant of God, Maxim, in the name of the father and the son and holy spirit, amen."

He blessed them both and then stepped back to Maxim again.

"Do you take unto yourself as your wife, Rachel, whom thou seeest before thee?"

"I take Rachel as my wife," Maxim said with a glowing countenance as he looked at his bride.

The priest moved to Rachel. "Do you take unto yourself as your husband, Maxim, whom thou seeest before thee?"

Rachel turned to the groom. "I take Maxim as my husband."

The priest blessed them again and stepped back. He placed a piece of fabric on the grass in front of them.

The couple stepped forward onto the square of rose-colored cloth, symbolizing their entry into a new life.

"Have you promised yourself to any other woman?" he asked Maxim.

"I have not promised myself to any other woman," Maxim answered, still looking at Rachel, tears forming in his eyes.

"Have you promised yourself to any other man?" the priest repeated once again, this time to Rachel.

Rachel gazed into Maxim's eyes, her voice almost a whisper. "I have not promised myself to any other man."

The priest blessed them and stepped back.

Valentin and Della reached for ornate crowns that had been placed on small velvet benches in front of them. The crowns were of gold metal and burgundy colored velvet with costume jewels adorning them. Valentin placed a crown on Maxim's head, and Della did the same to Rachel. Then they took the candles from them and set them back in the candelabras.

Holding hands once again, Rachel and Maxim followed the priest up the steps of the Gazebo where they stood before him as he blessed their marriage. He handed them a marriage goblet of wine to share. They both sipped from it and then handed it back to the priest.

A minister of a non-denominational faith joined the priest in front of the bride and groom. He spoke to Rachel first. "Please face the groom and repeat after me. *I, Rachel O'Neill, take you, Maxim Ballenchine, as my wedded Husband.*"

Rachel repeated verbatim. "I, Rachel O'Neill, take you, Maxim Ballenchine, as my wedded Husband."

The minister spoke again, *"And I promise you love, honour, and respect; to be faithful to you; and not to forsake you until death do us part."*

Rachel squeezed Maxim's hand as she spoke. "And I promise you love, honour, and respect; to be faithful to you; and not to forsake you until death do us part."

"*So help me God, one in the Holy Trinity, and all the saints,*" the minister added.

"So help me God, one in the Holy Trinity, and all the saints," Rachel said, almost crying.

Maxim steadied her with his grip on her hands. He was having a hard time holding back the emotions himself.

Then the minister repeated the same dialogue to Maxim.

Again, not a dry eye in the place.

The priest removed the crowns from their heads and set them on the table behind him.

"The rings, please," the minister said to Maxim.

Maxim reached into his pocket and produced two triple wedding bands of gold, the orthodox wedding rings. He gave them to the minister.

"Please place the ring on Rachel's finger," he told Maxim as he handed the smaller ring back to him.

Maxim did as he was told.

"Please place the ring on Maxim's finger," the minister said to Rachel while handing her the other ring.

She followed instructions.

The minister placed his hands on their hands. "I now pronounce you, man and wife." He looked at Maxim and said: "You may kiss the bride."

Maxim put his arms around Rachel and drew her to him. Their lips touched beautifully, lingering, not a kiss anywhere more romantic and precious than theirs. Then they turned towards the audience as the applause and squeals of delight began.

The minister said loudly, "Ladies and Gentlemen, I present to you, Mr. and Mrs. Ballenchine."

* * * * *

After the ceremony they mingled with the crowd, greeted family and old friends, made new acquaintances, ate, drank, and filled the halls of the mansion with music and laughter.

At one point, Rachel took the microphone from the singer and dedicated a song to Maxim. She completely caught him off-guard by singing the song directly to him while sidling up to him.

More than you know, more than you know
Man of my heart, I love you so
Lately I find you're on my mind
More than you know

Whether you're right, whether you're wrong
Man of my heart I'll string a long
You need me so,
More than you'll ever know

Loving you the way that I do
There's nothing I can do about it.
Loving may be all you can give
But honey, I can't live without it

Oh how I'd cry, Oh how I'd cry,
If you got tired and said good bye
More than I'd show
More than you'd ever know

Maxim couldn't believe his ears. He had no clue she could sing. "Why haven't I known about this?" he asked as he hugged her, beside himself with awe.

Rachel laughed. "I saved the best for last." She kissed his cheek and then handed the microphone back to the singer. "Oh wait! Can I have that back, please?" she asked. She turned towards the crowd and searched for Shellie. "We have another singer here, a very dear friend of mine. Shellie, where are you? Shellie-e-e-e, come out, come out, wherever you are!"

Shellie squeezed between the couples on the dance floor, pulling Adrian behind her. "Here I am!" She was in her forties and as petite as Allegra, only without the pregnant bump. Her thick, dark, curly, shoulder-length hair bounced as she hurried towards Rachel, and her short green dress fit her like a glove, one would never know she had birthed two children.

Shellie hugged Rachel and took the microphone. She took Adrian's hand, then turned to the band and said a few words to them, then stood facing the onlookers. "This is a song I sang on another New Year's Eve in Paris a few years ago. Rachel was there, Janet and Robert were there." She pointed to the couple standing nearby, grinning from ear to ear. "And my dear Adrian was there." She squeezed his hand. "This is to all of you, my dear ones." She turned to the band, snapped her fingers in a jazzy downbeat, saying in a quick tempo, "One, two, three, four."

> *What a difference a day made*
> *Twenty four little hours*
> *Brought the sun and the flowers*
> *Where there used to be rain*
> *My yesterday was blue, dear*
> *Today I'm part of you, dear*
> *My lonely nights are through, dear*
> *Since you said you were mine*
>
> *What a difference a day made*
> *There's a rainbow before me*
> *Skies above can't be stormy*
> *Since that moment of bliss*
> *That thrilling kiss*
> *It's heaven when you*
> *Find romance on your menu*
> *What a difference a day made*
> *and the difference is you.*

The crowd applauded vigorously as Shellie put the microphone back on its stand. Rachel grabbed her when she stepped down and hugged her so tight that Shellie couldn't breathe. They both started giggling.

"I love hearing you sing, Shellie. I needed that more than you'll ever know. Reminds me of Paris so much. Thank you, thank you, thank you."

Maxim put his arm around Shellie too, beaming. "You make my wife and me very happy. You must come to Moscow to visit us. We would love to be your hosts. And I want you to sing in Valentin's restaurant when you come."

Shellie blushed and smiled. "Did Rachel tell you that the river boat where I worked in Paris was called Maxim's?"

"Yes, and I would love to go there. We can all go together."

Shellie looked at Rachel with tears in her eyes. She hugged her again, whispering in her ear, "Be happy, my dear one. Be happy."

Chapter 61

After the wedding festivities, everyone went their separate ways, feeling thoroughly entertained, well-fed, and abundantly cheerful. Weddings tend to do that to people.

But before he and Allegra left, Connie invited Maxim's family to the New Year's Eve party at his home, starting at ten that evening, and also invited Rachel's friends from abroad. The day's activities weren't over yet.

Maxim and Rachel retired to their wing of the O'Neill mansion and changed into their robes.

Maxim reached for her hand and said, "Darling, do you mind if I take a nap for a few minutes? All of a sudden I am exhausted. I don't think I can stay awake a moment longer. I am so sorry."

Rachel smiled. "I'm exhausted too, my love. So yes, please, let's both nap or we won't be able to make it through the night."

Kellie soaked in a hot oil bath, touched up her fingernails and toenails, shampooed her hair and lazed in her room. Devin was snoring in the adjoining room, rejuvenating for the night ahead of them. He wasn't a late-night person, so a nap was required.

* * * *

Della and Valentin were full of energy. They drove into the village to find a few things Della needed, and she wanted to find gifts for Kellie and Devin for being such gracious hosts. She and Valentin were leaving early the next morning for Moscow.

At nine o'clock everyone gathered in the great room at the O'Neill house, dressed to the nines, and were served drinks before leaving for Connie's party.

"So, you are leaving in the morning for Moscow?" Devin asked Valentin.

"Yes, we must return. The restaurant could go bankrupt if I'm not there to watch over the operation." Valentin laughed, but believed in what he said.

"It doesn't run well without him," Della added. "We've gone away before and came back to disasters. But we have enjoyed our stay with you. Thank you so much."

"We loved having you," Kellie said. "And anytime you come to L.A. you have to stay with us. No hotels. Okay? We're family now."

"Thank you," Valentin said with a grin.

Maxim stood by his brother's side. "I'm sure she means that, Valentin. She speaks the truth, our little sleuth here." His grin was contagious.

"If you need a mystery solved, just give it to her. My little cupcake is good," Devin said, hugging her. "I have to stay on my toes around her. Can't pull the wool over her eyes. It doesn't work. She doesn't let me get away with anything."

They all laughed.

Rachel was quiet, still tired, but she was smiling, taking it all in.

"So you will be in Moscow when?" Valentin asked Maxim.

"We board the ship in Spain for the sixteen-day cruise, will disembark on the twenty-second in Istanbul and will fly out later that day for Moscow," Maxim said. "We sail to France, Italy, the Greek Isles, Croatia and Turkey."

Kellie squealed, "*Omigosh,* Devin, we have to go on that cruise too. I'm not kidding. When can we go?"

Devin raised his brows, amused. "Okay, okay. Maybe late in the summer. I'm pretty busy till then."

"I don't mean now, silly. I meant later. So that works. Yes, the end of summer."

Devin looked towards Rachel, who was still sitting on the loveseat. "Mom, will you still be in Moscow if we take the cruise in August?"

"We should be. Right, Maxim? Didn't we decide we'd go to Cornwall in September?"

Maxim nodded. "Yes, that is right. But if we go before then, for I don't know how long your mother will be able to stay away from England," he grinned as he glanced over at Rachel. "If we go sooner, then you must come to England to visit before the cruise."

"Yes, yes, yes. I want to see England again. Definitely." Kellie was ecstatic.

Devin looked at his watch. "We probably should be heading over to Connie's. Shall we?"

The New Year's Eve bash was exquisite. Connie Brown knew how to throw a party. His party-planner's staff of forty made certain everything went like clockwork; no guest was left unattended. Food, entertainment, games, hats, confetti, horns and balloons, they had it all.

As it turned out, Connie was already acquainted with Amanda's husband Richard. Amanda was Rachel's friend from Brussels. They had met when Rachel went to Brussels and Bruges to work on a novel and Amanda was there from California trying to make a new life for herself. Rachel invested in her lace and dress design business, and in fact, that was when Rachel met Richard. Richard had followed Amanda from the States, proposed to her in Brussels, bought a home there, and they married on Christmas Eve. The Christmas Eve

Rachel was to marry Pete. Rachel went to their wedding, and stayed through the following week before returning to England. It was on that New Year's Eve after the wedding when Rachel met Maxim in the square at the stroke of midnight during Brussels' celebration of fireworks.

So it was Providence how all that had transpired.

Now it was Providence again that Connie and Richard knew each other through Amanda and Rachel and Allegra. And of course it all connected to Maxim.

Rachel was thrilled to be with her dear friends from all parts of the world: Brussels, Paris, Zurich, and Moscow. She was so excited that they had come to the wedding and Connie's New Year's Eve party.

Janet and Shellie were always a delight, Janet with her crass sense of humor, Shellie with her sweetness. Their fellas, Robert and Adrian, were grouped with Paul and his new woman, Joanie, who seemed to be sticking close to Paul. She didn't venture very far away.

The Ballenchine family was drinking and laughing together in one of the parlors. Rachel had spent time with them when they first got there. Maxim, Valentin, and their sisters and brother definitely knew how to party too.

However, Della eventually strayed from the Ballenchines and hung out with Rachel as she left the group to find her other friends.

When out of nowhere, Janet and Shellie appeared, reaching to hug Rachel, Amanda was right behind them.

"Oh Rachel, I am so happy for you, I really am," Janet said. "But then on the other hand, that leaves just me to take care of the rest of the single men in the world, damn you." she laughed heartily. "Now how could you go and do that to me? Huh? Answer me that. What the hell!"

Rachel grinned at her dear friend. "Well, I bet you and Robert will be tying the knot pretty soon, and then you'll be out of circulation too. So I'm not sorry at all."

"It may be sooner than we think," Shellie added, winking at Rachel. "According to Robert, he's already bought the ring."

"What? When the hell did he tell you that?" Janet asked.

"Last week. You know about it, he told you before he told me. He's just waiting for the perfect time to pop the question, he said."

"Aha!" Rachel said. "So. We're going to be having us a wedding in Paris this coming year?"

"Hell, I don't know. I'm not sure I want to give up my freedom just yet." She lifted her glass and swallowed its contents. "I need another drink."

A passing waiter heard her and handed her another champagne off the silver tray he was carrying.

"You won't be giving up your freedom, silly," Rachel said. "I'm not giving up mine. And Shellie didn't give up hers. What about you, Amanda? Do you feel like you gave up yours?"

Amanda shook her head. "No, I don't. I actually gained more freedom. And I have a handsome man to go along with it, and a castle. Who would have ever thunk it?" She laughed. "I couldn't be any more happier than I am. I promise you." Amanda hugged Rachel. "And I hope you will be just as happy, Rachel."

Rachel looked at her four friends waiting for her to say something in response. Della hadn't said a word, but she was listening intently.

"Yes, I will be happy. I already am, in fact. We'll have to work out the geography as we go, but I'm sure it will all work out. I do love Maxim. I wouldn't have married him if I didn't. You all know that." She grasped Della's hand. "You all can believe me when I say that. I think you know me well enough to know."

Della squeezed her hand. "Sounds good enough to me." She raised her glass. "Now let's get down and party! I need another drink!"

At eleven-thirty everyone went to the roof of Connie's palatial estate to view the fireworks bursting in the sky over the beaches of Santa Monica and Redondo Beach. The view of the bay stretched from Malibu to Palos Verdes. The starry skies were clear as glass and there was a full moon. A beautiful sight. The rare second moon of the month, which made it a blue moon.

Rachel stood in Maxim's arms near the waist-high railing that ran the perimeter of the roof space. His hands were clasped in front of her, his chin resting on her head.

"This is magnificent," he said. "Reminds me of our New Year's Eve in Moscow on the roof of the Metropole. Although this is much more exquisite with the blue moon and the glowing sea instead of Red Square."

"It is, isn't it? Our third New Year's Eve together. Do you realize that?"

"Yes, and we will spend them all together in the future."

Rachel turned around, reached up and locked her hands behind Maxim's neck. "I love you, Maxim. Have I told you that tonight?" She stood on tiptoe and kissed his nose before pressing her lips upon his.

"*Ya palyubIl tebyA s pErvava vzglyAda,*" Maxim whispered.

"What?" She leaned back, grinning, looking into his eyes. "What is that?" She giggled.

"I fell in love with you from the first sight."

The rare blue moon, the stars, the glittering ocean, the fireworks, the mutual love, the mood of the moment . . . it all came together to enhance the embrace and kiss that followed at the stroke of midnight and the beginning of a new year.

Life was good.

It was perfect, in fact.

Chapter 62

The flight to Barcelona, Spain, where they were to board the cruise ship, was uneventful and comfortable in First Class. Maxim slept most of the way. The cab ride to the hotel from the airport was just the opposite. First the driver complained about the amount of luggage he was to transport for the newlyweds, and he was hesitant to load it into his trunk, as if waiting for Maxim to lift it.

Maxim immediately took control of the situation just as Rachel was about to step in and tell the driver to take a flying leap.

"This is our luggage," he said sternly, "please load it into your car." Maxim then turned to Rachel and opened the back door and ushered her into the back seat. Then he climbed in and shut the door. "He is very rude. I shall not tip him when we arrive at the hotel."

"If we arrive at the hotel," Rachel said.

The cabbie finally loaded the luggage with the help of another cabbie, mumbling and grumbling through it all, and then drove them to the luxury hotel in the middle of the city.

The hotel was beautiful and immediately erased any discomfort they had experienced getting to it.

"This is beautiful, Maxim," Rachel said as they entered the lobby. "So perfect."

"All for you, my love," he replied. He held her close and kissed her forehead and then they walked to the front desk.

After a candlelit dinner in their room, they both sighed and leaned back in their chairs, sipping wine.

"This is actually the first time we've been alone in— how long has it been?" Rachel asked. "I mean alone without someone, a relative, outside our door. And we're actually married now! I can't believe it. I think it just hit me." She giggled and grinned.

Maxim leaned towards her and placed his hand on her bare shoulder, stirred by the feel of her softness. "Yes, we are finally married. It is unbelievable, is it not?" His eyes were shining as he glanced at her voluptuousness.

Rachel set her glass on the table and stood from her chair. She took Maxim's glass, set it on the table, and then reached for his hand. "Come with me, husband." She pulled him to the gigantic bed with its canopy of brocade and silk.

As they stood before the bed in the candlelight, she undressed him first, and then he slowly undressed her while caressing her inviting curves.

Both standing naked in the flickering light of the candles had a sensuous effect on their senses. They ran their hands over each other, without saying a word, exploring, giving each other pleasure as passion levels increased with every movement. Their breathing became heavy, and they drew closer together until their bodies were entwined and they lost control of their feelings and actions.

If ever there was a more solidifying of love and desire, a commitment more serious, a true joining of two people, it was unknown to the universe, for at that moment Maxim and Rachel, Mr. and Mrs. Ballenchine, both loved each other with all their hearts, and displayed that beautiful love to the utmost, all through the perfect night.

* * * * *

They finally boarded the cruise ship on the morning of departure, but the second night of honeymoon lovemaking at the hotel had totally wiped out Maxim. He was tired all day long. Even Rachel yawned all day. They laughed about it, kidded each other about keeping up the pace at their ages.

When the ship left port, they immediately went to their stateroom, undressed and donned loungewear. They ordered dinner in, to dine on the balcony.

After a fine meal of lobster and salad, they raised their glasses together once more.

"Lovely, just lovely." Maxim whispered.

"Doesn't seem real, does it? It's a fairytale." Rachel grinned as she touched her glass to his.

"Darling, I hope you aren't disappointed that I'm not quite up to going to the first night's activities in the ballroom."

"Of course not, Maxim. We've partied so much lately, I just feel like reading a book. Right now that sounds like heaven to me, really. Do you mind?"

"The pleasure's all mine. I sleep, you read. Sounds like heaven to me."

It was morning. The sun was shining through the ship's porthole.

"Maxim, time to wake up, darling." Rachel held a glass of water as she sat on the edge of the bed. She took a swallow and set it on the bedside table, then looked at Maxim again.

He hadn't moved.

They'd both slept soundly and it looked like he wasn't quite ready to start the day.

She shook his shoulder gently. "Maxim, wake up, darling, it's nearly noon." She started to kiss the tip of his nose and noticed his eyes were slightly open. They seemed glassy.

She stiffened. Her heart pounded and the adrenaline rushed to her head, making her dizzy. She shook him again. "Darling? Maxim? Wake up now . . . time to get up. Maxim?"

267

No response. He didn't move.

She stared at him for a few more moments, then she braved touching his face. Her fingers shot up in the air when she felt his hard, icy skin.

She grabbed the stateroom phone on the table next to the bed. "Help me, please! Something is wrong with my husband. Please hurry!"

She dropped the phone and tried to awaken him again. His hand was cold too when she grasped it. She touched his face again.

"Oh darling, please . . . please . . ." She began to cry. She laid her head on his chest, listening for his heartbeat, then raised her head and looked into his stone-cold face. "Maxim, darling, *please wake up. Please . . .*" She shook him again. "Come on, wake up! *Wake up!*"

It was a fatal heart attack that took Maxim in his sleep. A blood clot had blocked a major artery. An autopsy revealed an advanced case of coronary artery disease. He hadn't complained of any symptoms to anyone. He never complained about anything, so it was a complete shock.

The ship's doctor removed him from the ship at the port of call in Villefranche. He was transported to the hospital in Nice where arrangements were made to fly him home to Moscow. Valentin and Della flew to Nice immediately.

It was a horrible nightmare for them all. How could it have happened? It wasn't thinkable or the least bit conceivable that Maxim was gone. He was infallible. He was everybody's rock.

Rachel collapsed the moment she saw Valentin and Della running down the corridor towards her at the hospital.

Rachel spent the next few weeks recovering in Moscow. The first two weeks she was literally out of it, then she contracted pneumonia. Her heart was broken to bits. Smashed to pieces.

Chapter 63

Nearly six weeks after Maxim's death, Rachel returned to Cornwall against doctor's orders and Della's wishes. She had developed a deep cough, but she went home anyway.

When she got there, she sent email messages to her friends and to her son, saying she wanted to be left alone. No phone calls, no visitors. She assured them she was all right, that they needn't worry about her. She just wanted to be at home, alone, where she belonged.

The day she arrived in Newlyn, feeling as if her insides had been ripped from her body, leaving a sick, empty dark hole where her heart had been, she opened up her big house on the hill.

A huge, black, billowing storm was moving towards land from the sea.

To her the storm was a final assault. An omen, a sign.

Death had entered her space once again, but this time it was different. Her will to self-destruct didn't last as long as before. She had wanted to die this time too, yes, but she didn't try to take her own life like she did when Pete died. Maybe the difference was Maxim's family, the sharing of the grief with them, the love and care they heaped on her, the protection. It was as if they absorbed some of her pain, sucked it from her. When she boarded the plane in Moscow the

269

day before, she felt relief somehow, in spite of the horrid emptiness she felt. His family was incredible, and she would miss them until she saw them again.

But now, she had to get her life back. She had to move forward. She could do that. If nothing else, she knew how to set aside pain and grief and get on with it. Her resiliency might seem callous to others, that she didn't care, but this was not true. There was a time for mourning; she wasn't stuffing away the feelings in some dark corner to fester, the feelings were near the surface, they were still there. She would deal with them in her own privacy.

Being a writer was a godsend, for she could express her saddest and most painful feelings through her characters. Plus, being a writer didn't require her presence with others. Being alone was the best part of her literary passion, and it was being alone that allowed her to sort through the feelings in her own way.

She stood at the bay window, beholding the dark skies. The lightning cracks and thunder booms filled her being. The chill of the air had seeped into the house through its crevices and seams, ironically making her feel invigorated and refreshed. She had turned on the heating when she first got home, but it wasn't doing its job yet. No problem, she preferred cool to warm anyway. What did the doctors know? Cold air was good for her.

With a knitted throw wrapped tightly around her, she watched the performance of the gods unfolding in the heavens, reminding her of how insignificant one person's life was in the grand scheme of the universe.

She coughed as she remembered something she'd read on the flight from Moscow to London: *The only true happiness is the joy of being, and that joy doesn't come from without. It doesn't come from another person or a place or a thing. It comes from within. From consciousness itself. Being one with who you are.*

"Accept the present moment and find the perfection that is deeper than any form and untouched by time," she whispered as she looked into the skies. The words of Eckhart Tolle, a spiritual leader of the day.

"You hear that, Lily?" She had always called her mother Lily. "I'm sounding more and more like you. Like mother, like daughter." She smiled at the fact that her own mother had been a spiritual leader. Seemed ironic.

Rachel grinned wider and gave up a chuckle as she turned from the window and began singing, *"No more sadness, or sorrow, or trouble I see . . . there'll be peace in the valley for me—"* Her coughs interrupted the singing.

She tossed off her wrap, and as she went through the house, fluffing pillows and cushions, opening draperies and blinds, straightening things, she continued to hum and sing and cough.

Finally, she poured herself a cold glass of champagne and stood at the bay window, watching a tiny sliver of sunshine pushing its way through the storm.

Yes, she would find happiness again, being one with who she was.

Lyrics to "More than you know"
by *William Rose and Edward Eliscu*

Lyrics to "What a Diff'rence a Day Made"
by *Stanley Adams*

Lyrics to "Peace in the Valley"
by *Thomas Dorsey*

Rebecca Randolph Buckley resides in San Tan Valley, Arizona, with her three feline beauties: Princie, Oreo, and Albee.

She spends her spare time gardening, reading, shopping for collectibles, and watching movies – mostly romantic.

Ms. Buckley travels around the world not only for pleasure, but to find new settings, story and character inspiration for her novels and short stories.

www.rebeccabuckley.com
www.rebeccabuckley.blogspot.com

rebeccajbuckley@aol.com

www.ingramcontent.com/pod-product-compliance
Lightning Source LLC
Chambersburg PA
CBHW030529030726
47495CB00004B/918